Praise for other books by Randall Peffer

Southern Seahawk

"A historian can give you the facts; a novelist can illuminate them. But it takes a historian/novelist/experienced sailor to bring nautical history to life. Randall Peffer is that rare combination."

—AMY ULLRICH, *Sail* magazine

Logs of the Dead Pirate Society

"A good book for armchair sailors and an excellent view of historic Buzzard's Bay, Peffer's account is recommended..."   —*Library Journal*

Watermen

"Gives the reader a strong sense that the heroism of early America did not pass away sometime around 1875 but flourishes right now."

—*New York Times Book Review*

Old School Bones

"Peffer submerges into plot and character from page one. His writing is vivid yet economical, carrying the reader along a fast flowing plot that doesn't let up until the end. In DeCastro, he has created a hero along the lines of John Baker's very human and very passionate Stone Lewis. This is a hero with fire in his gut and the potential to carry a strong series."   —*Crimespree Magazine*

Provincetown Follies, Bangkok Blues

"Peffer piles on the atmosphere until it's as thick as Provincetown pea soup in this seductive tale that, while obviously not for everybody, will appeal to those willing to cross over to the dark side."

—*Library Journal*

SEAHAWK
HUNTING

RANDALL PEFFER

SEAHAWK
HUNTING

A NOVEL OF THE CIVIL WAR AT SEA
BOOK II OF THE SEAHAWK TRILOGY

BLEAK
HOUSE
BOOKS

Published by
BLEAK HOUSE BOOKS
a Big Earth Publishing company
1637 Pearl Street, Suite 201
Boulder, Colorado 80302
www.bleakhousebooks.com

This is a work of fiction.
Any similarities to people or places, living or dead, is purely coincidental.

Library of Congress Cataloging-In-Publication Data:
Peffer, Randall S.
Seahawk hunting: a novel of the Civil War at sea / Randall Peffer.
p. cm. — (Seahawk trilogy; bk. 2)
Includes bibliographical references and index.
ISBN 978-1-60648-034-2 (alk. paper)
1. United States—History—Civil War, 1861–1865—Fiction.
2. United States—History, Naval—Fiction. I. Title.
PS3616.E35S43 2010
813'.54—dc22
2009053852

978-1-60648-034-2 (Trade Paper)

Printed in the United States of America
13 12 11 10   1 2 3 4 5 6

For Jacqueline ... with love

PROLOGUE

CSS *SUMTER*, MID-ATLANTIC
December 8, 1861

The gale's blowing hard northeast-by-east. Third straight day. Seas running 25 feet, sometimes greater. Pounding the bows. Loosening the planks, deck beams, knees, sheer clamps, mast partners. With wind screeching in the rigging, the *Sumter* heaves-to under reefed trysail. Most of the officers and men are locked below beneath canvassed and battened hatches. Waiting.

For deliverance or death.

Almost four bells into the forenoon watch. The captain, Commander Raphael Semmes, sits fully dressed—back to the bulkhead, legs beneath a quilt—braced in his berth, smelling the filth of a hundred men and the sea churning, rising, in the bilge. Listening to the jog, jog, jog of the pumps fighting to keep up. Losing. His ship is sinking under his feet. Just as surely as the USS Brig *Somers* sank beneath him exactly fifteen years ago today off the coast of Veracruz during the Mexican War.

He's prisoner to this endless gale, this harbinger of a tropical cyclone creeping closer. Prisoner to the memories of the *Somers*—half his crew drowned when a great north wind out of nowhere laid her down. These things are enough to make a man bite his lower lip until it bleeds. And he does.

Most Merciful God!

He tastes the sweet, hot blood. Thinks of family struggling back home in Dixie. Thinks of Maude, the Irish selkie lost to all but his heart. Thinks of duty, too. He has sworn to God, Jefferson Davis, himself. He'll go to the brink of oblivion and back to rend liberty for the Southern States and himself from the Yanks.

Well here we most surely are. In extremis, *the brink, Lord.*

He scribbles in his journal, the blue ink leaving blots on the vellum with each pitch of the ship. Writing because there is nothing else he can do. Writing to block out the howl of the storm, the memories of the cries of dying men from the *Somers*. Writing to block out fears that his life has been cursed in some devious, unnatural way since that day when he lost his ship. Writing to take his eyes off the slurry of water swirling over the sole of the great cabin—three inches of brine, sloshing starboard to port, back again. Getting deeper with each jolt of the ship, splashing as it roils against the chart table, settee, his sea boots cast in a corner.

The man's scratching at the page with his pen, unpacking the story of the *Somer's* death by white squall, retelling the catastrophe. Writing of things he has not dared to talk about since he was cleared of negligence by the court martial. He's sucking more blood from his lower lip when someone knocks on his cabin door.

"Sail up, right close, sir. Off the starboard bow, sir. Bit hard to see in this rain and blow. Could be a Yank gunship," Kell, the first mate, said, his voice deep with the struggle not to betray alarm.

"Beat to quarters, Luff. Tell the engineer light his furnaces. Get the funnel up. Clear the tompions from the guns. Keep the weather gauge."

He leaps from his berth, plunges his feet into the soaked sea boots and is surprised by the coldness of the water seeping into his socks. Thinks for some reason of Hamlet on the cusp of vengeance, glory, death. *Readiness is all.*

⚓   ⚓   ⚓

The bark's a Yank, but not a warship. She's the *Eben Dodge*, twelve days out of New Bedford, bound on a whaling voyage to the South Pacific. Battered by the gale, she's sprung one of her spars and is leaking badly. Her crew has been trying to nurse her to the Azores for repairs.

"I'm sorry," Semmes holds her captain in a steady gaze after he's been brought over to the *Sumter*. "But you serve my enemy. You light his munitions factories and oil his guns with the fat of the whales you kill ... and now you've had a change in plans."

The whaling captain returns Semmes' stare across the chart table where they sit in the great cabin, the water on the cabin sole swirling around their feet. He gives a broken, little smile and flicks his right hand into the air as if tossing something away over his shoulder.

"I'm a Quaker," he says. "This is not my war. What wouldst thou do with me?"

He looks at the grey-bearded Yankee captain, feels the man's helplessness, misery. The humiliation of a man who knows he's lost his ship. *The decks awash. The cries of the men in the water.*

A strange equivocation rises deep in his chest. "What would you do, were you me?"

"I doubt that I could ever be thee. I have not the hunger."

"What, good sir, is that supposed to mean?"

The whaler looks away to the floor of the great cabin, the seawater swirling around his boots. "The world paints thee as a man consumed with the act of destruction."

"So say the Yankee newspapers."

"Aye."

"They must reckon me a pirate and a villain to preserve their own deluded sense of righteous purpose ... to cloak their own dark enterprises."

The whaler looks truly confused. Where is this leading?

Semmes growls to himself. "Show me the rightness, the innocence, in your chosen occupation, sir. Show me how the Yankee Quaker can send a fleet of ships around the world to kill and butcher the great leviathans to extinction. Show me how you can destroy the very royalty of the seas, and then call yourself a man of peace."

"It is an honest living. And it brings light to the world."

"It is an abomination of nature." Words, insights popping into his head. "Rapacious Yankee greed, to fill the pockets of a few New England potentates with gold got from the blood of gentle and majestic creatures that have no fight with you."

"But ..."

Semmes stands up, fire in his eyes. "Just a moment ago I was feeling sympathy for you and your predicament. Wondering at the toll, the misery, the cost to my crew in our endless endeavors here on these stormy seas."

"But ..."

"Not now, sir. Not now. I see the devil in your work. My duty is clear. My resolve firmer than ever."

"So thou'st aims to burn my ship?"

"And every one like it ... as long as God gives me strength."

"What god would give power to him who supports the institution of human bondage?"

The Yank's words sting. Slavery, the old grievance. For a second Semmes feels off balance, steadies himself with a hand thrust down to the chart table. "Come again?"

"Pride goeth before the fall."

"We'll see about that, butcher."

"The tide is turning on your vigilante war."

"I highly doubt that."

The Quaker places a copy of *The New York Herald* on the table, the headline glaring from the page:

FEDERAL ARMADA CAPTURES PORT ROYAL SOUND

He bites his lip until it bleeds again, wonders if he will be a ghost before this struggle ends.

"Read it and weep, captain."

1

LIVERPOOL, ENGLAND
December 14, 1861

Nearly midnight. The bells started clanging from the churches a half hour ago, the din echoing up and down the Mersey. Across the river in Birkenhead, they're still at it.

Thomas Haines Dudley, the new American consul to England's most important seaport, doesn't need one of his spies to tell him that all hell has broken loose. He just needs them to tell him whether this means war. Whether he should catch the first boat to Ireland, and home. Whether the recent news of the Union warship *San Jacinto* snatching two prominent Confederate commissioners from the English steamer *Trent* has finally pushed Queen Victoria and Lord Palmerton to join forces with the South against the United States.

His boys—Maguire, Wilding and one he knows only by the code name Federal—will know. So he must get down to a pub on Hackins Hey in Merseyside to find them. As soon as he tells his wife that maybe she should start packing their "escape bags." As soon as he can get out of his nightshirt.

And into a disguise.

People say that at forty-two he looks like a young Abe Lincoln—big ears, big hands, beard, tall. This may have been a good thing when, as a leading delegate from New Jersey, he was brokering the candidacy of Honest Abe at the Republican Convention a little more than a year ago. But it is definitely not the look for present circumstances. Not in this city of Confederate agents and their hordes of sympathizers. So ... first things first. Locate his razor. The beard has to go. Then he needs to dig through the kit Federal gave him, put on the dirty overalls, the wool jacket speckled with sawdust, scarf, tweed flat cap from Donegal. Until he looks the part of an East Irish ship caulker.

⚓   ⚓   ⚓

"It's not quite war," says Matthew Maguire. He's a thick-chested man in a bowler, a private detective in the pay of the Yanks, and he's shoving a pint of ale into Dudley's hand, "... but it's just about as bad."

"The Royal Consort is dead. Just come over the wire, it did." Federal spits some tobacco on the floor, beckons to his mates with a flick of his head, calling them back from the throng at the bar to a quieter corner of the pub.

He's a Dublin-born ship framer whose sister in Boston could use a helping hand. An informer who the Yanks have been subsidizing at a rate of two quid a week. In exchange, Federal has been supplying the Americans with a steady flow of barroom gossip about guns and uniforms shipping out of Liverpool to the Confederates, about suspicious building projects at the shipyards.

Dudley feels his brain buzzing. "Prince Albert is dead?"

"Typhoid Fever. Ten o'clock tonight. The queen and England are in mourning."

"Worse than that," says Wilding. "The Union has just lost its most powerful friend, Thomas."

Wilding's the American vice consul and was acting counsel here in Liverpool before Dudley arrived less than a month ago from New York. Along with Henry Sanford, the American minister to Belgium, he has set up the beginnings of a covert network to spy on Confederate activities here. The Rebs have been in Liverpool since last spring. They are flush with money and in a righteous hurry to contract Liverpool shipyards to build them a navy.

Dudley hardly needs to be told what Prince Albert's loss means to the Union. Freeman Morse, the London consul, and Charles Adams, the new American minister to England, briefed Dudley on his arrival.

To wit: like most of the citizenry keen on Dixie cotton to keep the motherland's textile mills churning, England's prime minister, Lord Palmerton, and foreign minister, Lord Russell, are pro-Southern. They have great influence over Queen Victoria. Her husband, Prince Albert, a cautious pragmatist, has been just about all that was standing in the way of England going over whole-hog for the Reb cause.

"What do we do now?"

"This could mean full speed ahead for the Johnny Rebs," Wilding said.

"We need to watch their every move," says Maguire. "I need money to hire more men like Federal ... and maybe a couple of tarts."

Dudley feels his chest tighten, a gulp of ale clogging into a knot beneath his lungs. He's nearly spent all of the pounds sterling in the little chest that the secretary of state gave him before he left. This job, Lincoln's thank-you gift for support during the presidential campaign, is turning out to be less than a plum. Or more.

"What's the news from Fraser's?"

"I hear they have contracted for two new ships."

Dudley scowls. The prestigious Liverpool firm of Fraser, Trenholm & Co. seems to be fronting the Confederate's operations in England and France, bringing to bear its wealth and influence—rooted in plantations, cotton presses, railroads, shipping, hotels—to support the Confederate cause. One of the partners, George Alfred Trenholm, is a good old boy from Charleston.

"Something's up."

"Any sign of James Bulloch, yet?" Wilding sucks his cheeks.

"I ain't heard nothing on the docks." Federal tosses down the last of his pint, signals the bartender.

"That snake," says Maguire. "Bulloch's the last thing we need right now."

Dudley groans. It's an acknowledgment. He's never seen nor met the man. Only knows James Dunwoody Bulloch by reputation—a capable mariner and diplomat. Clever, sociable. A seasoned ship's captain with fourteen years in the United States naval service and eight years in commercial shipping. Bulloch's the man Jeff Davis has sent to England to be the architect of the Confederate Navy. But Bulloch vanished from Liverpool back in October.

Word has it that he has run the Federal blockade at Savannah, captaining an English ship called the *Fingal*, loaded with British Enfield rifles and cutlasses. That even now Bulloch is on his way back to England with a much bigger agenda than blockade running. He aims to build a fleet of cruisers and rams in English shipyards; predator ships to make Ráphael Semmes' *Sumter* look like nothing more than a pesky mosquito.

"Trust me, Bulloch could be a plague of torment to us," says Wilding.

"If he sets foot back on English soil, I could arrange for him to have an accident. Maybe for his next ship to sink." Maguire smiles over the lip of his pint.

"I will warrant no such thing!" Dudley feels his cheeks flush, hears an edge creep into his own voice.

He's not a man who thinks violence solves anything. He did not come here to Liverpool to start another war for his country by employing murderers and *saboteurs*. He came here hoping to end conflict, hoping to quash Rebel dreams, hoping to end slavery in America by exposing Confederate treachery to British officials.

"Let me ask you this," says Maguire. "How many of your American boys died at the Battle of Bull Run? How many more will die if the Confederates launch a fleet in the wake of that rogue Semmes? How many will die on both sides of your conflict before you use whatever it takes to stop the rebellion? Do not the ends justify the means here?"

"Not in my book, sir. Mr. Lincoln's government will not stoop."

Maguire wipes the froth from his ale off his bushy mustache, eyes this American with a sad little smile. "Maybe not yet."

2

DISTRICT OF COLUMBIA
Mid-December, 1861

Secretary of the Navy Gideon Welles wipes the snow from his eyebrows, his *toupee*. Feels the black news he carries freezing his heart. My god, if ever he were the wrong man, in the wrong place, at the wrong time, this is surely the moment, this evening at the executive mansion.

The spruce wreaths on the front doors and windows of the north portico, the tall spruce ablaze with candles in the vestibule, the scent of hot cider and cinnamon wafting through the house, the laughter of the president's boys, Willie and Tad, chasing a pet rabbit around the on the floor ...

These things mock me.

"Gideon. Tarnation, man. You look like Saint Nick ... when someone's gone and cancelled Christmas on him." The president ushers him into the Red Room. "Take off that snowy thing and go stand there by my fire."

The big, awkward man hands his wool overcoat to one of the uniformed guards at the door, and moves across the room toward the heat from the fire flaring beneath the mantle. Shakes the snow out of his long white beard onto the hearth apron. It melts into tiny diamonds of water, evaporates.

The president, it seems, has been playing on the floor with his boys and the rabbit. His shoes are off and the knees of his black suit trousers are wrinkled, scuffed. His white shirt tail sticks out around his pants hangers.

"Well?" says Lincoln when the guards close the door, leaving them alone. He circles the divan, parlor chairs, and the oriental carpet in the center of the room. Settles into his huge leather wing-back affair facing the fire and Welles. "Has someone cancelled Christmas?"

The secretary wipes the last of the melting snow from his cheeks, steps back away from the hearth. Closes his eyes, laughs aloud—a brief explosion rising out of his belly before he can stop it. Once again he's face-to-face with his own absurdity. And the madness of this drama surrounding him.

Good God! The president's cabinet is a nest of vipers. Treasury Secretary Sal Chase, a free-soiler from Ohio, one of Lincoln's rivals for the nomination, a bull-necked prize fighter. Si Cameron at the War Department, who may well get himself fired any day for passing out lucrative contracts to cronies. Ed Bates, another of Lincoln's political rivals, is ruling the Attorney General's office with the autocratic will of Caesar. Bill Seward, chief among Lincoln's challengers for the Republican presidential nomination last year, now Secretary of State. He keeps upstaging the president in front of the press ... or leaving him in the dark on issues of national security to look the fool.

And here I am, the bearer of bad news again. How will my president ever see I may well be his only friend? Me. His older, uglier shadow. The buffoon. Beloved of the political cartoonists.

"Speak to me, Gideon."

Welles opens his eyes, "I'm so sorry to intrude on your family on such a festive night as this, Mr. President, but ..."

"Plain talk is best with me, Gideon. You know that. What's so plaguing you that it cannot wait until the morrow?"

He reaches slowly for the paper he has folded into the inside breast pocket of his suit jacket. "I received a dispatch today from James Palmer, captain of the *USS Iroquois.*"

"Do I know him?"

"I don't think so. He was one of those captains I sent after Raphael Semmes and the *Sumter* ... along with Charles Wilkes and David Porter."

"Those billy goats again! How the names grate against my soul ..."

"Yes sir." Welles stumbles, settles with a crunching of springs onto the divan. He knows the president's distress has strong causes.

Porter is the officer who mucked up the re-supply of Fort Sumter last spring when he conspired with Bill Seward to divert his ship the *Powhatan* from Sumter to the Gulf Coast. Charles Wilkes, captain of the *San Jacinto*, has now brought the United States to the brink of war with England by seizing the confederate agents Mason and Slidell off the *Trent* a month ago. A move as counter to international accords as when the British seized sailors off American ships and started the war of 1812.

"What has this Palmer done?"

"It seems, sir, he found Raphael Semmes and the *Sumter*, middle of last month at the French island of Martinique."

The president rises on the edge of his seat, stiffens. "Do not tell me he has bumbled us into to a war with France. Do not tell me that, Gideon."

"Yes, sir. No, sir. He had Semmes boxed in and ... well ... I think you better read this ..." He hands over the dispatch.

> *Sir, as I expected, I have to report the escape of the Sumter, to the great dejection of us all, for never were officers and crew more zealous for a capture. At 8 o'clock on the night of the 23rd, the signal was faithfully made us from the shore that the Sumter had slipped southwards. Instantly we were off in pursuit, soon rushing at full speed to the southern end of the bay, but nothing ...*

"Mr. President ...?"

Lincoln seems not to hear him, settles back into his chair. He stares deep into the fire—says nothing, does not move for almost a minute. Then he leaps from his chair, grabs a poker, jabs at the logs, whacks at the fire until a shower of sparks shoot up the flue and out onto the floor.

The president pivots away from the fireplace, knots and unknots the heels of his jaw. "So ... we had the varmint ... and we lost him. Now what?"

Welles says that the evening papers are running a story. A brig from Maine, the *Montmorenci*, has got back home. The captain claims he came afoul of Semmes northeast of Antigua just a couple days after Semmes escaped from Palmer. Semmes let the ship go on a bond—twenty thousand to be paid to the Confederacy after a treaty of peace and Southern independence. He did not burn the brig because she was carrying neutral cargo, coal for the English.

"Semmes wanted this ship to get home. Wanted us and the English to see and hear how he respects English sovereignty. He's angling for legitimacy, sympathy, in the court of public opinion."

"I don't know what he was thinking, sir. But, yes, letting that ship go certainly helps the Rebel cause given present circumstances. Given the mess the *Trent* incident is causing us with her majesty."

"Where are those two Reb commissioners, Mason and Slidell, now?"

"Prison in Boston."

"I'm of a mind to release them and apologize to the Queen. Before this thing with England gets out of hand. One war at a time, I say. What do you think?"

He wants to argue against the release, but says, "I hear that England is sending almost eleven thousand more troops to Canada, and massing its fleet."

"And that rascal Semmes. How can he keep stinging us in new ways, and new places? What next?"

"I fear he may set his sights on the whaling fleet."

"We can't fight a war without oil."

"Precisely."

"You must catch him, Gideon. And stop the South before they can build a real navy."

Welles swallows hard. Wonders whether the Rebs have finished refitting the captured *Merrimac* as an awesome ironclad, capable of steaming up the Potomac to lead an attack on Washington. Wonders whether Ericsson's steel-clad floating battery, the one the designer is calling a monitor, perhaps just six weeks from completion in Brooklyn, will ever amount to anything.

"I'm going to need more money, Mr. President."

"And where will I find it, Gideon?"

3

RICHMOND, VIRGINIA
December 18, 1861

M aude Galway fears she'll burst into tears at any second.
      She's been to these parties every night for more than a week,
parties every bit as lavish and bubbly as Rose Greenhow's *soirées* back
in Washington. The streets and salons of Richmond are a constant
festival of Christmas cheer and secessionist optimism. But still
Maude feels the tears coming, pooling in the corners of her eyes, blurring her vision. Right here. Right now. In the atrium of Virginia's
beautiful Capitol, designed by the legendary Mr. Jefferson. Right
here in the reception line beneath the golden rotunda. Right here in
front of the President and Mrs. Davis, the luminaries of the Confederate States of America, their Christmas tree glowing with ornaments.

When she catches sight of herself in the large foyer mirror she sees
a young woman in the prime of her life. Emerald eyes. Thick, copper
hair pinned up on the back of her neck. A delicate pearl necklace.
Golden silk evening gown.

But she feels as dark and dead as the pall of coal smoke rising from
the chimneys of the Tredegar Iron Works along the James River, clot-
ting over the hovels of workers, the bars, the house of ill-repute in
Shockoe Bottom.

"Are you alright, *mon amie?*" Her escort's fingers tighten around
her own. The dank sweat of her palm seeps into her silk evening
glove.

She grits her teeth, tries to bully the tears, the sadness, the worry,
back into the dark cove of her heart. Squeezes Jean Claude de

Saunier's right hand, hoping she can tap into his confidence, his majesty.

In his *tricolor* chevron of red, white and blue evening coat, he looks regal. He's a viceroy through his father, a Rothchild by way of his mother. Tall, slender. Almost Raffy's age, with the manners of a prince, the firm, lighted-footed body of a man who can waltz her all night. It's a shame that he's not the man she loves.

"I fear I may have a touch of the grippe," she says, sees that there are now only five couples ahead of them waiting to be officially greeted by Jefferson Davis and his wife, the youthful Varina Howell Davis. "Just give me strength, Jean Claude."

"If you feel *mal*, we should take you home."

She shakes her head *no*. Does not want to go back to the town house de Saunier rented on Franklin Street at Linden Square when they arrived here a few weeks ago. She knows that tonight, this reception at the Capitol, is too important to miss. Knows that de Saunier has been frustrated, has been waiting anxiously for a chance to truly connect with the Confederate President. Tonight he's been told he will have his audience. This is his moment to make more than a first impression. And her night to help, to sparkle, to put aside her guilt over becoming this Frenchman's mistress, put aside her dark emptiness, her endless worrying about what will become of her dear, sweet Raffy. Tonight she must bloody well buck up and stand by the man at her side. Jesus, Mary and Joseph. He rescued her from that detective Allan Pinkerton, who wished to throw her in the Old Capitol Jail for treason with Rose Greenhow and Betty Duvall. He brought her South to safety. Has given her nothing but kindness and affection.

But her tears will not go away. They will not listen to reason, the demands of the moment.

"You look pale, Maude. I'm taking you home."

She sees that there are only two couples ahead of them in the official greeting line.

"No," she pulls back her hand from his—a strange, automatic jerk. Thinks of all that will be lost if she falls to pieces now.

Jean Claude was *chargé d'affairs* for the French legation in Washington. He's come here to Richmond on an unofficial mission to pursue French relations with this new government. This new country. These Confederates States of America ... who share his cavalier traditions. Who are rich in cotton for the textile mills of France. Who will certainly buy French guns, munitions, uniforms, ships in this fight for independence from the Yankees. If de Saunier can win the confidence of President Davis. Can arrange the subtle details, and help manage the clandestine flow of funds, goods, services, private correspondence.

Possibly de Saunier has ways and means to help keep her Raffy safe ... it is because of him and his diplomatic couriers that she has the letter. From French Martinique. The letter Raffy wrote her in November before he attempted his escape from the Federal steam frigate *Iroquois*. Even now the letter lies tucked against her breast beneath her corset, the final words ringing in her soul: *If you still love me, do all and everything that you can to keep yourself safe from harm. Try to get South where you will find friends. When this horrible conflict ends, if I survive, my first act will be to search for you. You are my sun, my moon, the star I steer by. The angel on my shoulder. Fair winds.*

Suddenly a gaunt, handsome man is introducing himself to her. Jefferson Davis himself, bowing. And someone has taken her hand again. A woman. Maude blinks to clear her vision, is looking right into the big hazel eyes of Varina Howell Davis.

"Goodness, my dear. You're crying." The words soft, sisterly.

"I'm afraid I've got something in my eye."

Madame Davis nods, says there's something going around. Pink eye or some such thing. She's been fighting it too. Seems to afflict women for the most part.

"I think our men folk want to talk about international relations for a bit after the caroling tonight. Maybe you would like to come back to the house and meet the newest member of the Davis clan. Master Willie arrived two weeks ago. And we can see what we can do about your pink eye ... after I've finished nursing the babe."

"I think I'd like that," she says. "Very much." Her words feel instinctive and unfiltered. Raw, right.

4

CADIZ, SPAIN
January 17, 1862

"They aim to throw us out, Luff." Raphael Semmes paces the quarterdeck, Lieutenant Kell at his side. "These blockhead Spaniards demand we settle our accounts and put to sea within six hours. Muddy-mettled rascals."

The commander glares off to starboard at the Spanish gig pulling away from his ship toward the white Moorish buildings of the port. The governor's *aide-de-camp* has just served him an ultimatum for breakfast. And he has just told the Spaniard that the governor and the queen may want to reconsider the implications of their precipitous, ungracious demand that he take his ship and disappear.

He bares his teeth. Takes no notice of the bright morning, of the golden haze that lingers like smoke over the Straits of Gibraltar, the twin towers of the cathedral, the distant hills of Andalucía. Only notices that there is just a ripple of wind on the water. Hardly enough to move a child's paper boat.

"We have no coal."

"Precisely, Kell. We are evicted *post haste*. And still, I have no money to buy coal."

Nor does he have money to pay for the oranges, bananas, beans, rice, beef, and goats he has taken aboard to feed his crew. No money to pay the dockyard for the repairs they made during the last two weeks to stop the ship's terrible leaks along the keel, around the propeller shaft. No money to pay the Jacks what he owes them. No money for the boys to spend on wine, women, song after more than a month at sea battling the constant winter gales of the North Atlantic. Not surprising the crew is in a pissy mood. Not surprising that he's had to issue orders for officers to carry loaded weapons when going ashore with the men, orders to shoot anyone who tries to run off.

"Surely the money will come."

Semmes growls. He wired Bill Yancey, the chief Confederate agent in England, two weeks ago requesting money to pay his bills here in Spain, to continue his hunt for Yankee merchantmen, to make a concentrated assault on Lincoln's whalers who will be homeward bound off the Azores. But he has heard nothing in response.

"I suspect foul play. The Yank consul Eggleston has been playing at all manner of hugger-muggery. The scoundrel has lured off over a dozen of our men, turned the Spanish officials against us." He doesn't need to say that by now Eggleston has called in the dogs of war, that probably half the Federal Atlantic fleet is heading for the Straits of Gibraltar to eat him alive ... as soon as he tries to limp out of this harbor.

"Do you think the Yanks have intercepted telegrams between us and Yancey, got off with a shipment of our money?"

Semmes pretends not to hear. Doesn't have an answer to the question. But he tells himself that Kell must have it right. The Yanks are to blame for his poverty, his lack of coal, for everything. The South cannot be out of money. The South must have a heap of gold and credit in England. After all, cotton is king. The South *is* cotton. The king can spend at will, is spending. He has read in the Spanish papers about this ship the *Fingal* that James Bulloch bought and sailed to Savannah loaded with munitions. Has read about a new Confederate raider, the *Nashville*, which seized and burned a Yankee clipper on the final leg of her journey to France. The Federal's victory at Port Royal was a setback, but what war doesn't have its foul tides?

"This too will pass." He tries to beam his most confident smile at his subordinate. "The South rises, Kell. We did not come this far to end our days as beggars or convicts, did we? We are warriors, and we have our duty."

Never must his loyal mate, his officers, his men see his fears, his doubt. Never must they know what worries have been rising to the surface when he writes in his journal of late. Never must they imagine how troubled he has been by the news that came a few days ago, news that Lincoln has released the Southern commissioners Mason and Slidell to join their families in England. News of England's shrinking back from taking up the Confederate cause, from joining the war. Never must they guess how every pretty woman he has seen in the streets and salons of Cadiz makes his heart ache for a West Irish selkie named Maude.

"Prepare the ship for sea, Luff. Ask the engineer if he can scrape together enough coal to let us steam the few hours over to Gibraltar ... with the help of sails."

⚓   ⚓   ⚓

Damn you. Just damn you and your two-faced, cowardly little country. This is what he's thinking as he stands his post on the horseblock and waves away the Spanish gig surging toward the *Sumter* from the Government House ashore. Waves away the *aide-de-camp* waving a letter in the air. He knows that after his haranguing the Spanish governor this morning, Spain is finally offering to extend his stay in Cadiz. But by a measly twenty-four hours.

He knows the Spaniards now fear that he may skedaddle without paying his bills. Which is exactly what he is doing. How can he not? Still no telegraph or money has come from Yancey today. His strongbox holds fewer than ten dollars. And, anyway, this country has not treated him with the respect—not to mention the honor—due a warship of a sovereign and belligerent nation. *To the devil with Spain, the fair ladies of Spain.* The ship's anchor is already aweigh.

He turns to the port pilot, tells him to take the *Sumter* to sea. *Pronto, hombre.* The heavily traveled Straits of Gibraltar lie just ahead. It is a bright, blue afternoon. There are sails on the horizon. He smells blood. Lord willing, it is Yankee blood—and he will have it.

⚓   ⚓   ⚓

The first ship he stops is the *Neopolitan*, a bark from Kingston, Massachusetts, bound from Sicily to Boston. She has a cargo of fresh and dried fruit ... and fifty tons of brimstone—sulphur—the root ingredient for gunpowder. No matter that her master claims the cargo belongs to the Baring Brothers of England. Semmes cares not a fig about the alleged English ownership of the cargo, brimstone is a contraband of war, illegal for a third nation to ship to a belligerent.

In the *Sumter*'s great cabin, his one-man prize court condemns the ship and her cargo. When his boarding party has taken the crew of the bark prisoner and confiscated drums of figs, cases of raisins and oranges, he orders the ship burned. Here. Within clear sight of that amazing pillar of rock called Gibraltar. Within clear sight of England's fortress and fleet.

Lieutenant Chapman has the watch as the *Neopolitan* goes up in flames. It's late afternoon. The winter sun casts a long shadow of the predator and prey on the nearly calm water. The sun already tending toward red, illuminates the puffy clouds to the west'ard. He stands by the starboard mizzen chains, his long glass trained on the shores of Gibraltar.

"The shore's crowded with all manner of people," he says to his captain, who has just joined him at the chains. "I think they have gathered to watch what we do, to watch the Yankee burn."

"Aye, let them watch." Semmes twirls the tips of his mustache with both hands.

Let the artists among them sketch the extraordinary spectacle. Let them see what will happen to fleets of ships because England is too cowardly to let us and the Yanks bring our prizes into her harbors. Let them understand by this spectacle that England's cowardice is emulated by the monarchies and absolute rulers around the world who fear democracy and revolution. Let them realize that I am but a reluctant executioner, an exemplum of their cowardice and failure to force the Yanks to bring this conflict to a swift and equitable conclusion. But though this duty cuts me to the core ... I have just begun to burn.

"Permission to speak, sir?"

He eyes the dashing young officer. "As you will. You have the deck."

"I was thinking that just yonder lies the legendary Cape Trafalgar. That Admiral Nelson sailed here to defeat the French and Spanish. We sail in historic waters. Nelson turned back a greedy empire at this place."

"And we must labor right much to do the same, son." says Semmes.

He turns away. Hopes that the lieutenant does not see the sudden spasm besetting his right cheek, does not know that when he thinks of Nelson, he thinks of the brave man's death here. And the deaths of so many other others. The families and lovers they left behind. Nelson, he has heard, kept a painting of his lover, Lady Emma Hamilton, in the great cabin of HMS *Victory*.

Another selkie. Another lonely mariner. Another pair of Fortune's fools.

5

DISTRICT OF COLUMBIA
Late January, 1862

"Stop!" The black man throws himself in front of Gideon Welles' cab, grabs the bridle of the horse. Jerks horse and conveyance to a halt.

The cabby tries to drive off the man, but the Negro feints, jukes beneath the flicking buggy whip, and charges the cab until he is face-to-face with the Secretary of the Navy. Through an open window, this bearded specter—this bundle in layers of clothes, tattered wool scarf swirled around his head—tosses the red envelope. As if it is a note from his mistress or an announcement of the apocalypse.

"Wait!" Welles' voice is full of desperation. He has money. He can pay. "Who sent you?"

But the messenger is gone, lost in a throng of carriages, cabs, the winter darkness. Smoke through a keyhole.

And this is not the first time.

This new round of threats started up again right after Christmas. No longer notes under the door of his room at the Willard, but always like this. Four notes so far, passed to him by random Negroes, beggars waylaying his cab on his way home to the Willard or back to his office on Seventeenth Street after a visit to the navy yard . . . as he heads up New Jersey Avenue toward the center of town. Always a different man or woman, always at different places along the streets. But always tossing him notes, the same red envelopes.

He tears open the envelope he's just received. The message, in black ink on the red card, is just like the previous three notes.

GO BACK TO LITTLE CONNECTICUT.
YOU'RE KILLING YOUR PRESIDENT!!!

Last fall, when hideous yellow notes began appearing under his door at the Willard, the president's new security man Allan Pinkerton—or E. J. Allen as he's calling himself now—helped him bring an end to it. The notes promised to show both Welles' wife Mary Jane and the president a bogus tintype of him kissing the Reb spy Rose Greenhow, unless he called off his squadron chasing Semmes. Allen had caught the messenger, the tart of the pirate Semmes, found her hiding in the kitchen of Mary Ann Hall's brothel on Capitol Hill. But the moll had escaped. Vanished. Well, good riddance. At least the threats had stopped.

Until now.

"Who's doing this?" he shouts out the window.

The cabby looks at him as if he's daft.

Who wants me out of Washington?

It's an open question. He's made a lot of enemies. Semmes' Irish tart seems of little consequence among the cast of powerful people who revile him. All he can think is that she must have been working for someone else. Someone powerful. Someone still very much in the national picture.

Since Lincoln offered him this post in the Navy Department a year ago, an obvious political plum for this Connecticut newspaperman and Republican organizer, he's crossed swords with some snorters. He and the Secretary of State, Bill Seward, have been at odds since Seward undermined the Fort Sumter relief effort. He's been clashing with the navy's senior captains and flag officers, the Curmudgeons, over war strategy and efforts to retire them to bring fresh leadership into the service.

In just the last week he has all but come to blows with General George McClellan, who has suddenly lost his will to support the secret plans for a joint land and sea assault on New Orleans. The man, it seems, has lost his nerve for everything except promoting himself as the next candidate for president. And now Lincoln has fired Si

Cameron in the War Department and appointed Edwin Stanton as Secretary. Stanton, along with McClellan, is another of Seward's cronies. A man who actually *sneered* when he talked to Welles at last week's cabinet meeting. A man whose public jokes about Lincoln just a few months ago seemed libel ... if not treason.

Sometimes Welles wonders if the whole crowd is not in league, conspiring against the president, and Welles himself. Trying to derail their efforts to bring this civil conflict to a quick end ... before America drowns in her own blood. Sometimes he wonders if he's up against a *cabal*. The word so perfectly expresses the breadth and depth of a mysterious enemy he senses in Washington. What he can't quite get his mind around is how these political players connect to a woman like Raphael Semmes' moll. Is this Southern-sympathizing Irish harlot a sign that he and Abraham Lincoln are facing more than political rivals; that his enemies in Washington work for the Confederacy?

He bangs on the roof of his cab with his walking stick, shouts, "Take me to Murder Bay."

It's Washington's most rough-and-tumble red-light district.

"Ever heard of a little ferret calling himself Major E. J. Allen?"

6

LIVERPOOL, ENGLAND
January 26, 1862

"Did I, or did I not, promise you a slippery monster?" A voice from nowhere. A husky whisper.

Dudley stiffens, feels the air rushing from his lungs. He hunches his shoulders, tightens his arms against his chest as if to protect himself from a blow.

A shadowy figure steps out from behind an immense wall of oak planks stacked for drying along the Brunswick Dock. A faint moon glows through the fog, turning the water of the Mersey and the air in Toxteth a murky silver. It's not even five in the evening, but already dark as the wee hours. The William C. Moore & Sons shipyard is a graveyard of still and cold. Proof of what the Secretary of State had warned Dudley before he left Washington on this spy mission: England in winter is no picnic.

"Matthew?"

"You weren't expecting the bloody queen, were you?" A man in a bowler sips from a flask, passes it to Dudley.

He takes the flask, drinks. Lets the single malt slide across his tongue, feels the heat spread from his throat to his lungs, his arms, fingers. The whiskey seeps into his core.

"You scared the stuffing out of me."

The detective shrugs. "Better you be on your toes, mate. The Capulets are abroad, so to speak. I just seen a couple of 'em back up there on Caryl Street."

Capulets. That's their code for Reb agents and their minions.

"Then we better be quick about this." In his dirty overalls, the wool jacket stinking of hard labor, scarf, tweed flat cap, the American consul looks a long way from tea parties, high church, his desk at 22 Water Street.

"Just look at her. She's a winsome slut if ever I seen one, eh?" The detective gestures to the ship in the slipway.

Dudley is no man of the sea, but even with this ship partially surrounded by staging, he can see she has the sleek lines of a thoroughbred. Thin-waisted, close to two hundred feet long, with three immense, raked masts, two raked funnels amidships.

"That ain't no merchantman, chum. Look at her. Spitin' image of a Royal Navy gunship. Stretched out a bit, too. Tall-rigged for wind work as well as steam, she is. And in her belly she got two big teapots from Fawcett, Preston & Co."

The consul eyes the black hull, black spars, black everything. *A sinister-looking thing, sure.*

"She looks almost ready to put to sea," he says.

"Within the month if we don't stop her."

"And you know she's a Reb boat?"

The detective rolls his eyes. "I got me this new top-drawer Jezebel, real friendly with a clerk at Frazer, Trenholm & Co. She said her fellow claims his agency bought it for the Rebs."

James Bulloch set up the whole business last summer. Frazer and the shipyard have been pretending that the vessel's being built for an Italian firm. They call her the *Oreto*. The plan is to run her out of the Mersey with a phony English crew. Not a speck of military hardware on her. Pure innocence. Somewhere down the road—maybe the Azores, Bermuda, the Bahamas—the ship will rendezvous with Reb seamen, merchant ships loaded with coal, cannons, Blakely pivot guns, shells, gunpowder, a year's worth of provisions. Thenceforth, she will be commissioned as a Confederate cruiser to make the *Sumter's* little reign of terror an asterisk to history.

"My God."

"Want me to have Federal and his mates burn it?"

"I believe in the rule of law, Matthew. Building this ship is a violation of the Foreign Enlistment Act against England outfitting warships for belligerent nations. I'm going to take my case against Frazer, Trenholm & Co. to London. To Lord Russell and Lord Palmerton."

Maguire closes his eyes, shakes his head in disappointment. "Yeah, have it your own way. But think on this. While you're off in London, there's another one of these little darlings abuilding over to the Laird yard in Birkenhead. Something even more menacing. Something you better hope Raphael Semmes never gets near.

"Can you take me to see it?"

Suddenly Maguire jerks his head, looks over his shoulder. Gets a strange look on his face. Wild-eyed, lip curling.

"Maybe not ..."

"Why?"

"Fucking Capulets." The detective nods his head toward a half-dozen figures coming toward them down the street ... with what look like barrel staves and chains in their hands.

"Now what?"

"Have you got a gun?"

He feels his stomach shrivel into a stone. "I've told you, I'm a lawyer. I believe in the rule of law, not violence. I'm going to protest the building of these ships with Lord Palmerton."

"Bloody shite."

7

DISTRICT OF COLUMBIA
January 27, 1862

Welles can see that his president's clearly not happy to be in his second-floor office, still working. It's dark. It's late. It's winter. Mary wants him in the residence. His son Willie has been riding his pony along that sewage-laden G-Street Canal again in the rain. And now the eleven-year-old has a fever.

"Let me get this straight. Someone has been sending Gideon here threats since last fall ... and you two are just telling me about it now?" Lincoln's right hand coils into a fist, releases, coils again as he paces in front of the two men seated on a horse-hair sofa, facing the fire raging in the hearth.

"That's not exactly right, Mr. President." The speaker's a short, slit-eyed man in a tight, brown suit. Heavy Scottish brows obscure cold, blue irises. Major E. J. Allen, *né* Pinkerton of Glascow. The short-cropped black hair and beard put Welles in mind of a muskrat trapper he knew on the Connecticut River.

He tells Lincoln how an Irish strumpet with ties to Rose Greenhow and the pirate Semmes had been trying to pinch Welles last fall. But he and Welles put a stop to it bloody fast. Sent the ruddy bitch packing. His informants place her in Richmond, keeping house for a Frenchy diplomat type these days.

"We thought we had taken care of the problem. I didn't know about this other thing until yesterday when the secretary sought me out, showed me that red card. Thought I had nailed Mr. Welles' mail problems in the bud."

"Apparently not."

"No ... it seems not, Mr. President ... I'm sorry." Welles speaks for the first time in minutes. There's a broken feeling in his chest.

Lincoln turns away, stares at the engraved portrait of Andrew Jackson over the mantle, sighs. "I don't want apologies, Gideon. I want honesty. I can't be constantly trying to claw my way out of piles of manure because people keep secrets from me. Do you understand?"

"The secretary made me think it was purely a personal matter with the trollop."

"Rubbish. You know better, Major Allen. Threats to extort a public official are never a private matter. I owe you my life, man. You got me through Baltimore last year when they planned to kill me on the train to the inauguration. Still ..." The president's lips move, trying to form words, but no sound follows.

Welles feels his scalp sweating. "I should do what these new notes say, Mr. President. I should resign and go back to Connecticut. You don't need me bringing more problems on you. You would be better ..."

Lincoln doesn't let him finish. He stands in the middle of the room, spreads his arms, the old stump orator.

"I cannot abide always being put on the defensive, gentlemen. It is no way to run a country, no way to preserve the Union. This is the last straw. You hear?"

Welles and the ferret nod stupidly, have no idea where Lincoln is going.

"I'm putting you two and this country on warning. Abraham Lincoln is nobody's fool ... and nobody's coward."

He says he is sick and tired of being jerked around like an ox in somebody's stocks. Tired of do-nothing, corrupt members of his own cabinet like Si Cameron whom he has finally fired. Tired of the squabbling among his secretaries. Tired of soldiers like General in Chief George McClellan, who can muster an excuse to delay any and every offensive. Tired of stewing over whether England and France will support the Confederacy. Tired of worrying if the blockade will eventually stop the flow of arms and cotton in the secesh states. Tired of fearing that any day the South will send a dozen Raphael Semmes–types to devour the whaling fleet, and leave the Union without light and gun oil.

The president scoops up a heap of maps cluttering his writing desk, carries them across the room. Drops them with a loud thud on the large walnut table in the middle of the room used for cabinet meetings on Tuesdays and Fridays.

"And I'm tired of hearing from Salmon Chase that the government is going broke with these war expenditures."

The men on the couch stare blank-eyed at their leader. The spy looks like a boy expecting a caning. Welles feels something stirring, some buzz in the air, some approaching lightning. He wants to cheer his president's rant, urge him on to glory.

Lincoln turns back to his desk. One sheet of paper remains. Loosely spaced phrases, sentences scratched on a piece of presidential stationery. He says that for some days, he has been at odds with himself as to whether to issue this order. Thought he should discuss it one more time with the cabinet even though many of them, like Stanton, Seward, Welles, are already for it.

"But enough! Tomorrow we go on the offensive. And we do not stop until victory is ours and the Union restored. If the Rebels want a war, we will give them one to remember."

For several minutes no one says anything. Finally, Lincoln speaks, says it's getting late. He has a sick son to attend to. Mrs. Lincoln is beside herself, hardly leaves the boy's side. Dear, sweet Willie. But, pay attention here. Tomorrow they launch the vanguard. Major Allen will henceforth commit his resources to finding the scoundrel behind these threats to Welles.

Welles reads the paper that Lincoln hands him. It's the President's General War Order Number One.

"Gideon ... you must send this order to your commanders, as Edwin Stanton will send it to his generals."

Executive Mansion,
Washington, January 27, 1862

Ordered that the 22nd day of February 1862, be the day for a general movement of the Land and Naval forces of the United States against the insurgent forces.

That especially—
The Army at & about Fortress Monroe
The Army of the Potomac
The Army of Western Virginia
The Army near Munfordsville, Kentucky
The Army and Flotilla at Cairo
And a Naval force in the Gulf of Mexico, be ready for a movement on that day.

That all other forces, both Land and Naval, with their respective commanders, obey existing orders, for the time, and be ready to obey additional orders when duly given.

That the Heads of Departments, and especially the Secretaries of War and of the Navy, with all their subordinates; and the General-in-Chief, with all other commanders and subordinates, of Land and Naval forces, will severally be held to their strict and full responsibilities, for the prompt execution of this order.

A. Lincoln

8

⌁

GIBRALTAR
Mid-February, 1862

Church over. Another balmy Sunday morning. Another secret liaison.

The captain of the *Sumter* hopes that the townsfolk, the Brits, his own men, will think he's just going for a walk to get some fresh air, to clear his mind this fine day. But the truth is he's following the woman again. Just as he has for the last three Sundays. Up-hill through the twisting streets of the ancient walled town until she reaches the switchbacks on the lower slopes of the Rock. Castle Road, climbing to Signal Station Road, mounting to the country-side—hummingbirds, olive trees, fields of clover.

The bells of the Cathedral of St. Mary the Crowned are still ring-ing as he watches her. She's almost a cable ahead, walking with easy strides. Her white linen parasol cocking left, then right, with each fresh step. Copper curls trailing off her neck catching the breeze. The pale green dress swaying from her hips.

With each new step—hers, his—he pictures Maude. Knows that if he's honest with himself, he must admit that he picked this woman because of Maude. Because from that first day at mass several weeks ago when he saw that burnished hair, the light freckles spreading over the nose, the willowy figure, he felt a tenderness, an aching at the back of his throat. An aching he thought he had lost almost a year ago when he left his sweet West Irish selkie in a dark, drafty board-ing house room near Capitol Hill.

Now there's this new girl.

He arrived here in Gibraltar near the end of January; was a man graciously received by the British Governor, by the officers of the Coldstream Guards. A man feted in the saloons and clubs of the town. A man greeted by bands with riffs from "Dixie." But a tired man, a worried man, a man who needs new tubing for his ship's boilers. A man with no coal, with stretched and patched sails, who has run out on his Spanish debts in Cadiz. A man with almost nothing but a smile and a bow at the waist to pay his bills, his men, his new hosts.

Here in Gibraltar he promised himself that he would no longer let the Americans sabotage his hunt with their pimps, spies and dirty tricks—as they surely had back in Cadiz. He cannot take on the Americans and their friends ashore alone. So now he has an ally. *Just look at her. She moves with an energy and grace that seems peculiar to the Irish female. She could be Maude's sister. A dream worthy of Queen Mab. A lass named Nessa.*

He credits the Lord for the good fortune. In this hour of his deepest need. Who was to know that most of the Queen's soldiers garrisoned at the Rock would be Irish? Or that some of the non-commissioned officers would have brought their families here? That the Almighty's mass would be a sea of ruddy Irish faces? Including the lovely Nessa's. Who in his wildest dreams could have imagined that this daughter of a master sergeant gunner would be drawn to a Southern seahawk, just as he was to her?

Who could have guessed that after his first mass in Gibraltar, she would greet him on the steps of the cathedral, look deep into his eyes? Implore him to tell her what she might do to ease his stay in this fair port. And help him hunt again.

"Would you be of a mind to take a walk," he almost choked on the audacity in his voice, "to someplace less public?"

⚓   ⚓   ⚓

"Is this what you've been waiting for?" She hands him her parasol, bends over, hikes up her dress, her petticoat.

A hot sea breeze gusts among the olive trees, taking the chill out of the shade in this hillside grove, a quarter mile off the Signal Station Road. The air's laden with the scents of fish, wet earth, something else. Oranges, maybe. For an instant he pictures Maude. Pictures her here with him at the very Gates of Hercules. His chest heaves.

He sees Nessa's knees, pale thighs . . . tries to do the noble thing and turn away. But his eyes are fascinated by those pink garters and what they conceal.

Under each garter is a telegram, each still sealed in its envelope. She removes one, hands it to him. Smiles.

"I really hope this is what you want, Captain."

He passes her the parasol, turns his back, pulls his spectacles out of his jacket pocket, reads. The wire is addressed to Miss Nessa O'Connor. It's from James Mason, the same James Mason who the Federal Charlie Wilkes had kidnapped off the *Trent* two months ago. Mason has finally made it to London, has superseded Bill Yancey as one of the South's commissioners there.

PLEASE FORGIVE DELAYS ON THIS END.
RECEIVED YOUR REQUEST.
I HAVE AUTHORIZED A DRAFT FOR $16,000 ON
FRAZER, TRENHOLM & CO.

At last, his money is coming. A small fortune. This subterfuge that he has worked with the fair Nessa has succeeded. The Yanks and their spies have not suspected that her telegraph correspondence with Mason is in any way a cover for the captain of the *Sumter*. They have not blocked or intercepted the wires. *Merciful God*. He can pay the damn Spaniards in Cadiz what he owes them. He can restore his ship's boilers, buy coal, pay the crew.

But how can he hunt again?

"What's the matter?" She must see his lips pursing beneath his mustache. "Surely this is good news for you."

"I fear it comes too late." He stretches out his right arm, points to the sea.

The USS *Tuscarora* lies anchored just a quarter mile from his cruiser. The USS *Kearsarge* lies across the bay in Algeciras. Both potent sloops of war that can outrun and outgun the little *Sumter*. Five miles to seaward the USS *Ino*, an armed fast clipper, is sailing back and forth, waiting.

"My enemy has penned me in. I am caged, Nessa."

She hands him the second telegram. "Maybe this brings better news."

He tears open the envelope, can hardly believe what he's reading.

NEW SHIP ORETO NEARLY READY FOR SEA.
SHALL I SEND HER FOR YOU?

He pulls off his spectacles, tucks them into his pocket. He feels his cheeks flushing, his lips spreading into an immense smile. His head swims with wild melodies, voices singing.

"May I read?" She moves so close to him. He can feel her breath on his cheek.

He hands her the telegram. "I need you to send Mr. Mason one more wire."

"What should I say?"

"Only this. *Do not send ship. I will come to England.*" He takes her free hand between both of his. It's an unconscious act. As if he's in another time, at another place.

"If you want to kiss me," she says. "Now might be a good time ... before you have to go."

He feels himself sinking into those green eyes, wishing for just a moment that his heart was free. "You are an angel."

9

RICHMOND, VIRGINIA

March 5, 1862

Oh bloody hell.

Fiona O'Hare has barely dismounted to the platform from the Richmond, Fredericksburg & Potomac Railroad coach when Maude Galway spies her, and does exactly what she promised herself she would not do upon finally seeing her friend again.

Ever since she got the telegram that Fiona was coming south, she has been a basket of nerves. Now she flies into her friend's arms, sobs rupturing the air. Breaking the silence of the light snow settling over Richmond, the soft hissing of the locomotive come to rest. On this gray winter afternoon with a harsh turn in the weather after the spring-like temperatures that came with the beginning of the new year.

"Why are you shaking, love?" Fiona puts her hand beneath Maude's chin, raises her face until the two have eye contact.

Oh bloody hell.

She stares up into that face. Her heart quivers a little. Fiona has a strong jaw, piercing dark eyes, bold nose, high forehead and straight, shoulder-length black hair. Almost boyish. But the easy crescents of the eyebrows, smooth pale cheeks, deep pink lips promise something more feminine and obscure.

"I feared I would never see you again and now ... " The sobs come again, a squall of tears.

"Oh, lass."

Just hold me. Make the world go away.

She presses herself against Fiona, remembers nuzzling her mom like this back in the little white cottage on Tralee Bay in the old country when she had come home from the convent school to hear that her father had passed on. She could not catch her breath then, cannot catch it now.

"I'm here now, Maudie ... tell me everything."

She clings. Just gives in to her pain, her troubles. Pays no attention that the driver of her carriage, other curious male eyes, are watching this reunion with uncommon interest.

There's so much she has kept bottled-up inside her. She tells Fiona that Richmond, like the Washington she left two months ago, has taken on the frightening aspects of a spectacle. That the capital of the South is festive at every hour of the day. The Christmas and New Year's celebrations have not yet waned. Southern gentry seem caught up in some kind of contagious euphoria, forever prattling about what they imagine will be a quick Confederate victory to end this civil conflict.

Then she really lets the demons loose. She confesses that she has sold her soul to a Frenchman whom she does not love. She sleeps with this man, imagines his body is Raffy's body, makes wild love to him as if she were a hay-yard beast. Forty-nine days have passed since she last had her monthly curse.

She's afraid to tell de Saunier. What hope is there for her in this strange city? Until now her one and only friend in Richmond is a woman of the highest moral principles ... the First Lady of the land.

"We must go see her," says Fiona. "For help."

$$\text{\small ⚓ \quad ⚓ \quad ⚓}$$

As the Negro maid ushers the two women up the sweeping circular staircase to the nursery in the family quarters of the mansion at Twelfth and Clay Streets, Maude can smell the distinct scents of Varina Howell Jefferson's world. Applesauce, rose water, fresh linen, baby.

Varina is sitting in a hickory rocker by the fire, her dark hair pulled up along the sides of her head with silver combs. She's nursing three-month-old Willie beneath a cotton shawl.

"Your reputation precedes you," she says to Fiona after they have been introduced and the guests have settled onto a loveseat.

"Beg pardon, Miss?" Fiona's West Irish brogue hits a high note.

"Maudie tells me she has much missed you ... and if I may speak a bit out of school ... I have heard that you, like Maude, have just barely escaped the fate of Madame Rose Greenhow and Mistress Betty Duval. I hear Mr. Lincoln's henchmen now have them both in the Old Capitol Jail."

"That's over and done with." Fiona's voice is oddly hasty, too loud. She shifts her gaze, looks askance out a window. It's the look of alarm that Maude has known since the days they first made friends on the bark from the Shannon River to New York. It's the look that means Fiona's not quite telling all there is to tell. The look Maude tried so hard to ignore after the two women decided to seek their fortunes together in the boomtown that's the American capital.

Fiona found a teaching job at the St. Mary's Academy for Girls first, brought Maude aboard shortly thereafter. Life for the young teachers was an adventure in teaching, homemaking, shared novels, candlelit confessions over glasses of peach wine. Museums, theaters, concerts. Lectures. Fiona took a keen interest in the slavery question and came to favor Southern secession from the union. Maude was infatuated with theater. She could not have imagined that anything was missing in her life ... until Raphael Semmes appeared.

And then when he was gone, when her soul had all but shriveled away with longing, Fiona rescued her again, introduced her to the socialite Rose Greenhow. They both joined Wild Rose's clutch of women warriors, both began using their beauty, their wit, to spy on the inner circles of Washington for the Confederacy. Then they went further. They hatched a scheme to blackmail Gideon Welles, to get the Secretary of the Navy to give up his hunt for Raphael Semmes. But Maude got caught.

"How do you know ...?" Maude says. She thinks back on her other visits to Varina. This magnificent woman has offered her tea, sympathy. But has never pried into her personal life. "I never told you ..."

The first lady smiles. "It's alright. I deeply admire you both. The South admires you. You are safe here."

Maude feels a sharp fluttering in her chest, feels stripped naked. "But how, Varina ...?"

"This is a big house ... but it has thin walls. I'm afraid I hear a lot of what transpires in Jeff's office."

"Then you've heard about Raphael Semmes, too?" Fiona.

"You mean that he's a national hero?"

"No," says Maude, suddenly feeling her shame rising in her throat. "That I love him."

Varina Howell Jefferson looks shocked. "But he's married. I can't know this."

"We hope you can help us," says Fiona. "Maudie's going to need some ..."

The first lady rises in her seat, lifts the babe away from her breast. "I don't see how ..."

Maude swallows hard, feels the tears in her eyes. "I think I'm pregnant."

"To Semmes?"

"To Jean Claude de Saunier."

"Oh dear."

Oh bloody hell.

10

DISTRICT OF COLUMBIA
March 9, 1862

Welles is watching the president stare out his office window toward the unfinished Washington Monument and the Potomac. Wondering whether this is the day when events finally get the better of Lincoln, the day he buckles beneath the weight. In three separate meetings since Willie's funeral, Welles has seen the grieving father break into tears.

The president's still wearing a tattered maroon dressing gown, slippers down at the heels. He holds a telegram in his right hand, has been keeping his back to the cabinet members he called here for this latest emergency. Welles and Secretary of State Seward sit on separate sofas. The new Secretary of War—chubby, stubby, bespectacled, long-bearded Edwin Stanton—paces the floor, waving his arms. Ranting. His face is red, the buttons on his vest look ready to pop.

"Today our navy is the laughing stock of the world," Stanton sneers at Welles. "And tomorrow it's likely that ironclad will steam right up the Potomac, destroy the Capitol, the White House, disperse Congress. Leading the way for the Rebel army to march in here with their rabble, seize the city and ..."

"Lord Almighty, Edwin, I bid you here for counsel, not ... not this sermon on the apocalypse."

Seward clears his throat, says that the gravity of this new turn of events cannot be overestimated.

Truly bad news arrived at the War Department an hour ago. The telegram the president holds tells how a Rebel menace called the

Virginia, built on the captured hull of the USS *Merrimac,* steamed out of its dock yesterday at the Norfolk Navy Yard, ambushing and destroying the massive Federal warships *Cumberland* and *Congress.* Driving the *Minnesota* ashore. Over two hundred men dead or missing. A monster's on the lose. A class of killer ship the world has never seen before. An ironclad ram.

Welles thinks of his wife Mary Jane, of her exceptional social and emotional acumen. Remembers what she always tells him to do in times of crisis. It may be the only way to help himself, to help Lincoln. *Deep breaths, Gideon. Still your body, calm your mind. Say nothing. Take stock. Watch. Listen. No matter what, do not speak until you can offer comfort.*

He does not flinch, scowl, arch an eyebrow, fiddle with his gigantic beard. He absorbs the dirty looks, the manic gestures of Stanton as the man blathers about impending doom.

"I must call McClellan back from his Peninsular Campaign or the Reb's Joe Johnston, with his Army of Northern Virginia and that infernal new ship, will have him cut off. Burnside will be overrun. And then ..."

Lincoln presses his massive hands over his ears. "Will you stop that noise, Edwin, and let us think? Let *me* think on this latest incarnation of mechanized madness."

Stanton pauses in the middle of the room, seems to shoot a quick wink, possibly some kind of signal to Bill Seward. Why? "This is no joke, Mr. President. Good people have died, are dying."

Lincoln drops into the chair at his desk. His cheeks are pale, even more sunken than usual. His eyes turn toward the window again, looking over the dark Potomac to the leafless woods of Virginia beyond.

"Willie," he says.

Stanton pretends not to hear, continues his bluster. "I must get off telegrams to Philadelphia, New York and Boston. Must have our people there start blocking their channels with logs, ships loaded with stone and anything they can sink to stop this Confederate ram before ..."

The president turns to Welles, tears in his eyes. "It is hard, hard, hard. My wife is paralyzed with grief."

The Secretary of the Navy braces himself, fights back his own tears. He and his wife had been at the side of the president and Mrs. Lincoln for brave little Willie's last hours. He had heard how Willie asked that his gold coins be given to the poor when he was gone.

Deep breaths. Still your body, calm your mind. Listen. Watch.

"How? How can these terrible trials keep descending on us like ..." the president searches his mind, "... like a plague of locusts?"

Welles sees an odd look pass between Seward and Stanton. He is usually a good reader of men, but this look baffles him. Is it simply impatience ... or is it conspiratorial? Are these men enjoying the president's misery? Could they be the scoundrels behind those threatening letters tossed in his carriage? They are insensitive bastards, sure.

Lincoln puts his elbows on his desk, holds his head in his hands. "Have I angered the Almighty? Shall I drown us all amid a sea of troubles? I wish Allen were here."

Stanton drops onto the sofa, looks at Lincoln as if he has gone round some treacherous bend in his mind, becoming thoroughly unhinged.

Welles feels the president looking at him. All of their eyes on him. He breathes deep. Takes stock. Breathes deep again. Sees.

Lincoln is not just a man torn open by the death of a son. Not when he brings up his spymaster Allen. He's a man wrestling in some dark corner of his mind with old fears. And he's sick, tired.

The Secretary of the Navy knows the litany. *Sick and tired of worrying that the blockade will fail. Sick and tired of do-nothing generals. Sick and tired of a Washington cabal that is selling Welles, the navy, the Union out to Jeff Davis.*

"Don't worry, Mr. President," Welles stretches for a note of comfort in his voice. "I will talk to Major Allen ... and Ericsson's ironclad, the *Monitor*, finally arrived last night at Hampton Roads from Brooklyn."

"That two-gun cheese box on a raft?" Stanton howls.

"It is hell afloat." Welles prays silently that what he is about to say will be so. "That cheese box will stop the *Virginia* before she goes after the rest of our fleet in the southern Chesapeake. Maybe as soon as today."

Lincoln jerks, raises his head, a man coming out of a trance. He smiles a little at Welles. "Neptune rises. He speaks!"

"The navy will not fail you. Trust me, sir."

For some seconds his words hang in the office's smoky air.

"You mean the navy may not fail us in the Chesapeake, may not fail us now. Today," Seward says.

The president scowls. "I don't understand."

"Just this." Seward rises to his feet, another furtive, ambiguous glance passes between him and Stanton. He says that he has received a dispatch from England. Dudley, the consul in Liverpool, fears he has not the means to stop the English from turning over a powerful new gunship called the *Oreto* to the Rebs. He has reason to believe that a second gunship is also near completion.

"One of these ships may well be going to our old friend Raphael Semmes," says Seward.

Lincoln shoots a hard look at Welles. "I thought we had that pirate penned up at Gibraltar."

Deep breath again, Gideon.

"I don't see how he could possibly escape."

11

RICHMOND, VIRGINIA
March 10–11, 1862

"Look at them. They think life is nothing but a snowball fight." Maude's voice sounds bitter.

Her students, the oldest ones—the fourteen and fifteen-year-olds—are romping street-side during their luncheon break in front of their little school on Linden Square. The academy for young ladies that Virgina Pegram and her daughter Mary keep in their town house here on Franklin Street. The school is bursting with new arrivals, with the daughters of merchant and professional families just moving to this wartime boomtown. The school where Maude and Fiona have found jobs. Maude teaching literature and Latin; Fiona, math and history.

"Can't you let them have their fun?" Fiona watches the girls tossing snowballs back and forth with a platoon of youthful recruits filing down the street in their long gray coats.

"They're flirting."

"Where's the harm in it?"

"I look at them," Maude takes a deep breath, "and I see a field of children lying dead in the snow."

Fiona takes her friend's hand. "Lass, what's got into you today?"

"I'm sick, just sick of this war. Sick of people pretending it is all just a game."

"These people are fighting for nothing less than their freedom from the tyranny of the North. It's intoxicating. Would that the Irish could rise up against old John Bull like this."

"Nothing but death will come of it." She drops Fiona's hand, steps away from her, kicks a mound of snow with her boot. The wet, fresh snow scatters without a sound.

"Is there something you are not telling me? Have you heard from Semmes?"

"No ... and no." Her voice is nearly a whisper.

What else can I say? I cannot put my shame aside and speak. Cannot say that the French lunar pills you got for me a week ago are still not working. Cannot admit that it has been more than six weeks since I last bled. Cannot say that I still have not told Jean Claude.

And there are other things. She cannot say she knows that even if this Frenchman accepts the coming of a child, there is another man—if he is still alive—who will likely not abide it. Not ever. At least, not in his heart. She cannot tell the secret that Raffy confessed to her. Cannot tell Fiona that while he was away in the Mexican War his wife Anne became pregnant to another man, bore a daughter named Anna. As sure as she knows her own torn heart, she knows that her captain has never truly made peace with his wife. Now what if he is to be cuckolded twice, how could he stand it? How could he ever forgive her? Better that he never comes home from the sea. Maybe better that she die, or commit her soul to immortal damnation ... than bring another bastard child into this violent world.

"I think I need to talk to a priest," she says at last. "And a midwife."

⚓   ⚓   ⚓

Maude's nuzzling with a chestnut colt, his head poking out above the gate to his stall, nibbling sugar cubes from her hand. The horse barn on this Appomattox River plantation is a long, whitewashed affair, bigger than the line of slave cabins. Heavy with the scents of straw, hay, manure.

"Are you sure you want to do this, lassie?" Fiona's voice sounds shaky.

Maude presses her forehead to the colt's, rubs his neck, says nothing. Her eyes watch the blossom of the colt's breath in the cold air each time he exhales. It's a gray afternoon, and the long ride out here into the countryside, over frozen, rutted roads, has left her with a queasy stomach, exhausted. Now she just wants to put this day behind her, wishes the plantation's Negro midwife were not so slow in boiling her flushing potion of tansy, black hellebore, juniper, malt. Wishes Varina were here too.

She promised she would come. But when?

She thinks about what the priest told her, that to go through with what she's planning here with Mammy Ray is a mortal sin. Nothing less than killing. But to bear the child seems a massacre—of a child, a man, a woman, a love.

"Do you think we could go back inside the house now?" Maude asks. "I want to get on with this ... and I would really like a glass of whiskey."

⚓   ⚓   ⚓

This is such a strange place, she thinks, *to conclude my savage choice.*

She has never been in a house this grand, not even the executive mansion where Varina lives, or Rose Greenhow's town house in Washington. This mammoth brick house with its steep roofs and gables, its three floors. It overlooks the half-frozen river like a laird's manor in the old country. The place belongs to long-time friends of Varina's family. Old gentry, free thinkers. With a matriarch known to have come to the aid of many of society's finest women. The slave midwife here, the legendary Mammy Ray, has been described to Maude as the best in all of Virginia. A bush medicine gal, known for her curative powers, her discretion. For twenty-five dollars she can rid a young miss or missus of the female blues. At least, if she is not more than three months along.

This afternoon the house has a lonely emptiness. The air outside feels like snow again. The fires are low in the hearths, the house a maze of shadows. The matriarch, all the house servants except Mammy Ray, are mysteriously absent from this place called Magnolia Ridge. And Varina's not here yet, either. Maude and Fiona have the mansion all to themselves. They are in the music room, still waiting for a call from Mammy Ray, waiting for Varina. Sipping Kentucky bourbon from crystal tumblers, seated on the bench before the new Steinway. Fiona trying to work her way through Beethoven's "Piano Concerto in G Major."

Just as Fiona gets stuck on a passage, just as she stumbles, re-starts, stumbles on the same eight notes for the fifth time. Just as Maude feels a scream for mercy rising in her chest. Just as she's slugging down a huge gulp of bourbon ... a tiny black woman appears in the doorway.

Crying.

Now what?

"Miss Varina here now ... and I be ready for you now, Missy," says Mammy Ray. "Healing bed all fix."

"But you're crying," says Maude.

The old woman wipes her eyes. "Miss Varina bring us some sad news. But don't you worry. I gone cure you of the female problems."

"What news?" Fiona asks.

Mammy Ray tries to speak, chokes. Tears are running down her sunken cheeks. "He done died."

"Who died?"

"Mister Lincoln's boy." Varina Davis sweeps into the room from the kitchen, pulling the winter bonnet from her head, her cheeks pink from the cold carriage ride. She wraps Maude in a hug, tells her she's so sorry she's late. The executive mansion was astir with news. She couldn't leave until she had overheard it all.

"Abraham Lincoln's son is dead?" Fiona asks.

"Willie."

Mammy Ray starts to weep again, says please forgive her. She's only a poor old woman, and this is a hard thing. A boy called to the Lord. Just eleven years old, consumed by fever.

"The sins of the father are visited on the son," says Fiona. There is a righteous note in her voice that grates beneath Maude's ribs.

"I do not believe the Lord meant that our children suffer for us," says Varina. Perhaps she is thinking of her own Willie.

The black woman presses tears from the corners of her eyes with the palms of her hands. "It a hard thing, sure, for a mother to bury her child. I know that."

Maude pictures children dead in the snow. Gray, frozen little eyes, lips. Pictures mothers tearing their breasts. Feels a chill shudder through her body. Something wraps itself around her heart. Squeezes.

"I have to go," she says.

"You're committed to this child?" asked Fiona.

"My heart won't let me do otherwise. My mind is settled."

"Then I should tell you," says Varina. "There was other news come to the mansion today besides the death of that poor little boy."

Maude feels her back stiffen.

"I heard Secretary of the Navy Mallory tell my husband that Raphael Semmes is alive and well. He's in Gibraltar. Then I heard the secretary say these next few weeks would be a good time for an attack."

12

LIVERPOOL, ENGLAND
March 21, 1862

"The slut aims to hike up her dress and run tomorrow if we don't stop her," says the detective Maguire. He holds out his hand, wants payment for the information.

Dudley grits his teeth, hands him five bob. It's yet another rendezvous with spies in a smoky little pub on Hackins Hey in Merseyside. Another night disguised as a west Irish ship caulker—the overalls, wool jacket, specks of sawdust, scarf. Tweed cap in one hand, pint of bitters in the other.

"*Oreto*'s leaving? You're sure?"

"On my word, mate."

"I thought your informer at Fraser said the ship was waiting for Captain Semmes."

"They can't wait. They know we're onto them."

Dudley says that he just got a note from Lord Russell saying he's looking into the matter, plans for customs agents to inspect the ship yet again. Dudley gets the feeling Russell sees the illegality of building even a bare hull for the Confederates, but ...

"Stalling is what the foreign minister is doing, Thomas."

The detective-agent sips from his pint. Says that an English captain named James Duguid's taking the unarmed gunship to sea tomorrow. An all English crew. Even putting a few ladies aboard for show. Everything on the up-and-up, so to speak. No obvious infringement of England's Foreign Enlistment Act. Duguid has filed papers with customs, claiming he's delivering the ship to Polermo, Italy. But it's all a dodge. Rifled cannons, shells, powder, rifles, sundry other weapons have been loaded aboard the steamer *Bahama*, which has already put to sea and will no doubt rendezvous with the *Oreto* at some remote location to transfer the arms and ship a crew of Rebel officers.

And that's not all. There's a fellow sailing on the ship named John Low. He's Scotch-English, but ... *but* he's been living in Savannah for the past few years, running a marine chandlery business. The man might easily be a Southern coast pilot or some kind of Confederate agent. Low has been seen of late around the docks and bumboats attending to the *Oreto* with James Bulloch.

"Bulloch's back?"

"Aye, the sneaky bugger."

"When?"

"Sometime in the last fortnight. Things was nearly stalled with the gunship until he come ashore again. Man has a talent for getting things done. His own way."

"I would much like to see my enemy at last."

"You need not look far." Maguire nods to his right. "Yonder he stands."

At the far end of the bar a group of four youngish men are clinking mugs, toasting, patting each other on the back, laughing. The Capulets. The clear leader of the group has the look of a mischief-maker. The dark whiskered cheeks and shaggy brown hair do little to hide the boyish bravura in that face with its twinkling eyes, smirking grin, proud, unshaven chin. The man may well be approaching forty years of age, but with that face, fit body dressed in the clothes of an ordinary seaman, Bulloch looks at least ten years younger.

"He most surely puts me in mind of a buccaneer." Dudley tosses off the rest of his pint. "Do you think he has any idea that we are on to him?"

"Mark how he looks at us now."

Bulloch has been watching Maguire and Dudley over his glass. Now that he has eye contact he says something to his mates. They all turn to look at the Federals, raise their mugs in toast. Nod their heads and smile wickedly.

"I must intervene with Lord Russell and Lord Palmerton to stop the ship."

"It would be faster and easier to wreck her."

Dudley feels something sinking in his bowels; his morals, most like. He fears that his reliance on the law will no longer serve his needs.

"Can it be done without violence?"

⚓   ⚓   ⚓

It's foggy, sneaky cold. Two in the morning. They are loading a rowing skiff with chain and cable at the Bramley More Dock at the foot of Boundary Street. Dudley, Maguire, the spy known as Federal, two men Dudley doesn't know, and a woman—a doxie girl named Lorraine who joined Maguire's crew as an informer six weeks ago and has shown an aptitude for the spy game. Maguire's plan is to sneak up on the *Oreto* tonight as she lies at a dock in Toxteth.

The tidal range here is almost twenty feet. It's nearly low tide right now, but rising. With the tide like this, exposing the rough stone face of the wharf, Maguire thinks his gang can slip up under the *Oreto's* stern in the skiff. Then wrap their cables and chain around the *Oreto's* rudder and her propeller, shackle and tie the whole mess together. Maybe they can even secure their snare to the shore by threading chain and cable through the crevasses between and around the rocks in the dock. Any attempt to leave the dock, engage the propeller or steer the boat will twist or break the ship's rudder ... if not her propeller shaft. She'll need several weeks, maybe a month, in a dry dock for repairs.

Dudley's in the skiff, guiding a shot of half-inch chain that one of Maguire's boys is lowering to him into a neat pile. He's just preparing to flake down another two yards of chain when he hears Lorraine.

"Jesus bloody Christ. The Capulets!"

From somewhere ashore comes a shout, then the crack of a gunshot. The man feeding him the chain, just a shadow really, buckles.

Falls to his knees. Groans. Drops the chain. It comes streaming down into the little boat with a loud rush of iron slipping over rock, crashing against more iron. The boat shudders, rolls abruptly. It's starting to ship water as Dudley loses his balance, tumbles backwards into the black Mersey.

The weight of his clothes drags so hard on him he is gasping for breath when he surfaces, cold crushing his chest. Maguire and Federal are in the river beside him and the swamped skiff. They must have jumped when he was underwater.

"Jump." Maguire is shouting up at the doxie, standing on the edge of quay. "Goddamn jump, Lorraine."

She's dressed like a man. Wool jacket, cap. "I can't swim."

A gun fires.

She begins slapping at her right thigh as if stung by a bee.

"Jesus, jump."

Dudley kicks off his shoes, peels out of his coat. Sees the woman's stricken face staring down at him in terror.

Another gunshot. Louder. Closer by. It makes a strange, hollow echo, rattling back and forth between the facing walls of the docks.

Lorraine's jaw drops. She falls, cart-wheeling before she hits the water face-first with a slap.

By the time Dudley reaches her, she has already slipped so far beneath the water he can barely reach her with his down-stretched arm and still keep his head above water.

She feels like nothing more than an armload of laundry as he brings her to the surface. Form without substance.

Up on the dock eight or ten men, some holding pistols, look down.

"Next time y'all be dead, Dudley."

13

———✦✦✦———

GIBRALTAR
Early April, 1862

Evening in the olive grove. The captain of the *Sumter* high up on the side of the Rock again. Watching the selkie climbing toward him up the path. Long, slow strides. Copper curls catching the hot air, trailing off her neck. The white linen dress blowing in the breeze.

The sun's just minutes from slipping over the horizon. The town below already settling into a haze of purple shadows. Tiers of puffy cumulus to the west, and high cirrus—he sees that a patch of blustery weather is coming. Rain. But right now the sun's lighting the nether regions of the clouds with tones of gold, crimson tending to purple.

"I've been worried that you could not come, that you had been followed." His voice aches in his throat.

Maybe from the dust, maybe from the orange and olive pollens in the air. Maybe because he knows the likely end of things approach. The end of these meetings with Nessa, which he has so much savored. And the end of the *Sumter*.

"Not even God knows I'm here." She's close enough now for him to smell the roses in her perfume, close enough for him to see the stain of tears on her cheeks.

"What's the matter?"

"Just hold me." She leans into him.

He wraps his arms around her, feels her chest quivering against his own. Feels her eyes looking up at him, asking for the kiss he has so far been able to avoid. Not because he feels nothing for her. But because he knows that his loneliness and desire do not trump the unspeakable longing he feels for Maude, the respect he has for Anne and his children. Because he knows this gallant young woman deserves more than a few stolen moments with an old sea dog. Because she has a perfection of which he would rather stand in awe than sully.

"I read the telegram. I'm sorry." She's still holding on, her cheek on his chest. The Rock, the olive leaves, the sea, the clouds—just moments ago golden—have turned a deep red.

"It's alright, Nessa. What's Mason say?"

Yesterday he wired the Confederate commissioner in London asking permission to lay up the *Sumter*. He sees no hope for her, penned in as she is with boilers gone all to hell, almost a third of the crew having deserted. He wants to pay off the rest of the crew and go to England with his officers. He's ready for the new ship, *Oreto*. He thinks he has a plan to sever the very aorta of Yankee commerce.

"Mr. Mason consents to your request. You must leave your ship and return to England. But ..." Her arms tighten around his back. "The *Oreto* has already sailed."

A blade strikes, twists somewhere behind his eyes. He can't help himself, he feels the need to hug her tighter.

"I'm sorry about your new ship," she says.

"I think there may be other ships."

"So do I."

"It just may be awhile. I could be on the beach, so to speak, for some time."

He detaches himself from the embrace, stares off to the west. The sky, the sea are now verging on a deep purple. Below in the harbor the *Sumter* and her nemesis the *Tuscarora* are nothing but shadows.

He feels her take his hand. Then, before he can so much as blink, she has her other hand behind his neck, is drawing him to her. Kissing him. A long, deeply rapturous kiss. One that part of him hopes will never end. A kiss beyond everything. A kiss offering him a life of sumptuous ease. A dream.

"I could go to England with you," she says at last.

"Please don't say that."

"Why?"

"It's not possible ... I have my duty."

She spins away from him.

"Fuck you!"

$ $ $

The girl, Nessa, is still stalking his mind when the mid-watch begins. There's no moon, just a quilt of stars overhead. The lights of shore all but extinguished now. A freshening breeze coming in off the Atlantic. *Sumter* tugs at her anchor in the mounting harbor swell, as if to call him to yet one more adventure. It has been months since he has climbed to the hounds, felt there the illusion of flight. Now he swings up on the rail at the starboard foremast shrouds, finds the ratlines, climbs. Climbs with the hope that he might leave below the sweet taste of a woman's lips, the rank scent of guilt that seeps from his pores.

Once again he's running. Running from a woman who wants nothing more than to shower him with peace and plenty. Running from a little ship that has given up her very soul for him. She has run him safely through two vigilant blockades, has weathered crushing storms. Has rolled him to sleep in the tropic loins of the sea. For the last six months she has been his bedroom, study, court of law, promenade, field of glory. Together they have captured eighteen enemy ships, quadrupled insurance and shipping rates for American vessels. Caused panic on both sides of the Atlantic, from Boston to Brazil, Calais to Gibraltar. Made Raphael Semmes and the *Sumter* household names wherever people read newspapers. Gained credence for the cause of Southern freedom. He and this exceptional little sea boat ... once as active and dry as a duck.

But now she's worn by hard use and age, like him. They are, he thinks, *hors de combat.* The war has passed them by.

He must let her go, post a midshipman as her keeper, be gone. To England. And who knows where else? Home? Dixie? Or into the fight again?

He grabs the futtock ropes, swings himself up on the foretop. Thinks about home. He can hardly imagine it without his two boys, who have both gone off with the army. Can no longer picture his daughters or even Anne. Can only remember how he describes her as his "stately handsome girl." But at forty-two, she is no girl.

Most merciful God, they have become but names to me, faint memories. And likely I to them ... to Maude too.

She too is no longer the girl she once was. Twenty-eight now, if he reckons right. In her prime. But no longer the girl outside the Smithsonian castle on that spring day in 1858. No longer that vision of budding innocence so like Nessa now. He had sliced a sprig of apple blossoms from a tree with his saber, presented them to Maude with a courtly bow. *Lady, may these blossoms bring your eyes some small measure of the pleasure that gazing upon you has brought to mine on this noontime in May.* Later he bought her ice cream, made with the first strawberries of the season, before she returned to her pupils at the little school on Capitol Hill. It was not long before she let him buy her dinner. Not long before he fell in love. Not long before she took his hand one evening and led him to her bed in that drafty boarding house on H Street.

Suddenly he slashes at the mast with his hand, curses himself for falling into this sailors' trap. These memories of hearth, home, love. These things that stall and rot a man with duties, rot a warrior.

"What an ass am I," he nearly shouts, finding Shakespeare on his tongue. Finding Hamlet. "Must I, like a whore, unpack my heart ...?"

"Who goes there?" A shout up from the deck.

"Kell?"

"Aye. May I join you, sir?"

He tells the luff to come ahead. When Kell has scrambled up onto the foretop, Semmes confesses, his voice a bourbon-soft drawl. He couldn't sleep. Needed a bit of exercise, needed fresh air.

"We'll be leaving the ship, won't we, sir?"

"A matter of days."

"I've been dreaming of home."

"Do you think any of it is still there?"

14

RICHMOND, VIRGINIA

Early April, 1862

She wakes with a start. The *su-weet, su-weet* of larks, the warmth of sunshine. The scent of wet earth, daffodils filtering through the open window of the town house on Linden Square. Wakes to the pressure of a man's arm curling around her torso from behind. His hand spreading over her breast, pulling her toward him. Feels something insistent in the way his muscles tighten against her. Knows what he wants.

Her eyes are still closed, her mind still half-submerged in a dream. She's imagining tending her mother's sheep outside the cottage on Tralee Bay in the old country. Imagining freeing a lamb caught in a thicket of brambles when she feels Jean Claude, smells his hot breath still heavy with brandy from last night.

Dry lips on her neck.

"*Amour.*" His voice is a low whisper, the hand that's not on her breast slides down over her hip, tugs gently at her *peignoir*. Searches for bare skin.

He speaks to her in French. She does not understand it all, but she hears the ache in his words. Knows the note of worry in his voice. Maybe he's asking why of late she has begged off to sleep each night with only a cursory kiss, with none of her old tenderness. Maybe he wonders if there's someone else eating her heart besides the ghost of the Confederate captain she carries with her. Maybe he's wondering why she would leave him so unsatisfied for so long? Or maybe he's bothered by something else entirely. Maybe he just wants to love his way out of his fears.

Cold fingers against her inner thigh, warming.

What can she say? That for the last two months she has been carrying his child against her will? That her mind denies the child's right to steal her from her old life, drive a bloody wedge between her and Raffy? But that half of her heart is already knitting infant clothes, already imaging those perfect tiny fingers like those of Varina's babe? Can she tell him that only her belly and breasts are growing now, that her arms and legs shrink daily? From worry, from her inability to eat little more than corn bread and peach jam? Can she say she doesn't love him? Needs to flee his arms, his bed, his house before he discovers her shame? Before he vows to marry her ... and tells the world they are having a baby?

She can't say that she writes to Raffy daily. That in her letters she pretends her life here in Richmond with Varina and Fiona, teaching, is all bloody warm and cozy. Can't say she sends off letters to her captain courtesy of a man named Mason in London. Can't say she would give her life to see Raffy ... if only one more time.

Fingers brushing back the hair from her cheek.

There's no chance she can say these things. The woman warrior she once was has all but disappeared from beneath her skin. Her waking hours have become nothing but a trial of fear, uncertainty. Emotions she cannot quell even when she throws herself into her teaching at the Pegram's school across the street.

Fingers tracing the edges of her eyebrows, nose, lips.

"You are so beautiful," he says.

She keeps her eyes closed, keeps still. Feels him draws back his face to look at her.

A hand tightening on her breast again.

She lets him roll her into his chest. What else can she do?

She pictures an afternoon in the District when she made love to Raffy. His broad back, the cords of muscle in his hips. How she loved to look at him, feel him against her. How the image of her lover as a Roman warrior popped full-blown into her mind and she called him her gladiator. How she bunched the top sheet into the warm wetness between her legs as if that could stop the aching in her throat or bridle her desire.

Lips against lips.

"*Je t'aime.*"

Chest against chest.

His weight, his quivering, hard muscles, settling onto her, into her. She feels something slipping away.

"Hold me." She knows she's calling to a different man, even as she wraps her arms around his shoulders, his neck. Cups the back of his long hair. Drinks his tongue from his mouth.

And as she drinks in her French lover, as she sinks into memory, she feels a kind of loss of traction. Fire spreads in her loins. A wild hunger. A craving for death. A yearning to ride her terror and Raphael Semmes' steaming body all the way to oblivion. To glory. With her child ...

When it's over, he nuzzles her chest, says there's something he needs to tell her. He's worried about their safety. The Yankee's Army of the Potomac under General McClellan, more than 120,000 men, are pushing toward Richmond. Whole legions and naval fleets are surrounding the Confederacy, pressing closer to places like New Orleans, Mobile, Charleston. With the onset of spring, there will be fighting like the world has rarely seen. Terrible, monumental battles have already begun. The Confederates are even now losing ground at Yorktown. Has she not yet seen the wagons of wounded trailing into Richmond? And just yesterday there came news of a two-day battle along the Tennessee River at a place called Shiloh. More than 20,000 men wounded or killed. Imagine. The South is not safe. Richmond is no longer a sanctuary.

They must leave for France before it's too late. Leave this very day. But will she marry him before they go?

She feels eels rising in her gorge. She almost says she needs to bloody find Fiona and Varina. Needs them to rescue her from this latest nightmare. Needs to run. Needs her Raffy. But what she says is, "I think I need to see a doctor first ... I'm going to have a baby."

15

DISTRICT OF COLUMBIA
April 25, 1862

Welles should be happy. Very happy. This is a day of triumph. Today, newspapers smuggled in from Richmond are announcing that David Farragut's fleet has broken through the Rebel defenses on the Mississippi River at last and seized New Orleans. The South's most important seaport is no more. The navy vindicated. When he gave Lincoln the news an hour ago, the man smiled for the first time since before Willie died. The president actually grabbed his hands and waltzed him once around the office, whistling "Camptown Races."

But now as he rides south toward the Naval Observatory in Foggy Bottom— despite the fresh, spring afternoon—he feels sweaty, feverish. Rotten. His lungs moldering with every breath he takes. Something foul is infecting him, and the man sitting across from him in the hack isn't helping. Washington's head rat and rat trapper, E. J. Allen. Pinkerton. Welles hates that he's even a little dependent on the fellow. The slit-eyed little Scot stinks of boiled cabbage, corned beef.

"It's the letters." The secretary says, staring out the window at an encampment of recruits, probably just off a train from Ohio or Maine. "The threats. They've started again."

"I feared this is why you sent the cab for me. Just two days ago I received strange news regarding your troubles."

Allen says that his informants in Virginia have been busy spying on Reb troop movements in the tidewater region of Virginia. He's got an old black gal, maid at a school for young ladies, who's keeping track of Richmond's gentry. Word has it that Raphael Semmes' ruddy moll has up and vanished again, just flat out left her Frenchy baron. Two rumors in this regard: One is that the wench Maude Galway has gone off to a backwater plantation to calve a bastard child. The other story claims that none other than the First Lady of the Confederacy herself has helped Semmes' harlot find dark employment with the Reb government.

"Do you think I still care about that woman?"

Allen looks at the Secretary of the Navy as he might stare at a chicken stuffed in a bottle. "Did she not hound you to distraction with a tintype of you kissing the Greenhow woman? Did she not threaten to destroy your career and your marriage until you enlisted me to put an end to her little reign of terror?"

"She may have been only the agent, not the demon, of my woes."

"Did she not put a knife in me and thrash me with a horseshoe late last November?"

"But she wasn't here when the threats began for me again."

"Perhaps ... still, her black-eyed girlfriend, the school teacher called Fiona, could have started in with the new threats."

"Major, I think such women are beside the point."

The Scot shakes his head in dismay. "Knowing how men dismiss women is exactly the recipe Greenhow's bunch used to gain access to our secrets and do us real damage. They smuggled out the Federal battle plans for Bull Run to the Rebs, you know? Good boys died."

Welles says that there are more dangerous forces at work in Washington than a few love-struck women playing at spy games. Says that he and the president both believe there may be one or more traitors in the government. Maybe even the cabinet.

"And you know it."

"I know no such thing. I have watched. I have detailed a half-dozen agents on this fantasy of yours."

"Good."

"They have nothing of interest to report beyond the usual gambling and drinking of your cronies."

"You must be missing something."

Allen rolls his eyes. "That's not in my nature. I really don't care how you and the secretaries have squandered your time, money and health. It's a waste of my precious resources to document such venal goings on."

"But ..."

"But this—only this, Mr. Secretary—you would do well to keep your feet on the ground. Avoid the soiled doves of this city. Set your mind on catching pirates like Raphael Semmes. Leave worries about a conspiracy to me."

Welles rubs his eyes with the palms of his hands, groans. "You are impossible."

The detective growls. "Take me back to my office. My agents and I have a war to stop."

"Can I just show you one thing?"

⚓   ⚓   ⚓

"This is it?" The chief rat kicks a piece of dried mule dung off the towpath and into the C&O Canal. "You brought me here to see a man of straw, a scarecrow?"

"Two," says Welles. He nods upward to a second stuffed figure hanging from a rope ten feet above the one propped against the base of a tree.

He and Allen are standing in a grove of oaks spanning the narrow spit of land between the canal and the Potomac. They are just fifty yards west of the new Naval Observatory on Camp Hill, the site of the American Meridian from which the survey lines of Western territories derive. Just fifty yards from the domed telescope building where a Negro courier left a sealed letter for the Secretary of the Navy yesterday.

"Red again, eh?" Allen waves a crimson envelope.

"Just like the last five."

"I don't see the connection between the note and these scarecrows."

The detective glances back and forth between the two men of straw. Both figures wear black suits, have gunny sacks for heads, painted faces. Immense, sad clown dolls. The one propped against the tree wears a flowing wig and a massive beard, both made of gray wool. It's a cartoonish version of Welles. The one hanging in the tree wears a stovepipe hat. Its black eyes blank. The mouth drawn as a large "O," a scream.

"I think you better look at what it says."

Allen withdraws a single sheet of dark red paper from the envelope, reads aloud, eyes growing larger with each word. "He will swing high in your own back yard, Neptune ... unless you leave the navy to the navy."

Silence for several seconds, except for the fretting of robins plucking worms from the soft earth.

"I don't like the looks of this."

"One of the marine guards spied the effigies on his way to work this morning, and asked that I come over here to the observatory. That's when I got the letter."

"What do you think that phrase means, 'leave the navy to the navy?'"

"Some people see me as an outsider in the department."

"Disgruntled officers?"

"A few senior admirals who know I'm planning to bring a bill to Congress asking for money to retire them."

"You think they are so disloyal as to write these treasonous words, to threaten the president's life?"

"I don't know."

"I need to find out if any of them buy this kind of red stationery."

"I'd have a look at the Cabinet members. Especially Seward and Stanton."

"Semmes' tart and her girlfriend, as well."

"I don't think this is the work of tarts."

"Who put the bite on you last time?"

16

LONDON, ENGLAND
Early May, 1862

Dudley closes the door of the hotel room in Mayfair and blows a deep breath as he looks at the woman posing before him. Lorraine's looking quite good. A lot better than when he last saw her, to be sure. Especially fine, considering that the doxie was a sputtering, bleeding sack of freezing laundry the last time he laid eyes on her. Barely alive when they fished her out of the river, pounded on her sternum to revive her, bound her wounds with her own soaking shirt.

An astonishing recovery, most certain. She, like him, had contracted a miserable grippe after the midnight swim in the Mersey. But he had not suffered a gunshot. She had two: one just grazed her left thigh, the other went clean through her right shoulder. Yet now she's back for more. In a silver gown of brushed silk, its high neck hiding the red scar tissue of the wound. She reminds him of the singer Jenny Lind when he saw her in *Sonnambula*. Except that Lorraine's hair is longer, a rich blond, twisted, piled, pinned on her head in a most becoming way. A Hackins Hey public Betty turned St. James princess. And tonight she's going to a ball.

"Are you sure you're up to this?"

Lorraine cocks her head at him, pure coquette. Winks. "As long as you pay me my three quid ... and the man can dance."

She's not talking about her escort, another Federal agent. A debonair London banker who plays the role of a Southern sympathizer for his weekly inducement. She's talking about the man the papers have been calling the Southern Seahawk since he arrived in England a fortnight ago. The famous sea captain come to town with his first lieutenant Kell, and ship's doctor Galt. Raphael Semmes.

Dudley and Maquire have spent over thirty pounds to costume, cast and buy Lorraine's way into this dance at the French Embassy. But the cost is nothing if Lorraine can work her magic. If she can get close enough to Semmes to find out what the man's up to. Word from Gibraltar and the Secretary of the Navy says that the pirate has a thing for young women. And Maguire's informers claim that James Bulloch came down from Liverpool just a few days hence to meet with Semmes. The gunship, called simply the *290*, is just days from launching at the Laird yard in Birkenhead. What if Semmes has come to take her to sea?

"Here's a little something for luck." He takes her right hand in his, bends, kisses it. Slips a little silver friendship band on the ring finger of her right hand. It's something he picked up on a whim from a vendor on the Mall.

"How do I smell, Thomas?" Lorraine holds onto his hand, shoots him a come-hither look.

"Like strawberries and honey."

⚓   ⚓   ⚓

It's after ten o'clock and Lorraine has not even talked to Semmes. The man has been constantly surrounded by admirers. Many regal ladies. Meanwhile, Dudley and Maguire, dressed as waiters, have been watching from an alcove near the service kitchen. Backs to the wall, bodies at attention, silver serving platters held across their chests like shields. Human statues.

"This is going nowhere, Matthew." Dudley feels his legs aching from the standing.

"Just hold onto your breeches, mate. And make like part of the bloody woodwork. Men are the doxie's specialty."

⚓   ⚓   ⚓

Another half an hour passes before she seizes her chance at the punch bowl. She follows Semmes there, asks him to refill her glass of champagne, brandy, dash of bitters, a cube of sugar.

The pirate's looking rakish. Clearly James Mason has treated the seahawk to a new uniform from a top-shelf London tailor. The gray, double-breasted coat, with its dazzling golden buttons and epaulettes, fits Semmes like a glove, highlights his trim torso. The deep tan of his face contrasts with the silver of the impossibly broad mustache. His hair, just slightly streaked with gray, is unusually dark and full for a man in his fifties. Truth is, Dudley thinks Semmes looks forty, younger than the Liverpool consul himself. Damn dashing.

And none of this is lost on Lorraine. Her eyes soften to a dewy glaze after the seahawk returns her glass, smiles full into her face, bows in a most courtly fashion, his heels clicking together. She looks dumbstruck, mouth gaping open.

Jesus. She's going to lose it. Dudley's starting to wonder why he ever signed on for this caper.

"Watch this," says Maguire.

It's as if a curtain suddenly draws back from Lorraine's face. She finds her smile, seems to rise inches taller, her shoulders arching back. Then she leans toward Semmes, pressing a breast against his upper arm. Says something confidential close to his ear. Puts her hand on his wrist ever so briefly as she speaks.

Suddenly, he's laughing, holding her at arm's length in both hands and beaming at her like a schoolboy. He's offering her his arm. Leading her toward the dance floor beneath the crystal chandelier.

Dudley leans toward Maguire, sighs. "Contact."

"That's me girl!"

⚓   ⚓   ⚓

It's after she has him talking to her nonstop. After she has him whirling her around the floor to the swish of her silk dress and the melody of violins. After she has him staring deep into her eyes. After she has moved closer to him, bit by bit, until his legs slide against hers with each new step. After her escort has come to stand just in front of Dudley and Maguire and nonchalantly sip his drink. During a waltz by Strauss called "Phenomena." This is when she stumbles, stops in the middle of the dance floor and bends down grabbing her right ankle as if she has just twisted it.

"That's it. That's her signal," says Maguire. "She wants out. Go."

Her escort, the courtly banker, hands Dudley his champagne glass, dashes to Lorraine.

⚓   ⚓   ⚓

A few minutes later the banker's escorting the limping Cinderella out the door to the carriage as Raphael Semmes watches from the embassy steps, a disappointed smile on his face, a hand raised in solemn goodbye.

What the seahawk doesn't see is that Dudley and Maguire are already waiting in the shadows of the conveyance.

"Well?" Dudley's voice is shaky with nerves and anticipation as she climbs into the cab.

"I need some bleeding whiskey, Duds."

Maguire passes her his flask. "What do you know?"

"What a charmer."

"Lorraine."

"Bloke's one hell of a dancer, you know?"

"Lorraine!"

"It's too bad."

"What?"

"He won't be dancing for long."

"He's going to take the *290* to sea?" Maguire asks.

She shakes her head no, slugs down another gulp of whiskey. "The man's booked on the *Melita* for Nassau in the Bahamas. Says he's heading home, says there are things in Dixie he needs to attend to."

"But he's a man of the sea. You believe him?" Now Dudley reaches for the whiskey.

"Without a doubt, Duds."

"He's not coming to Liverpool?"

She clears her voice, speaks quietly. "Man's carrying a torch for some Dixie dolly."

"How can you be so sure?"

She gives Maguire a look like he must be daft. "You know any other reason a sailor would turn down a free piece of pie?"

Dudley's suddenly wishing he were home, in bed, asleep beside his wife. In New Jersey, no less.

"So now where do we stand? The pirate king's abdicating for love. The future of the *290* remains a mystery. What do we do?"

Lorraine leans her head on his shoulder. "You still like the way I smell?"

17

NASSAU, BAHAMAS
June 13, 1862

Semmes feels his stomach tighten as the *Melita* eases her way down the channel toward Potter's Cay in Nassau Harbour, her canvas stowed, her stack spewing a gray haze of English anthracite. A harbor tug steaming in her lee. The crew flaking down lines for casting ashore. It's not yet mid-morning and he's already dreading the day.

He's about to be *on the beach*. A seaman without a ship. Possibly forever. A man whose mind can think of little but all that he has lost. And all that he desires, but fears seeing again. Dixie's just a twenty-four-hour sail away. Anne, the children. Maude.

But how will they know me? I am not the man who sailed away from them. He thinks on Tennyson's "Ulysses." Words from the poem wash through his heart, his soul. He knows the Greek's moods, his fears. Knows that sometimes a year gone to war and to sea can seem like Ulysses' twenty-two years away from hearth, family, loved ones.

Always roaming with a hungry heart.

He tosses the lukewarm coffee in his mug over the side, leans against the steamer's starboard bulwarks. Glares out at the newly sprouted boomtown that is Nassau.

"Exciting isn't it?" Kell's voice catches him off guard. "Being almost home."

He can't remember hearing Kell come up beside him. Wants to ask the luff if Dixie, too, will be so changed. Thinks better of it. Just nods. Exciting? Oh, yes. Most disturbing too.

The last time he was in Nassau, it was a backwater port lost in memories of its glory days as the capital of a pirate empire. The old wharves empty except for men and boys with fishing lines. A few coastwise packets of the Downeaster variety laying to the wharves or swinging at anchor. Conch smacks ghosting in from the eastern banks, the Exumas, Andros. Women in straw hats haggling over the price of grouper. Old men cleaning conch, throwing empty shells into piles. Shopkeepers along Bay Street closing their shuttered windows and doors until the shadows of late afternoon began to cool the town.

I am a part of all that I have met.

Now there are more than fifty ships here. Large steamers, mostly side-wheelers. A few screw boats as well. Full-rigged ships, barks, brigs. Dozens of schooners. He has not seen such a collection of Baltimore clippers since the closing of the slave markets in San Juan and Havana. Anyone who has been working on the water could see that the bulk of these vessels are Southern boats from the Chesapeake, Carolina, the Gulf Coast. But they now almost uniformly fly the Union Jack, hailed from places where they had never been, like Liverpool, Portsmouth, London. Everything these days, it seems, is masquerading as something else.

I sleep and feed and know not me.

The wharves are mounded over with cotton bales. Temporary warehouses rising all along the shore of the harbor between the wharves and Bay Street. Gigs and longboats creating a jam of traffic in the anchorage. Smacks circulating from ship to ship selling fish, chickens, goats, pigs, produce, rum. Passing out cards to proclaim the good times to be had in places with names like the Mermaid Tavern and the Silk Cotton Café. He can hear the jangle of harnesses and carriages, smell the sweet scent of horse dung blowing off Bay Street. The sounds of a *goombay* band filter in from a tavern or brothel that's already starting its daily party.

There gleams that untraveled world ...

"I must find our Confederate commissioner, Kell ... then a hotel," he says.

Kell suddenly snaps to attention, points to the wharf on Potter's Cay. "A woman yonder, waving at us. Is she someone you know?"

He squints at the shore, shades his hand against the sun. "Most merciful Christ!"

§　　§　　§

She really could be a selkie, he thinks, *appearing like this out of the blue.* His own Circe. The sweetest ambush.

He hails the first surrey he sees. Tells the driver to just go, head out of town. Holds her hands, barely speaks, just stares at those curls of copper hair, the light freckles across her nose, the moist emerald eyes. Until he has the surrey drop them at the east end of the island, past Fort Montagu. In a shady grove of fig trees by the edge of the sea. Only after the surrey has moved on does he see that the grove is an old cemetery with a small, random array of tombstones and a sarcophagus.

He leans against the moss-crusted limestone tomb, holds Maude tight to his chest, stares out at the vexed, dim sea. Suddenly he feels something catch in his throat. He's weeping. He tells her how he owes her his life. How her letter of warning that came to Martinique last November saved him and the *Sumter* from certain annihilation by Yankee warships. Says he has received a few of her letters via the South's commissioners in London. Still, he has tried to deny that this moment would ever come. Has told himself he would be a fool to imagine that she could still care for him. But he has never given up hoping—not for an hour—that somehow they would find each other again, would love. He has written to her every day.

She cries, too. Tells him about escaping to Richmond as he advised her in the last letter she received back in December. Tells him that none of his letters since have reached her. Tells him she, too, never gave up hope. She is now a courier for the South. Her friend Varina Davis having arranged for her to bring urgent correspondence to Nassau for Confederate agents here. She has traveled here with Lieutenant George T. Sinclair who at this very moment has orders for him from the Secretary of the Navy.

"To hell with Terry Sinclair," he says.

"What?"

"Run away with me." He hears a strange voice. A boy's voice, one he thought he lost sometime during the Mexican War, maybe when the *Somers* sunk beneath his feet. Maybe when he did not die with so many of his crew. "I have some money."

She kisses the tears from his cheeks. "Where would we go?"

"Anywhere. Could you fancy Brazil? I was there last year. I have a friend, Hernand, in a lovely little port called São Luís who ..."

Her fingers press his lips closed. "Make love to me."

"I must get a sheath."

She undoes his tie, bites his neck softly. "Not now. Not this time."

18

NASSAU, BAHAMA
June 15, 1862

She waits for her Raffy in the cottage she rented for them yester-day. It's a mile out of town on the Eastern Road, beyond the graveyard where they made love. Far from her official quarters at the Graycliff Inn, far from his own room at the Victoria Hotel. Far from those hosteleries full of Southern naval officers, agents, their families. All with prying eyes.

It's just one room, but it's clean, freshly painted in pinks and blues. Primitive watercolors of seashells hang on the wall. A fresh straw car-pet. The shuttered windows open to the cooling trade winds. Scents of acacia, bougainvillea drifting in. Lying in the double bed, wrapped in a light quilt, she can look out beyond the coral shore to the sea, its pale blue fading to air on the horizon.

Now with the growing shadows of late afternoon filling the room, she watches the hummingbirds darting among the blossoms outside the window. Watches the local smacks sailing back toward the har-bor, listens while the black fishermen strum banjos, sing wistful sea songs about homecomings. Wonders if she and Raffy could find a place like this in Brazil. A place to raise the baby she has not yet had the courage to tell him about. The baby she might not have to tell him about. At least not for awhile. By eating so little, she is still hardly showing her pregnancy. Maybe if she can delay the babe's coming a little, he will think it his child. *Holy Mary, Mother of God, blessed are thee, and blessed is the fruit of thy womb Jesus.*

⚓   ⚓   ⚓

Almost dark. The dinner, a calaloo stew of boiled grouper her elderly black landlady brought by, still sits in its pot on the little table. Cold, uneaten. The baby has been kicking, stretching in her belly for more than an hour. She has just pulled the shutters, just lit the citronella candles to drive off the mosquitoes. Just sat down on the edge of the bed when she hears the clopping of a horse on the coral road, the creaking of leather traces and wheels as a surrey comes to rest outside.

The moment her Raffy walks in the door, she knows he brings terrible news. His sun-burned face looks dusky, his mustache and shoulders droop. He tilts his head back on his neck, sighs. No longer the gladiator with the sinewy body of a Bantry Bay waterman. He's an old man. Her father stumbling home after too many hours at the pub. A defeated thing. Tortured. Spirit killed. Her father at the end of his life, when the bottle had him by the throat.

"You talked to Sinclair, didn't you? He gave you the orders."

He nods, says he's sorry. He owes it to his officers, Kell and Galt, who sailed here with him, to let them know their fates as dictated by the Department of the Navy. Kell, in particular has been so looking forward to getting home to his wife and children.

"And now he knows he's not," she says." None of you are to go home. There's more war for you, isn't there?"

He sits down on the bed next to her. Wraps her in both his arms. They feel frail, stiff. Sticks.

"You reek of whiskey."

"Sinclair and some of the others wanted to toast us."

"What happened to Brazil, Raffy?" She struggles out of his arms. Stands up, her back to him.

She can't believe she let herself even dream for a second about São Luís. She knew, more or less, that Sinclair carried orders that would drive yet another wedge between her and her sailor. But still she let herself imagine that Raffy might actually sweep her and the baby away to an Eden. She let herself believe his tears and the ardor of his love-making had the power to grow a whole new world for them, a new life.

"There's a ship called the *290*. I've been promoted from commander to captain. Ordered to go back to England to get her."

"Bully for you."

"I'm so sorry. I thought I could turn my back on the war ... but my country needs me. I've already written Secretary Mallory that ..."

"*I* need you!" She feels as if she's burning up, suffocating. Throws open the window shutters, the door. The trade winds rattle the room.

He tries to hug her from behind.

"Don't touch me."

"I have some weeks here, before I can get passage back to England. We still have ..."

She turns, both hands fists. Tells him he can wait for his bleeding passage alone. Then she swings on him, one hand after the other. Pummels him about the ears and mouth.

He does not even put up a guard. Just takes it, takes punches that make her knuckles and wrists ache ...

Until she is out of breath and sobbing. Dashing out into the moonlight, running over the jagged coral on the shore. Tripping. Falling. Her belly going into spasms.

⚓   ⚓   ⚓

Semmes is at her side. His physician Pills Galt eases her pain with a tincture of laudanum. The old black landlady is there, too, tending to Maude with cool compresses on her forehead, a tea of local herbs to strengthen her womb, staunch the blood leaking from between her legs.

Later, after she has told him about the baby growing in her, he walks silently beside her as she's carried on a cot aboard a schooner bound for the Savannah River. Her bleeding has not fully stopped. She has a fever. Keeping food down is difficult. Galt says she needs better medical attention than she can get here in the islands. She may yet require hospitalization, lose the baby, die from her hemorrhaging.

Just as Semmes is about to step ashore, she pulls him down to her on the cot. Embraces him, puts her forehead on his shoulder. Whispers. Does he want to ask her who fathered the child?

"I don't have the right," he says.

"You're giving up on us, aren't you?"

His eyes fill with tears, his voice shredding with each new word. "I do not think I could live even an hour without holding you in my heart."

The fire in her body cools just a bit. She kisses his ear, confesses the only truths she knows. If Nature permits, she will write to him every day, send her letters to Fraser, Trenholm & Co. He must promise to keep himself safe from harm. Above all, he must know that she will not stop hoping for another miracle to bring them back together. Selkies never do.

19

DISTRICT OF COLUMBIA
Mid July, 1862

How can this be? Yet another dead child.

Here in this carriage climbing the long hill out of Georgetown, heading for a child's funeral, Gideon Welles thinks the president looks as if he may tear his breast, throw himself into the dust and pray for deliverance.

"It's as if the Almighty has sent an army of avenging angels against America. As if we have angered God. As if the plague that smote the sons of Egypt has turned on this country with a vengeance." The president seems almost to be talking to himself as he stares out from beneath the canopy.

The brown pastures, the summer's leaves withering on the trees. The air brown with dust. The temperature over ninety-five degrees.

Today they are burying the infant child of Edwin Stanton and his wife. *But might well be all America*, thinks Welles, *my children. All our children.* He cannot shake a haunting tune from his mind. The lyrics of Julia Ward Howe, so recently published in the *Atlantic Monthly* echoing in his head. Words that are being sung around the soldiers' campfires. In the fo'castles of ships. Apocalyptic words. About the coming of the Lord. About fateful lightning. About a terrible swift sword ...

He's riding in the presidential carriage to the funeral with Lincoln, Secretary of State Seward and Seward's daughter-in-law. She weeps softly into her kerchief.

"I have about come to the conclusion that we must free the slaves."
Lincoln's voice is heavy, solemn.

"What?" Seward's head jerks awake. "What?"

Seward stares at the president, bug-eyed.

Welles feels the heat of the day descend on him, his skull beginning to percolate with sweat beneath his wig. Surprise is too soft a word to describe his reaction. Until this moment he has always heard Lincoln's prompt and emphatic denouncement of any interference by the federal government in the slavery question. The Cabinet has agreed that slavery is a local, domestic question for each state to decide. But now ...?

Lincoln stretches his arm outside the carriage, drums his fingers on the side panel. "I think it a military necessity, not to say a moral imperative, if we wish to save the Union. What say you, men?"

"The consequences are so vast, so momentous that ... that ..." Seward shakes his head in dismay. He cannot get his mind focused squarely on the idea.

Lincoln says that maybe Welles' blockade is working, slowly starving the South. God knows there have been some important naval victories of late. But the North is running out of energy, money, men to keep the land war going. During just the recent seven days of battle outside of Richmond, McClellan's army has suffered over fifteen thousand casualties and has retreated to the shores of the James River to lick its wounds. The Rebs have lost at least as many boys.

America is sacrificing its children at a horrible rate. Atlantic shipping is stifled by Semmes and those who follow in his wake. The country is going bankrupt. Meanwhile spies in Europe send dispatches with word of a squadron of new, deadly ships being built in England and France for the Confederacy. Major newspapers are calling for an end to the bloodshed and the devastation of international commerce. Baltimore is under marshal law. Protests against the war are breeding in the streets of New York.

"Tell me, Gideon. Would you free the slaves? Do you think it will help us stop this horrible bloodshed, the deaths of our children, of innocents?"

Welles pictures Willie Lincoln lying frozen in his coffin, pictures this new babe of Edwin Stanton's, too. Cold and gray. Pictures the carnage that may soon come if the Army of Virginia and McClellan's forces go toe-to-toe in earnest. He wonders how soon innocents will die at sea from attacks by Semmes and company. Wonders how long it will be before Raphael Semmes and his ilk develop a thirst for blood as insatiable as their lust for fire. Finally, he imagines the thousands of Negro slaves that Major Allen claims the South has forced to work as teamsters and laborers building Reb fortifications. Men he knows who bleed and die with each new Yankee offensive.

"We must study this more. But I think you have hit on something, Mr. President," says Seward. "We are losing our credence for carrying on this war. We need to show the people, show the world, that the government of the United States sees a higher purpose in all of this sacrifice. I think freeing the slaves would win us considerable favor with governments abroad."

"Gideon?"

He feels Lincoln watching him. Seward and the daughter-in-law, too. Feels the sweat now running down his cheeks, his neck. His chest cooking beneath his shirt, tie, jacket. If he could find the words, he would say that nothing is more important for this government to do. They cannot call themselves leaders at all if they do not now stand up for human dignity and the concept that all men are created equal and free. They must articulate a moral purpose for all this unnatural loss of life.

"Gideon?"

Something hot and dark bursts inside him. "Yes. I would do it. ... Yes, I would free the slaves. Yes, Mr. President."

Lincoln nods, gives a sad smile. "I hoped that was what you would say, old friend."

The president says he will begin to think on the drafting of an emancipation proclamation. But the country must have a victory on which to launch such a proclamation. The talented, aggressive Robert E. Lee has now taken over the Reb army in eastern Virginia. It does not look like George McClellan and his army on the James River will give the Union a victory any time soon.

"Can you give me something to crow about, Gideon? Do you think maybe your boys afloat could finally catch the pirate Semmes for us ... before he raises holy hell?"

"I have some men in mind for the job, sir."

Seward clears his throat as if he's skeptical ... or maybe jealous. Shoots the Secretary of the Navy a sharp look.

Welles feels something hot and sharp burn right through his left eye to the back of his head. Suddenly, he pictures threats in red envelopes, men of straw. *Figures in black suits, gunny sacks for heads, painted faces. The one hanging in the tree wears a stovepipe hat. Its black eyes blank. The mouth drawn as a large "O," a scream.*

"Just a word of caution, Mr. President," says Welles. "Freeing the slaves will bring packs of new enemies as well as friends. There may be plots."

"I do not fear for my own life, Gideon."

20

LIVERPOOL, ENGLAND
July 28, 1862

"What a whoreson, misbegotten, botched barney of an enterprise this has turned out to fucking be!" The volume and irritation in Maguire's voice is a sure sign he has been drinking for the better part of the afternoon and evening. "Where in bloody hell is Lorraine?"

Since the showdown with Bulloch and the Capulets that started in a Hackins Hey pub and ended in the Mersey some months ago, Dudley has shifted his rendezvous with his agents. They now gather almost nightly after sunset to hoist pints and share secrets at the pub in a doxie hotel on Endbutt Lane. Lorraine's half-sister, Bet, runs the place. Her clientele is a mix of men from the docks, seamen between ships, common-law wives, girlfriends, Jezebels.

All hell is about to break loose, and Dudley and Maguire's chief Jezebel is missing. She's been a key player in their secret war against James Bullock and his Capulets. Her absence on this crucial night is not a good sign at all.

"My man over in Birkenhead claims the *290* will sail tomorrow." Maguire licks the froth of ale from his mustache. "Bulloch has hired Captain Butcher of the Cunard Line to take her out of English waters. Butcher has demanded his crew report aboard tonight."

Federal says that he has been watching the ship all day as it lies to the dock at Lairds. Workers have been hanging festive strings of signal flags in her rigging. All manner of dignitaries and ladies have been invited aboard for the ship's sea trial. James Bullock has hired the tug

Hercules to shadow the ship. Probably to bring home the guests at the end of the sail tomorrow ... while the *290* escapes to sea to rendezvous with a ship carrying her munitions and her Confederate officers.

"All we need is to delay the ship a day or two more," says Dudley.

The British Attorney General, after two months of legal badgering from the American legation, has finally ruled that the building of the *290* is a flagrant violation of the Foreign Enlistment Act. The ship should be seized. But Foreign Minister Lord Russell, a known Southern sympathizer, has been conveniently out of town and unable to issue the seizure order. The head customs collector in Liverpool, a man named Edwards, is in the pay of Bullock and will do nothing. But the USS *Tuscarora* has left Southampton. She should be here any day now. The Federal man-of-war will hound the *290* to death if she tries to leave the Mersey.

"When I seen Lorraine at the market at noon," says Federal, "she said she was working something for us."

"Like what?"

"What could it be beside a man?"

"I have no bloody idea, but the moll should have been here an hour ago. We're running out of time, mates."

"Jesus. Maybe the Capulets got her." Federal.

"Or ... maybe she's been playing us. Maybe she's been working for them all along." Dudley feels sick to his stomach. *My god, what can I tell the president if the harlot has made a fool of me?*

"Don't bet your life on it." Maguire is smiling for the first time tonight. "That's me girl!"

"What do you mean?"

"Would you lookee what the cat just dragged in?"

Dudley, Federal, and three other agents follow Maguire's gaze to the front door of the hotel pub. There stands Lorraine with her arm around the back of a young man in a fine linen shirt and tailored pants. He's tall, thin, handsome. Smiling the drunken grin of a man who knows he's about to get lucky.

After she's given him a room key and sent him upstairs with two glasses of claret to await a tumble in the sheets, she sidles up to Dudley. Her eyes sparkle as she presses a thigh against his. She's such the tease. "How am I doing, Duds?"

"Who's the man?" Dudley tries to put a little space between his body and Lorraine's.

She leans back against him, her voice making a purring sound. "That, Duds, is none other than Clarence R. Yonge, of the Confederate Navy. He's just been appointed paymaster on the *290*. And he has a letter on him right this minute from our boy Jamie Bulloch to prove it."

"Bloody hell," says Maguire.

Lorraine helps herself to the fresh jar of ale in Dudley's hand. "He don't know it yet, but after Duds bursts in on us upstairs in about fifteen minutes, he'll be ripe to boink his little rebellion and his new ship right up the bleeding arse."

So this is what Maguire calls the "badger game." Dudley reads between the lines, sees how it will play out. Once he bursts into the love nest finding Yonge in *flagrante dilecto* ... once he announces that he's the U.S. Consul in Liverpool ... once he tells Yonge he'll go straight to Bulloch with the news if he doesn't play along ... once he says that Bulloch will surely have Yonge shot for compromising the South's secret navy ... *Yonge will most certainly agree to be my man on the* 290. *Especially after I take his appointment letter from Bulloch for safe keeping.*

"You love me now, Duds?" Lorraine bats her eyes, rubs her fingers along his overall hangers.

"You can be Queen of the Nile if your boy stops that ship."

21

TERCEIRA, AZORES
August 20–24, 1862

A mild morning. The air shimmering with considerable haze. An easterly wind stirring as the chartered steamer *Bahama* approaches the island. After a slow passage back to England from Nassau ... after tedious days arranging for financing, gathering a full complement of officers in Liverpool ... after a seven-day voyage from the Mersey ... Rafael Semmes is finally here. On the quarterdeck. At the starboard rail of the ship, scouring the shoreline with his long glass. Looking for the raked masts, yards towering above a harbor. Searching the coves of this island that Bulloch has designated as the place where the seahawk will rendezvous with his new ship. If the *290* has made it.

Bulloch stands beside him, his own long glass trained on the shore. "We should be able to see her by now, unless ..."

Semmes knows what Bulloch is thinking. *Unless the* 290 *has run afoul of the* Tuscarora. *Or succumbed to the brutal storm.*

Her life has been dangling from a thread since the day Bulloch and the Lairds conceived her. The Yanks pleaded with the English for months to seize the vessel. She escaped the Mersey under Captain Butcher just hours before a final decision to impound her arrived in Liverpool from the prime minister. Barely escaped a confrontation with the *Tuscarora* by taking the improbable northern route out of the Irish Sea. Then, after dropping Bulloch on a fishing boat off Giant's Causeway on the north coast of Ireland, she sailed smack into a ship-breaking gale. Bulloch has confessed more than once to

Semmes in their time together on the *Bahama* that he felt a sense of uneasiness about the untested crew and vessel sailing off into such a pounding storm along an unforgiving coast ... but so far there has been no news of a wreck.

As Semmes' eyes probe for masts against the backdrop of steep green mountains, his mind begins a silent prayer from the Rosary ...

HAIL, HOLY QUEEN, Mother of Mercy, our life, our sweetness and our hope! To thee do we cry, poor banished children of Eve; to thee do we send up our sighs, mourning and weeping in this valley of tears. Turn then, most gracious advocate, thine eyes of mercy toward us, and after this our exile ...

His eyes are aching from the searching, the iridescent haze. His will's beginning to swoon before this vision of Terceira. The sloping, cultivated fields, dark green beneath the clouds gathering over the mountain summits. The white cottages, red roofs. So like the paradise in Brazil he promised Maude, so like ...

"There, Captain! Three points off the starboard bow." Bullock has dropped his long glass from his eye, is pointing into the harbor of Porto Praya. "Behold the *Alabama*."

The name that Secretary of the Navy Mallory has picked for the *290* hangs in the air as Semmes catches his breath, squints. Focuses. Sees her.

Never has a ship looked so graceful with her long, lean hull, clipper bows, raked masts. Two hundred and thirty-five feet in length, thirty-two feet abeam, a thousand tons displacement. The short funnel fitting with the proportion and symmetry of all around it.

"She sits upon the water with the lightness and grace of a black swan," says Semmes. *My bride ... and my home.*

⚓　　⚓　　⚓

It's after nightfall. The *Alabama*'s steaming, heading into the bay at East Angra. Just now clearing the headland to port. It's so calm the only sound is the slow swooshing of the screw and the hiss of the funnel. Semmes is pacing the flying bridge, which rises forward of the funnel, a dozen feet above the deck. He's picturing how M. J. Freeman, the chief engineer he has brought with him from the *Sumter*, must be loving his new twin three-hundred horse-power engines when he hears shouting in broken English and Portuguese from shore.

"Soldiers, sir." Kell has the deck watch. "From that little fort yonder."

"What the devil are they saying?"

"Can't tell. But I do believe they aim to warn us off to sea."

"Pay them no never mind, Kell. Steady as she goes. Take her in." His voice is slow, calm.

How he hates officiousness. Reminds him of life with the flat-footed, curmudgeonly admirals of the Yank navy. Damn the tin soldiers. His boys are tired. He's tired. And he aims to anchor for the night. It has been a long twenty-four hours of excitement and toil. After assuming command of this ship that Captain Butcher called a *greyhound* ... after bidding Bulloch and the *Bahama* fair winds on their voyage back to Liverpool ... he has taken her offshore beyond the territorial limits of the Azores to rendezvous with the ship that Bulloch had sent as her tender, the *Agrippina*. Here beyond the authority of the Portuguese government, he has finished transferring the contraband guns and munitions, as well as coal, aboard the *Alabama*.

His mind is drifting back to Freeman and the engines, wondering if Bullock is right that his bunkers have enough coal for eighteen days of moderate steaming, when he hears the bark of a cannon.

Semmes turns around just in time to see the muzzle flash from a gun off the port quarter. The gun has the shallow cough of an antique, probably no more than an eight-pounder.

"Shooting at us," says Kell.

"Kind of a puny show of force ... but I guess it means we are indeed warriors again, Luff."

"Yes sir. It ain't Dixie. But it does feel kind of good, though, don't it?"

"How's that?"

"To scare the hell out of someone for a change. She's a grand ship. A new bride."

Semmes nods, wonders how it is that Kell so often knows just what his captain's thinking. *A bride. That she is. A savage bride. And the only one I've got now.*

"'Til death do us part." He's mumbling.

"Beg your pardon, sir?"

"What say we throw a party aboard tomorrow to christen her and sign the crew? Have Paymaster Yonge prepared to offer advances *in specie?* Then we'll go hunting the Yanks' whalers in earnest. Cut off the blood for their war machines."

22

RICHMOND, VIRGINIA
September 1, 1862

Her chest heaves, a cry almost escaping her throat. The face looking up at Maude from the litter is so broken. Only an eye amid a pulp of blood, bandages. Flies circling, dipping into the mouth to feast on the cud of the frothy tongue.

The leanness of his body. He must be little more than a boy. The skin on his arms and hands is heavy with grime from months in the wilderness and from battle. He's among the first wounded to reach the capital after the battle at Manassas Junction that started on August 28. A rifleman in the Stonewall Brigade.

"Please help me." The soldier's voice, low and faint, comes to her from all four corners of the room, not that mouth at all.

"Try to rest. You're in a hospital now."

She feels his hand on her wrist, clamping. "Don't let me die alone."

"I can give you a bit of brandy."

"Are you married?"

"No."

"I had a girl ... but I lost her." He tosses a hand in the air. "Somewhere."

She pictures a cottage by the shore of a tropical sea, a man wedded to that sea.

"She give up on me. Are you going to give up on me?" His hand a vice pinching her wrist to numbness.

"I don't have the right," she says, feels like she's had something like this conversation before. On the deck of a ship or in a dream.

Eyes filling with tears, Raffy's voice shredding with each new word.

She kisses the gauze where his ear must be, promises to keep him safe from harm. Says she believes in miracles. She has to. Without them what would this earthly life be?

"I'd thankee for the brandy now," he says.

His hand releases her wrist.

When she returns with a cup and a bottle, the soldier is dead. His mouth a house for buzzing blue bottle flies on this burning summer afternoon.

⚓   ⚓   ⚓

She's sitting on the side stoop of the Robertson Hospital at Third and Main Streets, watching the purple night spread over the steeples of Richmond. She's still wearing her nursing apron, the bloodstains on it already fading to a rust color. Fiona's at her side. They are sharing a large bottle of cool beer that Fiona has brought here from their room on this hot, windless night. The cicadas shrill against the chuff and rumble of a train staggering into town over the railway bridge.

Maude takes a long swallow of beer. "I wonder. Does it ever get any easier?"

"Dealing with death?"

"And the road to redemption."

Fiona shakes her head in a way that means she either doesn't know the answer ... or can't believe her friend is still agonizing over atonement.

But, yes. She bloody well is. She's only been back in Richmond, only been sharing Fiona's room in the rear of the Pegram's school for girls, for a week. She has lost about a dozen pounds since her accident in the Bahamas, but the baby is still safe in her womb. She can feel it move. Feel its strength. And its strength is her strength, maybe her spirit, too. Growing again. She barely remembers her home-stay with the doctor in Savannah, her bleeding spells, her fever. Only bits and pieces. Like the doctor's gray and shriveled face, the smell of magnolias and tobacco smoke. The sharp pains in her hips during the long train ride back to Richmond. The first time she felt the baby move again she wanted to shout *hallelujah*.

She entered the city by night. Found Varina Davis oddly gruff and cold when she went to see her. Only stayed in the city after Fiona told her that Jean Claude de Saunier was long gone. After Fiona offered to share her bed. Fiona told her that much trouble had come to Richmond since Maude left for the Bahamas. Every church and warehouse had become a hospital during this summer. The Confederacy was building clinics faster than forts. Still the wounded seemed to arrive almost daily by rail and wagon train. It had been while hearing this news that Maude felt a calling. As if something deep in her soul were being stirred by a sweet and terrible song. Something slow and shrill played on a pipe. Something heard in the dark ... back in Ireland. Carrying across the moors. A lyric from a lullaby or a funeral wake.

The next day—her abdomen now swelling with her child—she offered herself as a nurse to Sally Tompkins, the director at this small, private hospital.

"Can I say again it was hellish hard, watching a boy die like that?"

"Why don't you just quit, lass?" Fiona wraps an arm around her, pulls her close. "The Pegrams and the girls would much delight to have you back at our little school."

"This is my burden."

"How's that now?"

"I have sinned against God and man. And now I am called to help the suffering."

"Help the suffering if you must. But sinned? Not you, love."

She looks into Fiona's eyes, feels her tears coming. Tries to speak. Can't.

"You have done nothing short of giving your whole being for a noble cause."

"I've been a selfish harlot."

"Because of you, Raphael Semmes may yet bite the Yankees so hard they will stop this senseless conflict before more die."

She wants to shout. *Because of me? Because I have loved a married man. Because I slept with another I cared not for. Because I got with child out of wedlock. Because of stupid, girlish pride and vanity ... I have shamed my family, my love and my God.*

"That boy today probably died thinking you were an angel."

"That boy ... that boy was a sign of the horror I have made of my life." A sob breaks from her mouth. She buries her forehead against Fiona's chest. Feels her friend molding to her. Yields.

"This too shall pass, Maudie. Did I not tell you that Rose was here while you were off in the Bahamas?"

"Our Rose, Rambling Rose?"

Fiona says that bastard Major Allen finally let their old friends, the Confederate spies Rose Greenhow and Betty Duval, out of imprisonment in the Old Capital Jail.

"You saw Rose?"

"Before she took off for France and England ... with her daughter."

"She's working for the South again?"

Fiona shrugs.

"And you?"

"Am I what?"

"What haven't you been telling me?"

Fiona shrugs again. "Don't you think it's safer for both of us if you don't tell me about why you went to the Bahamas ... and I don't tell you about a little meeting Rose and I had with President Davis ... among others?"

"Fiona!"

Her friend gives the wave of a hand, changes the subject.

"I hear that Stonewall Jackson and Robert E. Lee have set the Yanks running for their lives."

"Just hold me."

"Like you are the rarest of all living things to me."

If only you were my Raffy, she thinks. "I don't deserve either of you."

"What?"

23

DISTRICT OF COLUMBIA
September 6, 1862

The wagons of dead and dying from the second battle at Bull Run have been rolling over the Long Bridge back into the city for a week. Wounded filling every vacant place that can take them, including the Corcoran mansion right next door to the house Gideon Welles has taken for his family. He can hear the moans and pleas of soldiers when he comes home from the office and tries to sleep. Then he thanks the Almighty that Mary Ann is away in Lewistown, Pennsylvania, tending to her mother. Thanks the Almighty that his wife and his young children do not have the sounds and sights of this growing catastrophe lodging in their memories.

And now, today, Saturday. The street's full of soldiers. Marching. In full battle gear. An endless legion of young men tramping up Pennsylvania Avenue, turning onto H Street, passing right by his house. Heading north. Twenty—no, thirty—thousand men. More. Possibly all that is left of George McClellan's Army of the Potomac.

Ed Bates, the Attorney General, has walked over from the War Department to watch the spectacle from Welles' front porch. The dust from the march has turned the sky a hazy gray.

"Where are they all going?"

"This is the beginning of the end. The country is in ruins," says Bates. He runs his sweaty fingers through the thick curls of his beard beneath his earlobes.

Bates says there is confirmation from scouts this morning that the Rebs have crossed the Potomac near Fredericksburg. Lee's fife and drum boys, it seems, are making a show of playing "Maryland, My Maryland" as they progress through back roads of the border state. It looks like Lee intends to enlist the support of all the secesh trash in Maryland and surround Washington. McClellan is taking his army north to stop them.

"That ass will destroy us all." Bates chokes on the dust, spits off the porch.

Welles says nothing. McClellan is no favorite of his. Six months ago the general's Army of the Potomac had a chance to sweep into Richmond and end the war. But he dillydallied until the Rebs dug in and reinforced the Army of Virginia. Then the Rebs pushed him back until he yielded the strategic advantage. Now Lee is bringing the war to Washington.

Many in the Cabinet, including Welles, have been exceedingly frustrated with McClellan's inaction. But recently some of the cabinet members like Seward and Bates, early supporters of McClellan, have made the general the scapegoat for all their anger. And all of their alleged guilt about the desperate course of the war, the precarious state of the Union. Some have even suggested executing McClellan for treason. Here's another place Welles breaks with his more political and self-interested colleagues. He can't fault McClellan for everything. The man's a capital manager. His men adore him. And his loyalty to the cause is beyond question. Lincoln has so far refused to dismiss McClellan. Says he may yet do something of note.

"Let's hope this will be the moment when George shows us why the president stands staunch by him."

"Bah! Sometimes, Gideon, your optimism flies smack in the face of experience."

He hears that apocalyptic tune in his head again. The one about the coming of the Lord. About fateful lightning. About a terrible swift sword. Imagines his own children cut down, frozen corpses like Willie Lincoln. Imagines Lincoln dead too, hanging in the tree, wearing a stovepipe hat. Eyes blank. Mouth in a silent scream.

"I struggle against my darker inclinations."

"I am packing up my household. I suggest you do the same. Go back to little Connecticut."

Bate's words hit him. Sharp, hot stings. He pictures the red envelopes. A threat.

GO BACK TO LITTLE CONNECTICUT.
YOU'RE KILLING YOUR PRESIDENT!!!

Bate's turn of phrase—little Connecticut—pierces his chest, draws blood somewhere deep.

"Gideon. You don't look well, man."

"I must excuse myself. I believe this dust is too much for me."

"Then I'll leave you to gather yourself together. I expect the president will want to talk to you *post haste*."

"Beg pardon?"

"There are rumors that new Reb raider the *290* is in Nassau ... heading for an attack on New York."

$ $ $

Almost sunset on the river. The navy yard tug pulls alongside the side-wheel steamer *Yankee*, a gunboat on river patrol off Alexandria where the Anacostia River joins the mighty Potomac. The funnels of both vessels trailing black swirls of smoke, looping slowly into the windless air. A fingernail moon and a planet, Mars maybe, hang low in the western sky. Gideon Welles hails the gunboat, beckons to an officer.

When the officer has joined Welles on the tug, the men walk aft to the idle stern-wheel, beyond the hearing of the tug crew.

"I suppose you have heard the news about the *290*, Mr. Secretary," says the officer. "That is why I am summoned here in such haste."

The speaker is Commodore Charles Wilkes. He's a naval officer of considerable age, half a head taller than Welles, with a booming baritone voice, chiseled face, and the sad, baggy eyes of a drinker. A few locks of gray hair fall over his forehead, quite possibly positioned there on purpose with spit or grease to add a look of youth or daring.

"I've spoken to Mr. Lincoln and the Secretary of State," Welles tries not to wince as he remembers the badgering he took from his boss and Seward this afternoon.

"Yes?"

"They have most earnestly requested that we mount a special Flying Squadron to hunt down and destroy the Rebel raiders."

Wilkes shrugs, slaps at a mosquito. "It's past time, don't you think?"

Welles feels a growl starting low in his chest. There it is again. The irritating, supercilious, nearly defiant attitude that has made Wilkes unpopular with his naval brethren. The attitude that compels Wilkes to ignore or exceed orders he disagrees with. The same *bravura* that led him to swoop in and seize the Confederate agents Mason and Slidell off the *Trent* almost a year ago. The *hubris* that nearly drew England into the war on the Rebel side ... but made Wilkes a popular hero among a host of citizens. Among voters.

Wilkes says he's heard that the New York and New England ship owners and merchants are raising hell with the president over the depredations of the Rebel pirates.

"I do not know what has become of the *Oreto*, the ship the Rebels are calling the *Florida*. But, yes, we have received rumors that the other British-built cruiser, the *290*, may already be in the Bahamas."

"Semmes is in her," Wilkes says.

"How do you know?"

Wilkes swats another mosquito, gives a sly smile as is to say *I have my sources*. The implication is that Wilkes is a friend and confidant of William Seward, maybe others in the Cabinet, and the Secretary of State has shared reports from his spies like Dudley in Liverpool.

Welles looks away to the western bank of the Potomac, tries not to growl. Tries not to think how Seward's cavalier dispersal of sensitive information compromises the workings of the government on a daily basis. He tries instead to picture Alexandria when it was a river port for the surrounding plantations, a sanctuary for George and Martha Washington, not a Rebel encampment.

"Semmes or no Semmes, Commodore, I will be writing orders tonight to place the five best steamers of your James River Squadron, including the *Wachusetts*, into the Flying Squadron. There shall be three other ships as well."

"And I am to have command?"

After Bates this morning, Welles has had enough of smug bastards for a day. He deflects Wilkes' question, his bid for acknowledgment and approval, with words of warning.

"Under no circumstances ... let no provocation induce you to invade the maritime jurisdiction of a neutral power or exceed the limitations of international law. You understand?"

Wilkes glares at him. "Am I to have this Flying Squadron or not?"

"Do you agree to the president's and my conditions?"

The tug's steam-relief valve opens, ruptures the silence with a loud burst lasting several seconds.

"The commander of a squadron should be a flag officer."

"Are you asking me to promote you to rear admiral ... a month after your promotion to commodore?"

"I'm the man who discovered and mapped Antarctica. I'm the man the papers call the 'hero of the *Trent* Affair.'"

You're an arrogant jackass, Welles thinks.

But what he says is "Perhaps the president would like to consider Farragut or Porter or Winslow for the post."

"Or, then again, since Semmes has slipped through your fingers for more than a year ... maybe Mr. Lincoln will make me acting rear admiral himself ... and send you home shortly."

24

CSS *ALABAMA*, WEST OF THE AZORES
September 8, 1862

Semmes bolts upright in his berth, hears the last of the eight bells chiming the end of the mid-watch. Four in the morning. He stares at the pool of moonlight beneath the skylight above his new cabin. Feels the dread tingling in his arms, a palsy in his hands.

"I smell a rat."

He's not sure he has slept at all tonight, despite the calmness of the sea, despite taking his second prize in just three days of hunting. Something feels wrong.

This is too easy by half, he thinks. *The ship's just here for the picking. I fear a Yankee trap.*

It's the end of the summer whaling season west of the island of Flores in the Azores. There are only a half-dozen whaling stations in all the world and this is one of them. The most accessible one to a cruiser from Europe or North America. Surely, any Yank with a brain would know that sooner or later a Confederate cruiser must set its sights on the New England whaling fleet. Must come here. With the current wartime price for oil so high, a loaded whaler can carry as much as $100,000 in precious cargo for the Union. Few prizes these days can be worth this much. Nothing can hurt Abe Lincoln more than cutting off his oil supply. So ... surely the Yank navy must be lurking here, about to guard this hen house of whalers.

Didn't the captain of the *Ocmulgee*, out of Edgartown, say as much when he seized her two days ago? Didn't that captain actually mistake the *Alabama* for a Federal cruiser sent to chaperone the

American ships here? Was it not the same mistake the young captain of the *Starlight*, from Boston, admitted to when Semmes seized the fit little schooner yesterday? These men know something. The Yanks, possibly the *Tuscarora* or the *Kearsarge*, must be here somewhere. They are just waiting for him to signal his presence by lighting up the night with one of these captured whalers. And then they will swoop in to destroy him.

He leaps out of bed, circles the chart spread out on his U-shaped desk. Glares at the constellation of splotches that are the cartographer's image of the Azores. Then he wanders to the sideboard. Seizes a decanter of brandy and a glass. He's just about to pour himself something to help him sleep when he decides against it. Slams the decanter down hard on the oak.

"I will not do it," he says. "Will not give them the satisfaction. Or myself."

He must deny himself his little pleasures. No more spirits. Not now. No more stirring nighttime bonfires on the waves. Only wit and discipline can save him. Especially discipline. He is sorely tempted tonight. There are three women passengers aboard the *Starlight*. Young, attractive women according to his boarding officer. Just what he doesn't need right now. He has refused to bring them aboard the *Alabama*. Tonight they remain on the schooner, with their men in irons. His ship keepers heaving-to the schooner off to leeward with a light at her masthead. He cannot be tempted by thoughts of the fairer sex. Cannot have his mind blunted by selkies, reminding him of that parting in Nassau. The brave heart he may well have lost forever. Maude.

She kisses his ear. Says she will write to him every day. He must keep himself safe from harm. And he must know that she will not stop hoping for another miracle to bring them back together.

The *Alabama* and her prize lie just beyond the marine league, west of Flores. An Eden of tall, steep mountains. Even now—especially now, it seems—the rich scents of the island's flowers perfume the air. Stir the most cloying memories of shore and romance. Memories that make him understand how the great Ulysses lost his way when he heard the songs of the sirens.

"I must get out of here." He slaps his face with both hands, rubs his cheeks. *And I need a disguise to keep the Yanks off me until I finish hunting.*

A knock on his cabin door.

"Is everything alright, sir?" It's Lieutenant Armstrong, one of the officers Semmes has brought to the *Alabama* from the *Sumter*. He's just coming off watch, heading for his own cabin beyond the wardroom.

Semmes opens his door. "I've been thinking. This morning we will put those women and the crew of the *Starlight* into their whaleboats and send them ashore. Now, let's get some sleep, man."

A plan is taking shape. A disguise.

When the women are gone, he will douse the ship's boiler fires, stow the funnel, hoist the stars-and-stripes. Sail in company with this schooner and other whalers he shall surely take ... as if the *Alabama* is indeed a Federal cruiser here to watch the flock. And when he is well out of sight of land and other shipping?

I shall make a fire of them to rival the sun.

25

SCHOONER *STARLIGHT*

September 8, 1862

West of the Azores.

Clarence Yonge, The *Alabama*'s paymaster, shakes the woman. Both his hands on her shoulders until she wakes. The second she opens her eyes, sees him, he cups his hand over her mouth and whispers in her ear. "Nod if y'all understand English."

He weaseled his way onto the ship-keeping detail aboard the *Starlight* yesterday. Now he has the chance he's been waiting for all night. Two chances, actually.

He's lank, boyish. With a rigging knife in his hand. And, just now, a bit inebriated on Portuguese *vinho tinto* pilfered from the schooner's galley. His body slides into the berth alongside the woman in this tiny cabin off the main saloon of the *Starlight*.

"English?" His voice is more insistent, but still more air than sound.

The false dawn is just breaking. In the dim light filtering through the deck prism, he can see her staring at him—at the knife—with large, fearful eyes. She nods. Yes, she understands English.

She is not as pretty as the wife he left in Dixie, not as game as the tart who snared him into this double-dealing for Thomas Dudley and the Yanks back in Liverpool. But he does love the ladies, and this wench seems just what he needs to put a cap on his spy games tonight. A dark Portagee maid, bound for the States to be some fucking Yank's bride. A maid with a tangle of thick brown curls to bury his face in.

"I don't want to hurt you."

He lifts his hand off her mouth, makes sure she sees him set his knife on the cabin sole as an act of good faith. Really hopes she won't struggle. He just wants a little loving, not domination. *Just a little of the Yanks' breakfast bacon, so to speak. A little chance interlude between two strangers at sea, darlin'. . .*

It takes some minutes with his body pressed to hers, his fingers laced in hers, before her breathing slows and her heart stops drumming against his chest. Eventually, he feels the stiff resistance start to ebb from her body. Only then does he kiss her. Pleasure her. Until the beast rises. And they go to town.

When it's over, he tries to pull away. But she holds him on her. Her arms and legs locking him while she looks into his eyes. Searching for something. His mortal soul, most like. The one the Liverpool drab and Dudley stole from him more than a month ago. The one Abraham Lincoln or some other Yankee bastards are squeezing just now. Well, he's getting even, isn't he? Now he's got her soul just the way they got his. He's shamed her, and now she'll do what ever he wants. Help him. For certain. Loving and hating every second of it … the way he does this double-dealing for the Yanks.

With a free hand he reaches for his jacket lying on the sole, fumbles with it. Comes up with a letter in a sealed envelope. The letter he wrote last night. The one that lists all the officers on the *Alabama*, all the armaments, all the powder, munitions, coal. The amount of gold Semmes carries in his strong box. The condition of the ship. The ship's position as of last night. Her apparent intention to ravage whalers here on the sperm whale grounds until the sea is empty.

He puts his lips next to her ear, whispers. "Once y'all are ashore, your men will want to find the nearest American consul in the islands to help them get to the United States."

"What you say?" Her first words. A thick Portagee accent.

"Give this to the American consul." He places the letter in her hand.

"Who are you?"

"A bastard."

"I ... don't understand."

"This letter can stop the hell ship that done made me what I am."

"Oh."

26

DISTRICT OF COLUMBIA

September 18, 1862

"Walk with me, Gideon." The president's voice seems rent with fatigue and a cold as he leads the Secretary of the Navy out the back door of the Executive Mansion toward the South Lawn.

Welles knows from experience that this invitation can only mean that news of something of a most shocking nature is about to be revealed.

"Has Wilkes sailed yet?"

It's a coolish morning for September. A blustery wind that makes the president turn into the stables for shelter.

"Yes, sir. Once you made him acting rear admiral, he finally took his leave. Eight ships. For the Bahamas and the West Indies."

"Do you think he has a prayer of catching Semmes?"

Welles eyes the well-oiled saddles and bridles through the open door of the tack room, thinks. "He's a maverick."

Lincoln grunts. "Let's hope he has some wit, too. It seems he's off to hunt a needle in a hay stack."

"Yes sir."

"Well, at least he's out there. Looking. With a squadron of good ships. That's something I can say today when those New England ship owners come knocking on my door again. I suppose they have been badgering you, too."

"Delano, Briggs, Howland. These whaling men from New Bedford are a persistent bunch."

Lincoln grunts again. Coughs a deep, barking eruption, then blows his nose. He says the whaling scions have done nothing less than insinuate that they could make or break his candidacy for re-election with the influence they have in New England. They are demanding Semmes' head on a pike, in the same fashion as their ancestors displayed the skull of the Indian rebel Metacomet during King Philip's War.

"Well they fear that Semmes and his fellow Reb pirates may take away all that is near and dear to them."

"We depend upon the oil their ships bring home."

Lincoln nods. "So we must do all that we can for them."

"Yes, sir."

"But re-election could not be further from my mind. Do you know that, Gideon? Do you know how this job does push down upon a man?"

"I can only guess."

The president pauses at a stall with two ponies, digs in his jacket pocket. Comes up with sugar cubes, which he offers with an open hand to the ponies. Then he presses his head to the forehead of the larger animal, closes his eyes.

Welles feels himself wince. Realizes that this was Willie's pony. Dear, sweet Willie. Taken so young. The president is still grieving.

"These are dark times." Lincoln, eyes still closed, seems to be talking to the animal, or maybe the spirit of his dead son. "Dark, dark times."

Welles feels the need to offer solace, says the first thing that comes into his head. "At least McClellan has kept Lee out of Washington."

The president coughs, chokes. Jerks back from the pony and stares at the Secretary of the Navy as if the man had hit him with a bull whip. Just yesterday a flood of telegrams—later, dispatches— arrived from the Army of the Potomac. McClellan threw his whole force of over seventy thousand men against Lee at a place called Antietam Creek near Sharpsburg, Maryland. After a day of tremendous fighting, McClellan turned Lee back. But he failed to pursue him and deliver the *coup de grace*. Now, the armies have called a truce to tend to the wounded and the dead. When the truce ends, the bulk of Lee's remaining army will no doubt have retreated south, safely across the Potomac into Virginia, to lick its wounds and re-gather strength.

"Our nation has never known such a calamity, Gideon. I badgered McClellan until he finally took some initiative. And now this. Dear God!"

"It was not your fault."

"I gave the order to advance."

"Lee forced you to it, sir. He would have taken Washington. He would have destroyed the Union."

"I hear there are tens of thousands of men lying where they fell. The fields are red with blood as far as you can see."

Welles doesn't know what to say. He has read the papers. They are saying America lost more men at Antietam Creek than it lost in the Revolutionary War, the War of 1812 and the Mexican War combined. September 17, 1862, is now the bloodiest day in American history.

"Maybe this will bring us all to our senses. Maybe Jefferson Davis will call for a truce," says Welles.

"I don't think so. If McClellan had pursued Lee back into Virginia, perhaps the South would have yielded."

"They are hurting. I hear most of Lee's boys who fell were so bad off they had no shoes."

"Yet they had the will to fight. And die. That's spit-and-vinegar for you."

Indeed. It seems to Welles that the audacity of the Southern warrior can hardly be over-estimated. Just this morning he received a dispatch from the Gulf of Mexico; one he does not think he will share with his president right now. The blockade has been breached in a rather spectacular way. A Reb captain named John Newland Maffitt has run his new English-built raider—formerly the *Oreto*, now the *Florida*—into Mobile. Right through a hail of persistent shelling by the USS *Oneida*. Maffitt doing all this with just a skeleton crew ... and while suffering from yellow fever.

"Where does such courage come from, Gideon?"

Welles feels the need to rub a hand over the soft, warm face of the pony. "I believe we are bred to it. I believe no place on earth values freedom as we do."

"Then it is surely time that we stand by that value. Don't you think?"

"Sir?"

"No more dilly-dallying. I am calling a special cabinet meeting. The time has come to free the slaves."

"You mean an emancipation proclamation?"

"I have begun writing a draft."

"Do Seward and Stanton and Bates know?"

"The moment has come for my freedom, too."

"Then you have not consulted."

"Not on the substance of the draft. Only here. Now. With you and the ponies."

He feels something like a current racing through his arms, legs. Maybe thrill, maybe dread. "Seward will be furious he has not been asked his opinion."

"I expect there'll be quite a few people who will feel like hanging me."

Red envelopes. Men of straw. One hanging in the tree, wearing a stovepipe hat. Its black eyes blank.

"Little Connecticut," Welles says softly.

"I beg your pardon."

"Remember what I told you once? There may be plots."

Lincoln shrugs, digs in his pocket for two more sugar cubes for the ponies.

"You're going to need a better security guard."

"All right, then. Let's see what Major Allen has to say, shall we?"

27

SHARPSBURG, MARYLAND

September 18, 1862

It has taken their caravan of ambulances two days and a full night of travel to get to this catastrophe. They had left Richmond when the combat here at Sharpsburg was only a rumor of things to come. Now, more than a mile from the battlefield, they can smell the rot and ammonia of death. The stink is nothing new to Maude after her work at the hospital. It's just stronger, more urgent. Maybe a sign that she truly needs to be here. To stop wallowing in her own misery. To help.

But the ambulances can go no further. A guard of a lieutenant and twenty infantrymen in soiled, gray uniforms has stopped them for more than an hour on the outskirts of Sharpsburg. Told them that the road ahead leading into town is closed. The truce to tend to the dead and wounded may not hold much longer. The Yankees are all around, and in, the village. This whole area could be a field of battle by tomorrow morning. No place for wagons full of women. They should turn around and go back across the Potomac, maybe to Harpers Ferry where they will be safe.

The nurse in charge of this wagon train is refusing to budge. Even now Maude can hear her badgering the lieutenant. She says she wants to talk to General Lee himself.

Nothing else is happening. Only two of the five nurses inside Maude's paneled wagon are awake. The other three lean together on each other's shoulders. Rag dolls. Scared. Exhausted. Asleep.

"We are not bloody stopping now." Fiona's words are fire. Brimstone.

Maude stiffens a little, feeling the heat of Fiona's body next to hers. She feels the vitriol of her friend's new, sudden conversion to nursing and—especially—this enterprise. This pilgrimage to the battlefield in Maryland. She wonders if Fiona somehow sees this as another mission, another chance to strike a blow for freedom. Whether Fiona is still secretly a Woman Warrior. Just as they both were a year ago back in Washington before that low bastard Pinkerton, or whatever he calls himself now, put an end to Rose Greenhow and Betty Duval's network of female agents.

The memory of her own capture and imprisonment by Pinkerton at that stable in Murder Bay makes her shiver. She pulls away a bit from Fiona so that her tremors can subside in private. Feels the baby kick in her, wraps her arms around it. Stares out the back of the wagon at the rows of field corn in tassel alongside of the road. Golden in the evening sun.

"If Varina were with us," says Fiona. "She would know how to make these ridiculous men see that we come here with a high purpose. Make them yield."

Another attack of shivering, her legs quivering as if the Earth itself has been pulled from beneath her with the mention of Varina Davis' name.

"It's too late to think about her."

"What do you mean?"

"She gave up on us, I think. Well, gave up on me, anyway."

"She adores you."

Then why, Maude asks, did Varina Davis turn her away the night she got back to Richmond after that terrible trip to Nassau? Why did she give her only a brief little hug and send her away saying "We must not be seen together just now"?

"I'm sure it had nothing to do with you, love."

"I felt ashamed, embarrassed. Stupid."

"The celebrated and powerful do not enjoy our freedoms."

"You mean, they are always under scrutiny. You mean it may not do for Varina to be seen with the common Irish tart of a Southern hero."

"Not if the affair is public knowledge."

"What do you mean?"

"While you were under doctors' care in Savannah, some officers' wives returned from being with their men in Nassau. They circulated rumors about you and your seahawk."

"Shite."

"Exactly."

"I'm stymied."

"Not if we do what Varina would. What she would want us to do."

"What the bloody hell is that?"

"*Carpe diem*. Seize the day."

"Get off this wagon?"

"I have to."

"This is about more than nursing, isn't it?"

"Don't you want to end the war, stop this terrible waste of life?" Fiona purses her lips, glares at Maude as if to say *let's move it along, lassie.*

She feels a jolt of courage tighten her muscles. A smile beginning to spread over her lips as she slings a sack full of medical supplies over one shoulder, a canteen of water over the other.

"If we stick to the cornfields, the guards will never spy us."

⚓   ⚓   ⚓

They have walked less than a mile to the east when they break out of the corn rows. Ahead, beyond a ruined split-rail fence, is a slight valley, a sloping field, and in it a lone woman wandering. First one direction, then another. Weeping. She's middle-aged, slender, in a full, brown dress, torn around the hem, and stained with dirt and blood and leaves.

She looks up at Maude, stares at Maude's pregnant body pushing out her dress. The woman holds her shaking arms out at her sides, gesturing to the field. "He's here somewhere. My baby's here somewhere."

At first, it looks to Maude as if the corn has already been harvested, the stalks cut down. But on closer examination she sees that the corn is still on the shocks. The plants, a fading green, have been broken off between knee-high and waist-high by what could only have been a persistent fusillade of musket fire and artillery bombardment. The air stinks of shit and sulfur ... along with the ordinary odor of death. Among the broken stalks lay bodies—hundreds of them, as if sleeping. Except for the deep purple holes in their faces, bodies. Some dressed in gray, some blue.

"I can't find my Charlie, find my baby."

Maude thinks she hears something slow, shrill, playing on a pipe. A lyric from a lullaby.

Holy Mary, Mother of God, blessed are thee, and blessed is the fruit of thy womb Jesus.

"You know he's here?" It's a dumb question, but she feels the need to engage this woman.

The mother speaks in bursts between sobs. Her son is Charlie. In the Pennsylvania 51st Regiment. From Norristown, out to the east. Just a boy. Just fifteen. She had followed him. Along with a group of women called "regimental mothers." To look to his needs, you know. For these two months he has been in the service. Yesterday, General Burnside sent the 51st into this sloping field. The soldiers tell her. Sent Charlie from across the bridge down yonder.

"Now ... where did he go? Where did you go, Charlie? Where did you all go?" The woman looks around her as if she's blind or in a thick fog.

"Hey." Fiona has walked off forty yards to the edge of a wood. "Bloody hell, Maudie. This one's alive."

"Come on." She grabs the mother's hand. Breaks into a run.

The canteen and the sack of bandages, soap, whiskey, laudanum pounding on her shoulders as she goes. She's imagining great billowing wings on her back. Sails. Duty. Raffy.

Right before someone pulls a gunny sack over her head and drags her to the ground.

28

CSS *ALABAMA*
September 18, 1862

Northwest of the Azores. Alone on the bridge. Five bells into the noon watch. Semmes turns his face sou'west, squints into the half-gale. Looks aloft. More than thirty knots of wind pressing at the topgallants, the topsails, courses. A sharp whistling in the rigging.

From this perch amidships, a dozen feet above the deck, he can see the *Alabama* as he has never seen a ship before. See every corner of her aloft and below. See the quartermaster and two seamen back aft on the wheel, see the luff Kell at the taffrail just now eyeing the stern wake to judge just how fast they are sailing. See the two men on bow watch shielding their eyes against the spray with hands extended over their brows. See the rest of the watch gang, too. More than thirty Jacks and their officers hunkered down out of the wind, backs to the weather bulwarks near the main chains. Every man opening his eyes and ears and heart to the galloping of the ship as she reaches to the north before the building storm.

All three masts are bowing under the strain of wind on canvas, the weather shrouds tight as violin strings. The sky roiling clouds. Spears of lightning flashing off to port. But no rain yet. Seas gray, rolling heavily. Cresting, breaking in large white patches of foam. He feels the wind stinging his cheeks, lifting the wings of his mustache. Feels his upper lip curl up instinctively. Thinks, *this must be what a hound feels when he's right hard on the scent of fox. Nothing at all in your mind or heart or soul besides the thrill. The blood lust. The prize.*

A renegade thought seizes him. *Would that this would never end.*

He stares off the starboard bow, sees the whaling bark he's been chasing most of the afternoon. She's no more than two miles ahead now. One second she's hull up, another hull down in a trough between these building waves. She's got everything but her stunsails set. Trying to outrace him. Running for her life. Somehow knowing that this sleek, black hound chasing her, this ship that came out of nowhere with no name on her bows or transom, is an angel of vengeance ... even though the *Alabama* flies the false flag of Great Britain.

"Is my lady a sea boat or not?" Semmes speaks to the air, the gods. His words proud, as much challenge as question.

This is the cruiser's first encounter with heavy weather since he has been aboard, and he's eager to learn how she will react in all of her moods. What better way to test her than to go charging after this Yank whaler in an angry sea? His tenth prize in twelve days. But never has he had a chase like this. Never in all his life. Never aboard such a gem of a ship. Something tells him he may never have such a moment as this again.

Don't let it end.

The *Alabama's* so different from all the other ships he's been in. The *Sumter*, the *Somers*. The old Connie when he was her sailing master. This lady does not grow sluggish, unpredictable, leaky, dangerous in the gale. She rises to it. Takes its energy. Makes it her own.

This is as close to a true ecstasy of spirit as I have ever known, he thinks. To ride her now, this brave, young thing ... to feel her surging forward, pushing the immense waves aside ... to hear the call and response from the song in her rig and the hiss-and-crash of her hull in its element is to know the insane glory of some winged beast of prey. Yes, she has engines. But now, with her fires out, her screw raised into its bay, she schoons, as the old sailors used to say. *Good Lord Almighty, see how she schoons.*

If he can just make this last a little longer ... if he could bottle the sights, and sounds—the levitation in the knees, the lightening in the boots—of this moment ... if he could distill this schooning into a tonic to ward off the dark hours of toil, misery, loneliness, loss, war.

An elixir against the pathetic and insignificant death that he must surely face, too. Better to meet his maker drunk with this moment, to pass boldly into that other world in the thrill of schooning, than to drown slowly beneath the thousand troubles and disappointments of a landsman: the failed husband, absent father, restless lover.

Kell mounts the bridge and approaches Semmes. Turns his back to the wind so he can speak to his captain. The man is beaming a huge smile through his thick, curly beard. "She's making twelve to thirteen knots, sir."

"Look how she carries her canvas."

"A different breed from the common, certain."

"It's like walking on water."

"I've never been in a faster ship. That bark there is no slouch for speed and we've come up some seven, eight miles on her in the last two hours."

"I hate to end this. What a ride!"

"Aye ... but this storm may yet be but half-grown."

"You think we may have some trouble trying to board the whaler?"

"Aye. We could be hard put right soon, the way things have begun to ..." Kell motions off to windward. The waves building and collapsing on themselves. Foam everywhere.

How Kell's voice does sometimes seem his inner conscience. Acknowledging or questioning, as the situation warrants. Always with the utmost prudence. The perfect counselor. The tempering, patient friend. A man to wear in one's heart.

"Could we but race with the Yank for yet another hour or so, though, eh, Luff?" He feels the longing in his chest. Hears it in his voice too. Buzzing in his head. Almost like champagne.

Kell has his long glass up to his eye, staring at the whaler. "Dark's coming on fast."

Dark? And he had so hoped the day would never end.

He pictures the island of Flores. That night he lay off to leeward of the green mountains. The scent of flowers perfuming the air of his cabin. The songs of the sirens. Addicting. Diverting. Destructive.

This schooning, so different, yet the same. A craving of the highest order.

"I can read her name," says Kell, his voice almost too neutral, too washed of color. "*Elisha Dunbar*, New Bedford."

The name slaps him in the face. Cold, wet, salty. The enemy's handmaiden, his very whore.

The yearning wavers, starts to fade.

"She may give us the slip if night falls and we don't take her."

"Yes, sir."

The song in the rig now seems a screech. A war cry.

"Lincoln's bully boys must soon catch wind of us here, Kell. We have played hard with their harem."

"Aye, right hard."

"Then ... gunners to the ready. Prepare to fire across her bows. Let's snatch and burn the Yankee drab. This is no time for boyish games. We have an ocean to cross tomorrow."

29

DISTRICT OF COLUMBIA
Late September, 1862

"Would you look at this?" The Secretary of State, William Seward, waves an overseas dispatch in his hand.

It flashes in the bright morning light blasting through a window. The paper is as thin and frail as onion skin. A nearly impenetrable collage of pale blue scribbling. Floppy as it moves through the smoke-laden air of Gideon Welles' office.

"What? What now, Bill?" Welles can't hide the suspicion in his voice. Almost asks, *What new torture and deceit have you designed for me. What new threat? Is it me who will be hanging in that tree by the observatory next?*

"Is there even the slightest chance that you remember who Thomas Dudley is, Gideon?" Seward has his hands on his waist, pinching back his jacket. Pushing out his little pot belly beneath his shirt as if to underscore his haughty disrespect.

Welles doesn't back down. He turns on Seward, steps toward him. Looks down on the man who he thinks must surely be the slipperiest snake in Lincoln's cabinet.

"Of course I remember who Dudley is, Bill. I just can't figure out what in heaven's name our consul in Liverpool has done to set you twitching like a rabid hare."

"You better read this damn dispatch from Dudley."

"Put out that blasted cigar and leave off marching around my office. I can't abide smoke, and you're making me nervous." Welles opens a window.

"Are you trying to bully me?"

"Me? Bullying you?"

"Can you for once imagine that you and I might be on the same side in this government and trust me?"

Welles continues looking away out the window.

"I bring you critical fucking intelligence from one of our best agents and you treat me as if I were ..."

The disloyal, power hungry, conniving, theatrical fox that you are, Welles thinks. But what he says is, "Take a seat, will you? How about a cup of tea? Then ... let me tell you about how we do things in civilized, little Connecticut."

The Secretary of State gives him a black look, throws the dispatch on the floor. Stomps out the door.

$ $ $

Welles is still standing at his window and staring down at the morning dew sparkling on the grass below. He's feeling a little bit of alright about how he put Seward off balance for once, ten minutes past. About how he did not let the Secretary of State fluster him with a lot of hyperbole and drama. Or this flimsy little dispatch in his right hand.

He's also thinking how he cannot wait for his wife and younger children to return from their long summer with family up in Pennsylvania. Washington can be a lonely place, a mad place. If it weren't that he thinks the president needs his loyal counsel more than ever— and that Lincoln is now on the right track by having signed the Emancipation Proclamation on the 22nd—he might gather his family and head right back to little Connecticut ... might say to hell with this whole mess. The war. The threats.

But he can't put aside his suspicions. Or his curiosity. That nagging sense of duty either.

"So ... what? What now, Seward? What now, Dudley?" he asks, looking at the filmy dispatch from the U.S. consul in Liverpool.

In truth, he admires Dudley. Maybe the man couldn't stop the escape of the *Oreto* or the *290* from Liverpool into Confederate service. But he has been sending a constant stream of information about Rebel and English naval plans for months. This dispatch seems no exception. It unveils a plan that a fleet of English blockade runners are hatching to overrun the Federal blockade at Charleston. This dispatch is just the kind of information he needs to light a fire under the Secretary of the Treasury to commit more funds for his ironclad-building program, to rush the new monitors to completion and set them up as sentries on the Carolina coast.

But it's Dudley's final two sentences in the dispatch that have really got him thinking, got him wondering if here in his hand he holds a time bomb that Seward intends to destroy him ... or whether, in fact, this dispatch is a key to a weapon more powerful than Wilkes' Flying Squadron to catch and destroy the *290*.

> *Before the 290 sailed, I was able to secure the services of a turncoat Rebel officer aboard the ship to help our cause. The man has strict orders to pass ashore to us every chance he gets any and all information about the operation, location and intentions of the 290.*

The words are still echoing in his brain—he's still wondering if Seward is somehow baiting him with this dispatch—when a soldier appears at his office door. Lincoln wants to see him. Immediately.

⚓　　⚓　　⚓

"What have you found out about these threats, Major Allen? Gideon's red envelopes? Who's behind them? Do we have cause for concern, sir?"

Lincoln's leading Allen and Welles across the east lawn to the stables. This seems to be his favorite route when he has something delicate to discuss. Just now he claims he needs to check on Tad's nanny goat that's giving off signs that she may drop her kid momentarily. It has evolved into a perfect September day in the capital. Warm. Crisp. Redolent with the scent of ripening apples ... and a golden pollen that makes Welles' nose run.

Allen clears his throat in a pretentious way that makes Welles feel like giving the ferret a whack with his walking stick.

"I believe we will have our answer shortly. My agents in Sharpsburg have sprung a trap."

"I don't follow." The president stops walking.

"I hear we've bagged an old friend—of Mr. Welles and mine—and her sister in crime."

"Come again." The president has not moved.

"We've told you about Raphael Semmes' West Irish strumpet who was trying to put the bite on Secretary Welles a year ago. The one who consorted with the Greenhow widow and Mistress Duval. The one who snuck off to Richmond."

"She's back?" Welles can't believe it.

"Remember what I told you about women, Mr. Secretary? Once they get onto something, they do not give up."

"What's she doing in Sharpsburg? On a battlefield?"

"That's the big question, ain't it?"

Lincoln rubs his forehead between his thumb and fingers. Asks his top agent to stop beating-around-the-bush.

Allen says he's got this old darkie gal in Richmond who has been watching Maude Galway for nigh on a year. Says the tart's a close friend of the First Lady of the Confederacy. So close it seems she got herself a job smuggling dispatches overseas for the Rebs. Possibly to Raphael Semmes himself. Of late, Jeff Davis and his Secretary of State Judah Benjamin have been using women as secret couriers. Including a friend of the Galway drab, another Irish school marm named Fiona O'Hare.

Sometime last summer Galway returned from courier service to find that she had been socially destroyed by public rumors of her affair with the married Semmes. Madame Davis necessarily had to hold the slut at a distance, but Benjamin may have retained her services. Set her up nursing in a hospital for wounded veterans. And now both these Irish lassies seem to have been using the pretense of nursing to gain access to the battle lines and cross into the North with a secret message.

Lincoln paws the ground, his shoe raising a cloud of dust. "What message? For whom?"

"That's what I'm going up to Sharpsburg this afternoon to find out. All I know at this point is that the O'Hare woman had an odd thing hid in her small clothes."

"Excuse me?"

"She was carrying a folded page of script ... from Shakespeare's *Julius Caesar*."

Welles feels something burning in his guts as his mind connects the dots.

"I still don't get it," says Lincoln.

"The play, Mr. President," says Welles. "You know? It's about assassination."

"You think these women and that play, Major Allen, have something to do with those threats to Gideon?"

30

CSS *ALABAMA*
October 9, 1862

"To hang or not to hang? That's the question, gentlemen." Semmes eyes the officers at this impromptu court martial. A flinty, frozen look right now on the face of the captain who has become known to his crew as Old Beeswax.

It's one bell into the evening watch. Not yet sunset over the Grand Banks off Newfoundland. The air heavy with the damp warmth of the Gulf Stream, despite the fresh breeze. The ship silent now, laboring westward against a headwind, foul current.

Paymaster Clarence Yonge is trying to avoid his captain's gaze, staring at the wardroom table. Feeling the sweat trickling down his back. His hands claw at each other in his lap.

"The man deserves to die," says Lieutenant Armstrong, the second luff.

"Desertion is punishable by death." Kell says. "It is the naval code."

"It might make a potent lesson to the more unruly of the crew," Lieutenant Beckett Howell says. He's the ship's marine officer, the other on-board celebrity beside the captain. Varina Davis is his sister.

"What say you, Mr. Yonge?" That flinty look from Old Beeswax again.

Y'all are a bunch of self-important hardasses. That's what the brandy in Yonge's stomach is saying, the brandy he stole off the *Starlight* in the Azores. But his mind is just clear enough to reach for reason. His soul just lonely enough to crave an ally.

The paymaster—the Yankee's penny boy, the spy—lifts his gaze and looks across the table at the seaman seated before the assembly of officers. George Forrest. A man still in the bloom of his youth. Heavy bearded. Tan. A bit shorter than average ... with the shoulders, arms of an ape. Hands like claws. A man clearly accustomed to the sailor's life. Yonge doesn't know him from Adam. He just knows the poor fellow has had the misfortune of coming afoul of Semmes, the captain he deserted in Cadiz, back when Semmes sailed on the *Sumter*. Forrest came aboard the *Alabama* among the crew from the New York grain carrier *Dunkirk*, seized and burned two nights ago. Kell recognized him. Semmes has branded him a Judas. The poor bastard.

There but for the grace of God sit I.

"What say you, Mr. Yonge. Hang him?"

Yonge swallows a mouthful of saliva, tries to collect his thoughts. Looks for a means to save a potential ally's life. "Was this man an able hand, sir, on the *Sumter*?"

"Kell?" The skipper defers to his luff, supervisor of all things having to do with the daily management of the Jacks.

"Reliable topsman, rigger, steady on the helm. Some decent carpentry skills, too. As I remember."

"What are you driving at, paymaster?" Semmes asks.

"As I understand the code of military justice, capital punishment is not our only option here. It's a last resort ... and a hard sentence for both judges and defendant."

"Permission to speak, sirs?" Forrest shoots a quick look at Yonge as if he recognizes a comrade, knows what he must say now.

"As you will, man."

"I throw myself at the mercy of your generous hearts, good sirs. I only left the *Sumter* because I had news in Cadiz that my wife had birthed our first child, was some sick. She needed me home."

"You could have come to me with your problem." Kell's voice is flat, neutral.

"If you but give me another chance to sail with you, Captain Semmes, I will do this ship as good as any man Jack aboard." Forrest casts another swift glance at Yonge for approval.

"We are still short some twenty men for a full crew, captain," says the paymaster.

The flint softens in the captain's cheeks a bit. His mustache twitches. "Can you make good use of this man, Kell?"

"Aye, sir. Long as he minds his Ps and Qs."

"I will be your willing servant. On my honor." Forrest vows.

Something in the sailor's voice sounds too ready to Yonge. More like optimism, or pure balderdash, than certainty. More like his own voice back in Liverpool when Thomas Dudley was threatening him with exposure for his whore-mongering. When he would have said anything, done anything, to save his own neck. Even betray the Confederacy.

But, blessed are the fucking gods. The captain seems too lost in his own thoughts to hear the false note in Forrest's voice.

Semmes presses his hands to his lips in prayer, exhales audibly into them. Then he turns his gaze on each of his officers seated at the table, one man after the other.

"Gentlemen. I propose we sign this man to the crew. His punishment for desertion shall be to work for no pay. But if he finishes this cruise in good standing, he shall have the pay and prize money due every man before the mast. Leave hanging to the Yanks and the old navy."

Yonge looks to Forrest. The seaman blinks back at him. A bond, a debt acknowledged. His first recruit.

The only questions now are how to use Georgie Boy ... and when. Yonge is still pondering his new ally, his rising fortunes, when the call comes from aloft. "Sail ho. Another Yank. A freighter, sure!"

This will be the fifth prize in six days as the *Alabama* closes with the American continent. Just as Yonge thought. Raphael Semmes aims to seize and burn his way right down the coast. Unless someone can put a stop to this mayhem.

31

FREDERICK, MARYLAND
October 9, 1862

"What does 'J.W.B.' stand for, you slut?" Allen holds a page of script from Shakespeare's *Julius Caesar* in his hand. It's the page the soldiers found folded and hidden in Fiona's small clothes when they bagged her and searched her on the battlefield. The page with the letters J.W.B. written on the outer face of the folded page as if it were an address.

The Federal agent seizes Maude by the hair and yanks her head back on her shoulders until her throat closes. She thinks it will rip open from the strain.

The child in her belly feels heavy, quiet. She's on her knees in a bare room kneeling before a vat of freshly pressed apple cider at a place known as the Hessian Barracks. After the battle at Antietam Creek, this old Revolutionary War barracks served as a hospital for wounded soldiers from both the North and the South. But the wounded are gone now. Only she and Fiona remain—prisoners in separate rooms of this two-story fieldstone building with is gallery porches. She has not talked to Fiona for twenty-one days. Can only hear her cursing, ranting since the day they were both captured while trying to help that crying mother on the battlefield. Captured by Yanks who used the soldier's mother as a decoy to catch suspected Southern spies masquerading as nurses and doctors.

"Is this script from the play some kind of code from Judah Benjamin? Or Jefferson Davis? Is there a plot against my Caesar, Mr. Lincoln? Or is it against Gideon Welles like before with you? All to save your pirate lover? What do you know about threats delivered to Welles in red envelopes?"

She tries to force her throat open to breathe. Tries to shake off the dull sting of these same questions that Allen has been badgering her and Fiona with since he arrived three days ago. Over and over. The bloke never stops. She has no idea about red envelopes or a plot. Had only the vaguest suspicions that Fiona might have come to Sharpsburg's battlefield for a reason other than nursing. Didn't know about the concealed page of script from Shakespeare.

But she does know that Judah Benjamin is Jeff Davis' dirty tricks man. Not just the Secretary of State, but the head of the Confederates' secret service, too. Knows that not long after Rose Greenhow was released from the Old Capital Jail, and she made her way to Richmond, she visited with Varina Davis and Benjamin. Quite often. Before she undertook her sea voyage abroad to see someone named Boolard or Bullot. Something like that.

"Tell me what you know hussy. Is 'J.W.B.' someone's initials?" Allen lifts her off her knees by her hair. The roots burn.

She doesn't know what or who J.W.B. stands for. Doesn't know about threats in red envelopes. Wouldn't tell now, even if she did. Unless it could save her baby. Maybe she will have a son. Maybe Raffy will love the child against all odds.

She closes her eyes, reaches in her mind for Raffy, for his strength. The last time she was with him. Deeply tan, handsome in his new gray uniform as he saw her off from Nassau to Savannah. Tears in his eyes, his voice whispering that he does not think he could live even an hour without holding her in his heart.

She kisses his ear ... he must know that she will not stop hoping for another miracle to bring them back together.

"Speak or drown, girl. Have you been pestering Mr. Welles again with threats?" Allen shoves her face down into the cider again. It's cold and sticky. She has been dunked so many times on this chilly morning that all the sweetness of the apples is long gone. What remains is an acrid gas rising out of the tub, burning her eyes, nose, lips.

"I'm just a nurse," she says when he snaps her head out of the cider again.

"Like hell you are, lassie. You're a bloody Reb agent. Just like you always was. You and your tomboy girlfriend."

As if on cue, Fiona shouts from somewhere in the barracks. "Just fuck you, you bleeding arseholes. Let her alone! She doesn't know anything!"

Allen drives her head into the cider again. Holds her under as she struggles to rise.

"Maybe we should lay off her a bit, major," the Union captain with Allen says when he finally pulls her sputtering, gagging, coughing to the surface. "She looks to be about ready to pop that baby in her."

"Damn her. This wench and I have a history. Isn't that right, Maudie?"

She glares at him. Pictures a knife in her hand. A knife driving through his tight little tweed jacket, his chest.

"Tell the good captain how you tried to blackmail the Secretary of the Navy, a year past. How you put a paring knife right through me hand. How later you nearly blinded me with a horseshoe to the head before you ran off to Richmond with that Frenchy."

"Bugger off."

"Get her mate out here to watch her die. Watch the baby die, too." Allen shouts at the officer. Then he drives her down into the cider again.

"She can't take much more of this," the captain says. His voice sounds booming yet distant.

"I want O'Hare!"

When she comes up from her dunking, Fiona's bound to a porch post. She's in the same soiled, gray dress she was wearing on the battlefield three weeks ago. Her face is streaked with dirt. One eye is swollen shut. The corner of her mouth is bloody, looks torn. Her good eye reaches out to Maude. Her lips move with soundless words. Some sort of silent supplication. Apology.

"It's been days you've been wasting me time, Fiona O'Hare," Allen is shouting. "I ain't a man to squander away me life on the likes of you two."

"Fuck you."

Allen roars. "One of you two hussies better tell me who this script was meant for ... or I swear I'll drown this bloody tart. Then I'm going to fuck you up the arse with a piece of porch rail until you beg for death ..."

Down into the vat Maude goes again. Deeper this time, until her shoulders and breasts are submerged too. He nose and lips pressed so hard against the bottom that she can't keep the cider out. Feels it streaming into her sinuses, mouth, throat. *Jesus, Mary and Joseph.* Her lungs.

I'm going to die, she thinks. *My child.*

She's been under the cider so long that Allen's voice, his threats to Fiona, are fading out. A buzzing in the ears, a blackness growing in her head. She's seeing her baby. Silver, shimmering just beyond arms reach. She's relaxing. Reaching out for the child when she hears Fiona. Her voice almost impossibly faint. Far away.

"Wait! Let her go. I'll tell you everything."

32

===~~~===

CSS *ALABAMA*
October 11, 1862

It's as if a spike pierces Semmes' heart when he spies the letter addressed to Fraser, Trenholm & Co. When he recognizes the graceful, looping script. When he fears to hope.

The letter has been buried beneath a pile of newspapers, magazines, letters that his postmaster spilled onto the floor of his cabin during the first dog watch. Mail for England carried aboard the *Alabama's* sixth prize since October 3. The *Manchester*, from New York bound to Liverpool. Stopped and seized this very afternoon. Even now awaiting his verdict, just as is the *Tonawanda*, taken two days ago. His prize crews sail the two Yanks in the *Alabama's* wake while he contemplates whether to burn them, what to do with *Tonawanda's* many passengers who are children. And their mothers. Young women.

It has become his habit—almost immediately after seizing a ship—to go through all its mail bags for news and information that might give him clues as to the progress of the war, the movement of the Yanks' ships, any references to Gideon Welles' pursuit of him. Before he passes on the newspapers and magazines to his officers in the wardroom, he scours them. He's continually astonished how open the Northern government is in reporting the movements of its troops and warships. This information is so specific, so timely, that he wonders if Lincoln's boys are sending out false signals to the press to delude the South. Delude him. He must be doubly careful as he closes with North America.

The newspapers he has been examining for the last hour are just a few days out of New York. They contain news to twist his guts, to make his cheeks burn with anger. News again of the terrible battle at Sharpsburg, Maryland; over twenty thousand casualties. News that Lee's army, except for J.E.B. Stuart's cavalry, has retreated back into Virginia. News that Lincoln has issued his Emancipation Proclamation to free the slaves. Nothing good.

And news of an even more relevant character. Charles Wilkes and a so-called Flying Squadron have been sent to hunt and destroy the *Oreto* and the *290*.

But, surprisingly, there is still no news of his seizures of the whalers in the Azores. His movements are still invisible. The *Alabama*'s a phantom. The world does not yet even know her name. And according to the papers, Wilkes squadron has already headed to Nassau and the West Indies by way of Bermuda to search for him. Fools. Do they actually think he would cross the Atlantic at the lower latitudes, or dally in the tropics, during this season of the great storms?

Maybe they are willing to chance coming afoul of the cyclonic typhoons the Spanish islanders call *Jurakán*, after their Indian god of malevolence. But the captain of the *Alabama* would rather avoid such a risk. He'd rather plow slowly west against the Gulf Stream current and the prevailing westerlies at this high latitude, harvesting east-bound merchantmen. If, as it seems from the Yank papers, Gideon Welles and his minions are so unaware of where he actually is, he might hunt his way as invisibly as a phantom all the way down the East Coast.

He had been picturing how he might charge into New York Harbor and bite the Yank in the nose ... when his foot—stirring the mail at his feet—uncovered the blue envelope for Fraser, Trenholm. The letter that must surely be from Maude.

⚓   ⚓   ⚓

His hands shake as he tears open the envelope, finds a letter inside, sealed in wax. Her seal. A shamrock. The letter addressed to him.

Most merciful God. She's alive. After Nassau he had so feared ...
He wipes his spectacles clean with his kerchief before he breaks the
seal on the letter. Takes a deep breath, tells himself before he begins to
read that this letter may bring even worse news than the papers.

17 September, 1862
My Dearest, Sweetest Captain,
My hero. I love you. I love you. I love you. Never forget, my
Raffy. Never let me go. No matter what.

He feels a jolt in his chest. Not the steel spike from before, but a
cascade of shudders, rolling bursts. And with them the tears. A fissure
opening in his chest.

Those terrible days in Nassau seem like a bad dream to me ...
the child I so feared to tell you about ... my sin against God
and you ... all seem something from a nightmare that I ...

His hips seem to buckle, break as a sob rises in his throat. His guts
are tearing apart. Legs crumbling into dust. Into the ship, the sea.

But somehow I have survived. The child, too, still grows
within me. Maybe because what I try to remember about Nas-
sau is the way you held me in your arms all night long. Until
I imagined nothing could destroy this love I feel for you. This
love that keeps me warm and smiling eastward toward your
ocean every day as I write these letters to you. Everyday I hold
you to my breast and kiss you in my mind, my heart, my soul.

He can hear the rise and fall of her throaty Irish brogue, see the
sparkle in her green eyes, the freckles on her nose, her broad smile.
As she tells him, as she must have done already in many other letters
that he hasn't received, about having been nursed back to health in
Savannah. How, maybe as a result, she found this new passion for
nursing.

She has spent most of her waking hours of late working at the Robertson Hospital. It's run by a woman named Sally Tompkins, who Jefferson Davis has made a captain in the cavalry to support her ceaseless work for the South. Her friend Fiona has joined her. Now there has been news of an immense battle up north at a place called Sharpsburg in Maryland. She and Fiona are joining a wagon train of doctors and nurses leaving this very morning for the battlefield to see if they can save lives.

Wish me God speed, Raffy.

She writes, too, about the misery of the wounded that have come under her care in Richmond. Called her angel, love, daughter, wife. Wounded who have died in her arms.

He does not want to imagine such scenes. Still, he sees. A dingy room, a man of bandages, a soldier with no face, stumps for arms. Sees his sons. Oliver, Spencer. Torn and broken. Hugging her. Weeping as he weeps now. Smelling the lavender powder on her shoulders, neck. Beside themselves with wonder. Even as death stalks them. Begging this goddess for one last kiss before ...

He tosses the letter onto his floor. Swears. Rises from his chair. Kicks the pile of correspondence on the cabin sole into a flock of twisted paper.

Damn the Yankees. Damn the women ... look what they do to us. When all we want is our freedom. And some sense of our own worth. "Damn. God damn me. God damn it all."

His heart is a bloody fist, pulsing on the heaving sole of the cabin when a knock sounds twice on his cabin door.

"Is everything alright, sir?" It's Yonge, the paymaster. The busybody.

Doesn't he have anything better to do?

"Sir?"

"What, man?"

"Dr. Galt wants to keep a Negro boy off the *Tonawanda*."

"What?"

"To serve him. Name of David."

Jesus Lord Almighty.

"What next?" Semmes leans his forehead against a bulkhead, closes his eyes.

Kell wants to know what the captain plans to do with the prisoners, the prizes—*Tonawanda* and *Manchester*. It looks like dirty weather coming before daybreak.

Burn them all, he almost says. *And burn my heart too. It lies yonder on the floor. In the blood. In that letter. In that selkie's mouth.*

"Captain?"

He picks up her letter. Clutches it to his chest. The tears coming again as he wonders where all this anger is coming from.

"Put all the prisoners on the *Tonawanda*." He says when he finally finds his voice. "I will send them off to England under a bond signed by their captain. The other? Light up the night with her. Until we wake Neptune and make him roar!"

33

LIVERPOOL, ENGLAND
October 13, 1862

Endbutt Lane. Another night of bitter ale for Dudley at the pub in the doxie hotel. Another night to see what's come into the pen from Maguire's agents dogging the Rebs who now have several new ships building in England. Two, the *294* and *295*, right across the Mersey at the Laird docks. Turreted rams, iron-clad with four-inch-thick plate. Ships to destroy any blockade. Not fleet corsairs like the *Oreto* or the *290*. But ships to lay siege with impunity to New York, Norfolk, New Orleans, Washington. Ships that must never leave England.

Another night of Lorraine asking if she's still Queen of the Nile. Another night of her offering him a tumble.

And who wouldn't be tempted? That hair. Burnished blond, twisted and clasped up on the back of her head, baring a long, creamy neck. Its wisps of golden hairs. The immense, blue eyes. The bow of pink lips. The easy curves of her slender body beneath the close-fitting green bodice; the tawny dress, tight at the waist, flowing over shadows of hips, thighs, ankles.

Lord.

"What have you done for me lately?" He tries to seem coy, disinterested as she leans into him. Presses her breasts against his arm as she takes a sip from his pint. He thinks that it may only be because he holds himself just beyond her reach that he maintains his leverage over her. Keeps her fishing for the Union.

"I know a secret."

"What?"

"I'll tell you if you come upstairs with me."

"I'm a married man."

"Are you trying to break my heart?"

"No, I ..."

She takes another swallow from his pint. Stares up into his face with a ring of foam on her lips. "Haven't I been loyal?"

He nods, thinks how many ways she's laid her life, even her soul, on the line for a cause that is not even her own. Imagines that it is partially because of him, what she feels for him—longing, confusion, challenge—that she risks herself again and again. But he also knows that there is something else possibly even more powerful in her soul that drives her ceaseless taking of risk upon risk. Not just on midnight spying missions at the docks or at courtly balls. But the other. What he tries not to think about. Romantic liaisons with all manner of beasts. Like the turncoat Yonge. For money. For information. For Blackmail. Power.

And yet she always smells as fresh as summer strawberries and honey.

"Duds?" Her hand slides into his free hand.

He thinks of his wife, his children. Tries to pull away ... but gently.

She tightens her grip, pouts with her full lower lip.

"What would you do if I went over to the Rebs?"

He feels slapped in the back of the head. Pictures nearly a year of work. The network of more than two dozen agents that he has put together. Exposed. Torn apart.

"Are you serious?"

"Some of them are nice to me."

"No doubt."

"There's a new bloke in town."

"Who?"

He's younger than you. Handsome as a fairy prince. Rich. Charming."

"What's his name?"

"I know a lot more than his name. I know things." She swills the last of his pint, turns away. "Things even more dangerous to your Secretary of the Navy and President Lincoln than Raphael Semmes and his new ship ... but I can see you're not interested."

"Lorraine!"

"What?"

He suddenly reaches after her. Grabs her by the elbow. "Don't be difficult."

"Me?"

"Haven't I given you money beyond your wildest dreams?"

"I want more. Maybe Lieutenant George T. Sinclair can give me more. You know, he served briefly with Semmes. He knows Yonge." She shakes off his grip.

He can feel her sudden fury as she stomps toward the stairs leading to her room upstairs. By the time he catches her by the waist, she's reached the landing at the top of the steps. Some of the dock workers, sailors, Jezebels, are watching them. He's calling too much attention to himself. This is not acceptable. But he has to settle this thing with her.

"I truly hoped that I would never have to say this."

"Leave me alone, Duds."

He spins her on her heels until they are eye-to-eye. His hands holding each of her wrists now. "If I ever really thought you might go over to the South ... I would kill you first."

She looks away, trying to hide tears boiling into her eyes. "Maybe that's what I want."

He can't help himself. Her honesty, vulnerability, desperation, brass. They tug at something in his core. He throws his arms around her, pulls her to his chest. If he had the stripes of a military man on his shoulders, he might well rip them off. Right now. With everyone in this Endbutt pub watching. Bill Seward and Abe Lincoln want too much. He thought this job was going to be all about loyalty, persistence, intelligence. Not this. He's just a man. A tired man, a scared man. A lonely man. With her sweet, hot breath on his neck.

"Can we go to your room?" The question comes from him.

"Are you sure?"

"You're my Queen of the Nile ..." *And who can say how soon before one, or both, of us is dead?*

34

CSS *ALABAMA*
October 14, 1862

The Jacks have queued up just forward of the bridge. It's the end of the first dog watch and time for the daily rum ration. It has been thick fog on the Grand Banks all day. Now, with sunset, it's thicker. Dark. Except for the lamp hung low to cast a circle of yellow light over the grog barrel. The ship's a thing of shadows, magnified sounds. The creaking of the standing and running rigging. The slop of waves on the starboard topsides. The shuffle of men. Pills Galt trying to cajol the Negro boy David to dance a jig for the ship's company. Harmonica music. Bits of laughter too.

Yonge sees Forrest leaning against the bulwarks to leeward near a gun port. The man is looking up at him on the bridge where he's lounging along with a number of the officers who are off watch. There's a question on the Jack's face.

It's that 'tween time after the mess when the Jacks relax with their grog and pipes of tobacco. The officers have their cigars and glasses of French *vin rouge* brought to them by the wardroom steward. Twilight. When the crew shakes off the tedium of the day for an hour before eight bells sound the start of the evening watch. And the ship goes dead quiet for the night.

It's nearly dark when Yonge dips deep into his hidden bottles of brandy from the *Starlight*, too. Until the heat rises from his belly and the bitterness and guilt he feels about his betrayal of the South grow into something else. A dream. The first tendrils of a plan.

Tonight the fog makes the air damp, cool. It's as if there's a shroud over the *Alabama*. A man cannot see farther than twenty feet fore or aft along the deck. The sea is out of sight altogether. The ship's sailing in a cloud. Still, there's gaity. The boy David is dancing a hornpipe to "Oh, Susannah" amid a circle of clapping crew, when Yonge descends from the deck, walks forward. Passes Forrest with a subtle beckoning nod, keeps walking until they both are alone in the sail locker.

"I thought we should talk," says the sailor.

"Indeed."

"I know that I owe you my life."

"I did what I could. You seem a useful hand."

"And now ...?" Forrest's voice echoes with expectation. He is a man of the world, and he understands fully that the gift of his life will come with obligations to the paymaster.

"I heard some of the Jacks talking when y'all first came off the *Dunkirk*. They said George Forrest was a blackguard on the *Sumter*."

The seaman bristles. "Not so, sir."

"They said George Forrest led a whole gang in the fo'castle to jump ship in Gibraltar."

"It wasn't like that. I ..."

"Listen to me, man. I see y'all as a man of uncommon enterprise."

"Sir?"

"There's a good lot of money to be made if a man can keep quiet and go about some private business. Are you that kind of a man?"

Forrest puffs out his barrel chest a bit. "None other, sir."

Yonge hands the Jack a ten-dollar gold piece pilfered from *Alabama*'s war chest. "Then here's what I want y'all to do. Just one little thing to start. To see how you get on."

"Anything, sir."

"Sound the crew most quiet-like for tough, able seamen and coal stokers—especially stokers—who would like to end this voyage sooner rather than later. And set themselves up in a tropical paradise as kings."

Forrest's eyes are suddenly large as oysters. "You aim to take this ship from Old Beeswax?"

"Just bring me names, man ... and give me a drink of your grog."

35

NORTH OF BALTIMORE

October 16, 1862

"At least we're together, Fi," says Maude. She clutches the hand cuffed to hers, leans her head on her friend's shoulder. Tries to ignore the two grisly soldiers, the guards, sitting opposite on the facing bench seat. One fishing into his tobacco pouch for a chaw, the other picking his nose, examining the booger between his fingers.

Fiona doesn't answer, doesn't even move. Just stares out the window through the one good eye in her ruined face as the train ambles north from Baltimore on the tracks of the Pennsylvania, Wilmington & Baltimore through the pastures north of Aberdeen. Over the Susquehanna River at Havre de Grace. Even with the windows in their carriage closed, soot and ashes from the locomotive are being sucked inside from the open door to the vestibule, making the afternoon even more gray than the thick clouds obscuring the sun.

"You know, these bloody bastards aim to kill us, love," Fiona says.

She doesn't seem to care that the guards hear her. She treats them like they don't exist. A habit she has with men in general. But now her disregard has gained a cavalier, imperious edge. As if she thinks what more can these bastards do to her that they haven't already done, twice?

Maude knows there may well be truth in what her friend says about murder. Really, what good are she and Fiona now to Major Allen? Fiona gave up all that she knows. The actor Booth. And the name of the doctor in Richmond who sent the page of script. No doubt those men will soon meet with an accident. Unless they have connections in high places that can save them from Allen.

When Lincoln's head agent put her and Fiona on this train in Baltimore, handed them over to these two guards, he made a spectacle of himself. He announced to all that could hear him at the station that *Right here before God and the good citizens of Baltimore, I wash my hands of these two Rebel harlots and spies.* He then actually soaped and rinsed his hands in a basin a black woman held for him. Like he was bleeding Pontius Pilot or something. *Jesus, Mary and Joseph!* Allen just wanted witnesses. Just wanted people who could say that whatever happens next to the two of them, Allen is without blame. Above suspicion. That's why he didn't kill them in Frederick after Fiona confessed. After Allen raped her anyway with a riding crop. Just for the hell of it. He wanted to be blameless in any killing. It seems Allen is squeamish when it comes to actually pulling the trigger.

Supposedly Maude and Fiona are going north to prison. But to where, Maude hasn't a clue. Once Allen said they were going to Fort Delaware on Pea Patch Island in the Delaware River. At another moment, he said they were going to Eastern State Penitentiary in Philadelphia. It really doesn't matter. She knows that neither place has accommodation for women. And quite possibly she and Fiona will never get there.

She's pressing her face tighter to her friend's shoulder, her chest. Wondering if she could have ever foreseen this failure of a life ending this way when she left her poor mom back on Tralee Bay to come to America.

Could this short, ignoble end be the Devine's judgment against a simple lass who gave her heart and soul to a married man? Who carries another man's baby? Who has no husband? Is there something too rambunctious or romantic in her Irish nature to make a successful go of this immense, wild, rude country? Was it something in the early death of her own dad—the military man and dreamer? Did that somehow make her so vulnerable to Raffy's charms, color her other devastating decisions?"

What would Raffy say to her now? She's wondering where he is ... but then she remembers. Allen told her. Raffy was all over the papers again. He and his new ship *Alabama* had raised hell with Yank whalers in the Azores. Now, it seems, he's crossing the Atlantic. Coming home to spit in the very face of the Union. And, Allen says, the Union is more than ready. This time she cannot send him letters to warn him away as she did last year when the Yanks almost caught him in Martinique. She has not been able to write at all since she was captured on that field of death near Antietam Creek. This time she's helpless, just about as good as dead. And Raffy's heading right into a trap.

"I'm so sorry I got you mixed up in all of this again," says Fiona. The train has begun to slow as it starts to clatter onto a trestle over a marsh opening into a bay. There are men, like the watermen of Bantry Bay back home, tonging for oysters in small, white boats.

"I've made my own choices."

"I wish we could just leap off this train and end it all."

Fiona's words flare in Maude's head. A series of arcs, sizzling little connections. Then a searing blaze. An insight. A vision of escape. "Holy Mary."

"What?"

"Help me." She raps one of her guards on the knee. "I'm going to have my baby."

36

CSS *ALABAMA*
October 16, 1862

"You better have a look, sir." Kell, the ever-steady luff, cannot keep the concern from his voice, the pale hue of fear from his face. "The glass has fallen an inch in the last hour."

Semmes rises from his desk where he has been all but lost in his journal entry about seizing and burning his eighth prize in twelve days. The *Lamplighter*, out of Boston for Gibraltar, with a load of Connecticut tobacco. He still has one foot in the memory—the scent of tobacco smoke sweetened the air as the Yankee burned last night—when he follows Kell topside, breathes something totally different.

The breeze comes in heavy, whistling gusts from the southwest, withering with equatorial heat. So moist his skin erupts with beads of sweat. Off to the south, a wall of gray clouds surges toward the *Alabama* with the visible haste of a squall line. But this is something altogether different. Taller. A curtain of fuming vapor draping down from the knees of God. Already blocking the sun. The sky overhead still clear, but not blue. A sickening, deepening green, tending toward black.

For just an instant in the captain's head it is December 8, 1846, yet again. The Mexican War. Aboard the *Somers*, on blockade duty off Veracruz.

A torrent of salt air laying the brig down on her side. The starboard rail awash. The tips of the lower yards snagging in the waves. The mainsail dragging in the water. Filling like a pool. Jacks tumbling into the sea, hugging the rigging, anything else to anchor them. A cannon breaking loose from its breaching ropes to windward, skating across the deck. Crashing through the lee rail. Shrill shouts from men trapped below decks as the ship starts to fill, sink. As he loses his ship, nearly half the crew.

"Hurricane," he says.

"I've already rigged jack lines fore and aft."

"Beat to quarters, Mr. Kell. All hands on deck. Take in the fore-topsail. We must reduce top-hamper. Send down the topgallant yards. Rig your heaviest storm staysail."

"Yes, sir."

"Batten all hatches ... I want every man—Jacks, officers, prisoners alike—to remain on deck."

Kell gives him a confused look. The whole crew on deck? In a hurricane?

"A man on deck has a chance, Luff, if our girl should falter. A man below has none at all."

Kell's gaze begins darting randomly in a half-dozen directions.

Semmes senses his first officer's sudden loss of bearings, knows the feeling. But also knows that this is no time for misgivings. Only preparation, focus. He inhales. Holds the breath. Gathers himself.

"Look sharp, Kell ... Our God aims to test the *Alabama*, and us, right shortly. This monster cometh."

⚓　　⚓　　⚓

With the rest of his men, the captain huddles beneath the port bulwarks to stay out of the worst of the weather. The ship heels hard to starboard even as the two men at the helm try to ease her a bit up into the storm to spill some of the air from her remaining sails. The wind now a deep roar, driving rain like buckshot. The seas are broken mountains. Avalanches of foam. The ship shuddering, bucking from the pounding. This howling behemoth of air and sea presses down on the *Alabama* until the leeward longboat is torn from her davits, smashed, by a sea sweeping the starboard side of the ship from stem to stern. It's all Semmes can do to hold fast to a belaying pin beneath the mizzen chains to keep from tumbling down the deck to leeward ... to be washed off into oblivion.

He's looking up at the main topsail, shielding his eyes from the rain. Thinking the sail is putting a horrible strain on the mast, the main yard. Thinking that he must start the topsail's sheets and let the canvas blow to pieces, when he hears something like the crack of a cannon. The seamen lashed to the mizzen mast, wrestling with the ship's double wheel, look aloft with jaws dropping. The eyes of the rest of the more than one hundred souls on deck follow.

Overhead, the main yard—a timber over sixty-feet long, three-feet around—its windward brace parted, has snapped from its slings. It cartwheels into the clouds, vanishes with the topsail tailing behind.

"Jesus fuck," mutters somebody.

And then another gust hits with a force like nothing any of these men has ever felt before. A ship-shattering blow. The *Alabama* lurches, gets away from the quartermaster and his mate at the helm, rounds up into the wind. Stalls. Her bows plunging into a wave that rises fifty, sixty, seventy feet as it rushes down on the ship.

"Bear off." Semmes hears himself scream.

Sees the helmsmen spinning the wheels hard to starboard. But nothing's happening. The *Alabama*'s failing to answer the helm. All the air's gone from the storm staysail. Ship wallowing as the immense wave towers. Sky quiet in this valley before the wave. Men gasp as if all the air in the world has been sucked from them ... just before the wave sweeps over the ship, and everything and everybody is buried beneath black water.

When he comes up for air, Semmes is holding onto the port jack line that Kell rigged as a handhold for such a case as this. One by one, men start popping up out of the water all along the length of the jack line. All of them waist deep in the sea. Wind roaring again. The *Alabama* a spongy ghost somewhere beneath their feet.

This is it. This is the nightmare he has woken to a thousand times in the last sixteen years. The death of the *Somers*.

Hills of foam raking his ship. The starboard side lost below the surface. Men cursing, calling the names of their mates for comfort. Begging their God for mercy.

He claws his way forward along the jack line, hoping for a miracle, shouting that this will not happen again. Willing the bows buried in the black water to rise and shake off the seas. Willing the staysail to catch the wind, to restore steerage. Yelling into the faces of his men. Encouraging them. Spit at the devil in the storm! Proclaim that this ship—this beautiful dream, their bride—will rise again.

"She will rise. By all of God's good grace. Let her rise!"

By the time he has reached the foremast boys clinging to the jack line, the entire ship's company—prisoners and crew alike—are shouting. Let her rise.

And she does. *Alabama* does rise, her handsome clipper bows lifting from the deep.

Alive again. Like a selkie he knows.

At least for now.

37

❦

DISTRICT OF COLUMBIA
October 18, 1862

"How do I have even a minute to give a pig's poke, Gideon, about threats and plots? About Semmes' misguided girlfriend? When we have that pirate to stop." Lincoln's voice has a gruff edge.

"Can we continue this talk privately?"

Lincoln nods. Looks out his office window, possibly thinking it's time for another walk to the stables. Sees a hard rain soaking the White House grounds. He leads Welles into the shabby little office of one of his secretaries, John Hay, in the northeast corner on the second floor of the executive mansion.

But just as he seems ready to speak, he shakes his head as if even this place is too public. He waves Welles back down the hallway through a doorway that the Secretary of the Navy has never noticed before. It leads to a flight of stairs rising to the attic. Even before the two men have mounted to the top of the steps, Welles can hear the rain drumming on the mansion's roof.

"Raphael Semmes has resurfaced with a vengeance," says Lincoln, standing amid what looks like the costume shop for a theatre. "A true hell hound now with this new ship called the ... the ..."

"The *Alabama*."

Lincoln hands him a copy of the *New York Times* from Wednesday, October 17, pokes at a front-page story with his index finger.

THE PIRATE ALABAMA

Her Operations in the Track of Vessels Going to England. The Ship Brilliant, of Boston Destroyed by Her. Another Ship, Name Unknown, Burnt. Eleven Vessels in all Known to Have Been Destroyed. Statement of Capt. Hagar, of the Brilliant ...

Welles has not seen the article before, but he knows the contents. That's why he's here to see the president this morning. The news of Semmes began to filter in a few days ago when he received a telegram from B. F. Delano, a shipbuilder. A naval contractor born to one of the prominent whaling families in New Bedford, Massachusetts. The telegram spewed the stories of whaler crews just arrived back in New England with news of the *Alabama's* seizing and burning their ships off the Azores. Yesterday evening Welles had a visit from the senior senator from Massachusetts demanding action. And now there's this news from the captain of the *Brilliant* that Semmes is off the Grand Banks, westbound toward New England, raiding grain ships carrying wheat to Europe.

"Bill Seward says we should sue England for damages," says Welles. "They built Semmes' new monster, and the other raider, the *Oreto*, for the Rebs."

"Lawsuits won't stop Semmes."

"Exactly."

"I thought we sent Wilkes off with a whole pack of ships to stop this madman." Lincoln.

"That's why I thought we should talk in private."

The president looks around him in the dim light. Seems distracted by a half-dozen women's dresses thrown over chairs, an old sofa. "It appears Tad and his friends Bud and Holly Taft have been playing dress-up again, putting on another one of their gaiety shows up here for the help."

"Beg your pardon, sir?"

Lincoln waves his hand as if to dismiss his last remark. "What are you trying to tell me, Gideon?"

Welles says he doesn't hold out much hope for Wilkes. The man seems more show than substance. And exceedingly contrary.

"So what do we do?"

Lincoln fears the nation is losing patience with him. It does not look like the November elections will go well for his administration. The Copperheads are growing in strength, gaining support, especially in New York City and among the Irish immigrants. More citizens are turning against this war every day. And now Sal Chase has persuaded Congress that the country must go off the gold standard just like the Confederates. Switch to paper money to pay the war bills. The United States will become a nation of debtors.

Welles says he sees a hope. He tells Lincoln about Yonge, a Reb turncoat on the *Alabama*.

"I'm in possession of a letter that Yonge sent to Bill Seward a few weeks ago from the *Alabama*."

There's a flash of lightning through a skylight, almost immediately followed by a thunderclap. The rain pounding so hard on the roof it sounds as if it may have turned to hail.

"Has Seward seen it?"

"Not yet."

"How did you get it?"

"Yonge sent it with a Portuguese mail-order-bride who was a passenger on one of the vessel's seized by Semmes. She was supposed to give the letter to our consul in the Azores, but she never got the chance. She gave it to one of my officers when she reached America some days back."

Lincoln has wandered over to a make-shift fort created by Tad and his friends with pillows, logs, condemned rifles. There's a rocking horse corralled here, and the president has begun to stroke the mane.

"This was Willie's horse," he says. His voice sounds far away.

Oh God, I'm losing him again to his dead son.

Welles doesn't know what to say, knows his president is once again sinking into a memory of the lost boy. Hopes that Lincoln does not dissolve into the blubbering and weeping mourner that Willie's poor mother has become.

"Life is a precious thing, Gideon. Maybe more precious than the Union."

"Your trip up to Sharpsburg with Major Allen must have been very difficult."

"Great fields of graves, of dead boys."

Welles says that they must make sure that such a terrible battle never happens again. The government must stop the killing of America's children. Must show the South they cannot win. That the days of J.E.B. Stuart's pesky raids in Pennsylvania and these predations of the *Alabama* are coming to an end.

Lincoln's fingers caress the wooden horse's mane.

The Secretary of the Navy takes a deep breath, holds it as if it may be his last. Waits to see if the president can come back from the land of the dead. Prays for it.

The tall, gaunt man leaves off fiddling with the mane of the rocking horse. "Can this turncoat help us stop Semmes?"

Welles exhales. The story told by the captain of the *Brilliant* confirms Yonge's reported belief that Semmes intends to sail westward at the high latitudes, toward America, to catch and burn the grain carriers and whalers riding east from New York and New England on the Gulf Stream. Semmes' ultimate goal is to make a clandestine attack on a prominent Yankee port.

"Seward told me this morning he is convinced Semmes plans to come right up the Potomac for us. He said we must concentrate our naval defense here."

Welles shakes his head. "Seward is either an imbecile ... or he aims to send our ships on a fool's errand. Only an idiot would risk bringing his ship up the Chesapeake and the Potomac—days of dangerous travel under our guns. And Semmes is clearly no idiot. I expect him to hit somewhere between Boston ... and New York."

"We have to set a trap."

Welles says he has sent dispatches to the naval commanders in Portsmouth, Boston, Newport, New York. They have shore batteries on twenty-four-hour alert. They are posting every ship they can spare to sentry duty. The steam sloop *Mohican* under Captain

Glisson has orders to head for the coordinates where the *Alabama* was last sited, where she burned the *Brilliant*. The *Vanderbilt* will join the hunt soon. But the ships have been delayed putting to sea. There has been a monumental storm traveling north just off the East Coast during the past week.

"Maybe that storm did our job for us," says Lincoln. "Maybe it dragged Semmes right into Davy Jones' locker."

"We can always hope."

"But hope is a vain thing when faced with this piratical sod."

"Indeed."

"So, Gideon, assuming Semmes survives this storm ... what help can we get from our man on the *Alabama*?"

"I'm not sure. His letter made a vague offer of delivering the pirate Semmes to us in exchange for twenty-five thousand dollars. But who knows what the man actually intends to do? The Portuguese bride said he was a rutting goat and a drunkard."

"Don't tell Seward about this letter. We don't want him interfering."

"I was hoping you would say that."

38

LIVERPOOL, ENGLAND

October 19, 1862

Dudley can't make himself get out of her bed. He stares up, watching the play of candle light on the ceiling of Lorraine's room while he strokes her head. The dancing of the light on her blond curls, her tawny cheek too. Downstairs in the hotel he can hear the sailors and doxies singing a shanty called "Rolling Home," accompanied by a concertina. It's not yet even seven o'clock of the evening.

"Maybe you shouldn't see Sinclair tonight."

She lifts her head off his chest, looks up into his face. "Are you jealous, Duds?"

"It's just that what you're doing is so dangerous ..."

A little kiss on his neck. "Haven't we been through all this a dozen times? Your Secretary of the Navy and president could be in real danger."

It's true. In the last week or so Lieutenant George Terry Sinclair, while wining and dining the lovely Lorraine in some of the more gentrified restaurants of Liverpool, has bragged that the war will soon be over, a Southern victory a near certainty. Little by little, Sinclair has let slip vague references to a plot. Persons high in both the Federal and Confederate governments are conspiring to drive Gideon Welles and Abraham Lincoln from power. Sinclair's female cousin, a Washington socialite, has been a messenger traveling between Judah Benjamin's people in Richmond and Washington. There may be a ranking Union officer, or officers, involved in the plotting, maybe someone in the navy. Others in the capital area as well.

The details are shadowy. Lorraine is convinced that Sinclair knows more than he's told her. The difficulty in getting Sinclair to reveal more about the plot is that he suddenly prefers to talk about Clarence Yonge these days. As if he suspects Lorraine has been involved with the *290*'s paymaster. As if the idea of Lorraine as another man's moll scratches some itch in Sinclair.

"The man makes me nervous," Dudley says.

"He's a lonely bloke."

"He's a rogue. He defies Bulloch and the rest of the Capulets at almost every turn."

Lorraine thinks "rogue" is the wrong word to describe Terry Sinclair. He just likes to work alone, without the help or approval of James Bulloch and his boys. While Bulloch and the official representatives of the Confederate Navy seem to be losing credibility with each new Federal victory, and running out of money to pay their ship-building bills, Sinclair has floated an ingenious financing scheme. He's gotten seven British cotton manufacturers to accept paper certificates for cotton not yet delivered—cotton futures—in return for their investing in the construction of a new cruiser like the *Alabama*. The new ship, *Canton*, will be owned by the cotton merchants, but captained by Sinclair. Bulloch seems annoyed with Sinclair's independence and envious of his initiative. Annoyed that Sinclair reports to someone in Richmond, not the Capulets.

"If he's willing to disregard senior navy officers in his own government like Bulloch, what do you think he's capable of doing to the likes of you?"

She draws back from his chest. "What's that supposed to mean?"

"I'm worried."

"Because you think Terry might find out about us?"

"What if he did? What if he suspects what we've turned Yonge into? What if he follows you back here some night? Or what if James Bulloch is following Sinclair? Spots you, follows you to me?"

Lorraine sits up in bed, turns away from her lover. Wraps her bare body in a wool blanket. "You're afraid someone's going to expose us to your wife, aren't you?"

"That's not the point. There's a war going on. This is combat. We have a network of our people to protect."

"Tell me something I don't already know, love."

"Do you remember our forced swim in the Mersey last March? You've seen what the Capulets are capable of. Don't you know what they would do if they could get their hands on soldiers like us?"

She turns to him, her mouth gaping in agony. "Is that how you think of me? You think of me as a soldier?"

Oh Lord, what have I said?

He tries to wrap her in his arms, but she pushes him away. Turns her back on him and gets out of the bed. Draped in the quilt she moves to the window, stares out into the foggy night.

"Don't be like this, please," he says.

"Why not? I'm a soldier."

"Lorraine." He follows, circles her waist with his arms, pulls her back against him, kisses her check.

"Don't touch me," she says. But she makes no effort to escape his arms now.

"What if I told you I've fallen in love with you?" He can't believe he's just said this. Can't believe it could even be remotely true. Yet ... there it is. Not an attempt to keep this exceptional agent loyal and working for the Americans. Words from the heart. Feelings that have been hiding in there since the night he first fished her out of the river, growing since that night when she played Cinderella to Raphael Semmes in London. Blooming since they first made love six days ago.

"Don't say things like that."

"I think about you day and night."

"Last week you threatened to kill me."

"Last week I was trying to pretend I didn't care."

"Please. I can't hear this."

"I love you."

She turns slowly into the harbor of his arms. Kisses him. "I'll be back. I just promised Terry ..."

"Can't we forget about Sinclair for tonight?"

"Don't you want to know who's dealing double with Lincoln?"

39

———∽✎∾———

BRANDYWINE VALLEY, DELAWARE
October 29, 1862

The walls of the dark, smoky room swim around Maude. She hugs the child in her swollen belly, shivers. Hardly ever stops shuddering. Even though she huddles together with other torn and tattered souls. All trying to press their backs to the fieldstone chimney, which radiates heat in faint waves. Eleven black men, women with children. Some of the females young, some older. And her.

They've been hiding here for days. A concealed room, between a walk-in fireplace and a wall of the carriage house of a Brandywine Valley farm. The weather outside stormy, wet. Cold seeping in through the carriage house walls. So cold she cannot remember what day it is or when she came here. Sometimes she thinks she's on that train north of Baltimore ... or up to her breasts and thrashing in the murky water of the Christina River again.

But it was more than ten days ago when she surprised her guards on the train with her announcement that she was in her labor. A lie, of course. But just the right lie to get the soldiers to free her cuffed wrist from Fiona's. To fluster the two soldier boys. To distract them long enough for Fiona to grab one of their pistols and hold the men off. While she and Maude tried to escape the train, which had begun to slow along the banks of the Christina River south of Wilmington, Delaware.

"Go, Maudie, just go." Fiona holds a gun on the soldiers who have begun to stalk them as they flee out onto the vestibule of the railway carriage.

*The train still moving faster than she can run. The crossties, the
ground alongside the tracks, only a blur. The river, the oystermen in
their boats off to the right, things from another world.*

"Just hang from the steps until your feet touch. Let yourself go."

*She climbs down the steps, hangs onto the handrails. Her feet frozen
to the wooden step. Thinks about the child in her womb, fears she will
crush it in her fall. "I can't."*

*One of the soldiers is pointing his pistol at Fiona. The two of them eye
to eye in the doorway to the vestibule, guns in each other's face.*

"Now, Maudie." Fiona's voice shrill. "Go, love!"

*Fiona kicks her in the chest. She falls. Splashes into the reeds on the
river shore.*

*Gunshots, two of them, are still echoing in her head when a pair of
watermen fish her out of the river onto the pile of oysters in their boat.
No Fiona to be seen.*

*And no Fiona when the watermen take Maude to a Quaker named
Thomas Garrett in Wilmington. No Fiona when she's smuggled out
of town to this Brandywine farm in a hay wagon with the blacks. In
the dark.*

⚓   ⚓   ⚓

"I have to get to New York," she tells the tiny black woman who seems
to be the shepherd for this Negro flock.

The woman the blacks variously call Minty and Miss Harriet looks at
her with watery eyes. "Peace, Missy. You with child. You weak. In no condition. The soldiers looking for you ... looking for us all. We safe here."

Maude squeezes her eyes shut as a wave of nausea rolls through
her. Tries to understand what's happening to her. What's happening here. Who these people are. These people who share their
peanuts, beef jerky, and water with her. These people just as scared,
tired, weak as herself. But people who look on her with soft smiles.
From what she can gather, they are escaped slaves from plantations
on the Eastern Shore of Maryland. Like her, refugees of war. Rene-
gades of prejudice. Fugitives from the law, too, in a border state

where the Union is not enforcing the Emancipation Proclamation. The Fugitive Slave Law remains something to dread.

Right this minute her mind can't focus for long. Her heart can't help itself. It tugs on her soul. Wants to run to New York at any cost. On the chance she might find Raffy there. Because with Fiona gone, her best and last friend, lost ... with no money ... with the baby coming ... where else can she turn? What other hope does she have?

This morning, when she had a spell of clarity, she read the newspaper the farmer dropped through the trap door into this crowded room of fugitives. Read the story about Raffy. Read about his recent attacks on shipping. Read speculation that he and the *Alabama* are heading for New York. Rushing to support mobs of anti-war Copperheads who aim to cast out Abe Lincoln's army and navy, liberate the city from Federal rule.

It sounds absurd, New York breaking from the Union. But then again this whole war has been absurd. What could be more mad than those fields of the dead on the banks of Antietam Creek? Or the way she and Fiona were brutalized by Allen? What could be crazier than these half-remembered days in a dark, spinning room among people who smell like earth?

The baby kicks her hard beneath a rib. Almost takes her breath away.

She closes her eyes to crush the strange pain, reaches out for the shepherd's hand. "I must try for New York. This may be my last chance ..."

"To what, child?"

"To find a man."

"What kind of man?"

She opens her eyes. Looks into the coffee-colored face of this Minty, this Harriet, this Miss Tubman. Knows that she cannot say Raffy's name. Not to this woman. Not to these people. To them, Raphael Semmes is the right hand of Satan.

"He's a sailor," she says.

"Sailorman? He some lucky to have a gal like you." The shepherd tucks a blanket up around Maude's neck. "Try and get some rest, Missy. Dream on that baby. The Promised Land just over yonder ... New York coming, sure enough."

40

CSS *ALABAMA*

October 29–30, 1862

Rain pelts Semmes' oilskin slicker, his sou'wester hat. Heavy hobnails of water hitting so hard he cannot hear the whir of the headwinds over the deck, the rush of the wake as the *Alabama* beats southwest into the gloom along the edge of Georges Banks east of Cape Cod. From the bows comes the faint shouts of the leadsmen sounding for the banks. The captain's feet are cold fish as he paces the *Alabama*'s quarterdeck in soaking sea boots.

He's reeling from the intermittent sea-sickness that began with the hurricane, has plagued him off-and-on for more than a week now. Reeling from that lack of sleep that comes with *mal de mer*. Comes, too, from the worry, the careful scrutiny of merchant captains and their ships' papers attendant with stopping an average of two vessels a day in this kind of weather, condemning and burning three since October 23rd. The bark *Lafayette*, schooner *Crenshaw*, bark *Lauretta*. Ashes on the dark sea now. Their crews crowded aboard *Alabama*.

Just a half hour past, he had been face-down on his desk, pen in hand. Having finished a letter to his wife Anne and family. A letter full of righteous sentiments about the Southern Cause and his own achievements with this new and able ship. A ship that has proven not only her speed, but her stoutness in surviving a hurricane and a nearly endless parade of gales that would have doomed most vessels.

Hell is the North Atlantic in winter.

But the writing, holding up the brave face of the cavalier mariner and family patriarch, has exhausted him. Left him unable to finish more than the first sentences of a letter to Maude. His first words *Forgive me, my dearest angel* setting a tone that descended into anger, self-pity—worst of all, guilt—over having left her time and again to endure her misfortunes alone. Left her to day after day of nursing the sick and wounded, left her to the battlefields of Sharpsburg. Carnage and suffering like she should never see.

My God, she's with child. May already have the baby ... if it lives.

He has come here on deck to put the guilt, the terrible longing for Maude, the personal worries aside. *Rain and fog and selfish cares be damned.* He must bring his mind, and what energy he has left, to bear on his ship ... and her extreme overcrowding with prisoners on what has become a violent ocean.

Most of all he must think carefully on how he will deliver on the bold promise he has made to his crew. The promise that he will take the *Alabama* right into New York Harbor and set it howling with Southern thunder and Yankee blood. The city lies just two hundred and twenty miles off. He could be there by the middle of tomorrow night. By Halloween.

Never before has he made his cruise track or destination known to officers and men. But after two months at sea, he knows his shipmates are no longer satisfied with tallying their conquests and estimating the prize money they may get in some distant future, if and when the *Alabama* pays off. He can feel the tension in the wardroom, the petty fights over tobacco, the back-biting when his young officers think he's not around. He knows from the daily discipline reports Kell provides that there is more abuse of liquor stolen off the prizes, more fighting among the Jacks. They crave new action. They crave some bold enterprise to unite them. Crave glory. And the sight and smell of land. Of women, too.

Sweet Jesus, so do I.

The latest newspapers from New York, seized off the *Lauretta*, announced that the *Vanderbilt* and *Mohican* are out here looking for him. Charles Wilkes and his Flying Squadron may be too far afield in the West Indies to worry about, but they too will soon be threats. New York's batteries and patrol boats are on alert. The papers make it sound like New Yorkers are expecting the *Alabama* with the same enthusiasm they await streets full of goblins on All Hallows Eve.

He must not disappoint. New York may well anticipate he's coming. But only he knows how and when. He has played the ghost ship for two months. Eighteen hours more of invisibility should not be impossible. Not in this wretched weather. Not if he veers further offshore, out of the shipping lanes for the next day. Then comes at New York from due east. A dark thing, breathing fire in the middle of the night when ghosts roam free.

The problem is that this phantom he sails is loaded with prisoners. He must somehow send them ashore before clearing the *Alabama* for action. Before the sound of the enemies' cannons and his own.

Lord Jesus, show me a way.

⚓   ⚓   ⚓

Semmes is feeling very much on the right side of the Almighty as the *Baron de Castine* falls off on starboard tack.

Blessed indeed art God, wondrous in his works.

Seven bells into the evening watch. Eleven-thirty. The mid watch just about to begin. He braces himself on the leeward wing of the bridge and watches the antique, heavily laden brig out of Bangor, Maine, lumber away into the drizzly night, her bows rising, falling in a heavy swell as she vanishes. Her course southwest-by-west for New York City. An answer to his prayers. Her decks now loaded with his former prisoners. Leaving him free to show the Yanks what a Confederate phantom can do.

He can hardly believe his good fortune, spotting and capturing the *Baron* in this murky weather just hours before dark fell. Her cargo, Maine oak, bound for Cuba. With ship and cargo of little value to him or the Yanks' war effort, he has made quick work of having her captain sign a bond of debt. Then charging the *Baron*'s master to take his prisoners to New York. Would that he could send his mail, too. But the Yanks would have a picnic combing his correspondence for signs of his intentions, his weaknesses. So the mail, all his plaintive letters to his selkie, must wait for a neutral port.

Right now Semmes must prepare his ship for combat. For New York. Must go below to study his charts. Must set a skeleton watch for the next eight hours to rest his men. Tomorrow the deck officers will want to drill their men on the guns. Beckett Howell will want them practicing with small arms and pikes for repelling boarders. There are a thousand details to attend to. He's going to need a word with the chief engineer.

If *Alabama* is to successfully sneak into New York Harbor, hit-and-run, she is going to need her engines like she has never used them before. Most of the last two months, the ship has been under canvas, her propeller hoisted up into her hull, the boilers only keeping steam on to run the machinery, the water-maker. To give a little heat in the high latitudes. But tomorrow night, facing the currents at Sandy Hook, the Narrows, the Hudson, the East River ... Freeman must have his teapots in top shape.

So Semmes has engines on his mind as he descends to his cabin and starts peeling out of his slicker. That's why it seems as if a kind of collective prescience is at work on this ship when his steward says that the chief engineer, Miles Freeman, begs a word with him.

⚓　　⚓　　⚓

The captain motions his engineer to the couch in the great cabin, raises a decanter of brandy as an offering to the dark-bearded Welshman. The man he thinks of as the "magician." The man who nursed the old *Sumter*'s leaky tubes and crusty boilers from Brazil to Gibraltar.

Freeman shakes his head. "Afraid I ain't in a drinking mood, captain."

"Just a dram?" Semmes has never known his engineer to turn down a nip of Napoleon's finest.

"We're going to have right much need of my engines in the days to come if we aim to give the Yanks a Halloween surprise."

"Most certain."

"I just had me a look into the bunkers yesterday, sir. We had enough coal for eight or nine days of hard steaming."

"Good."

"No, sir."

"What are you getting at?"

"I just checked the bunkers again. Half our coal is now missing. Nothing but coal dust, where before we had tons."

"Where'd it go?"

Freeman says he found some torn-up planks on the bunker sole. The coal settled down through the holes during all the ship's pitching and rolling. Tons of fuel is now down in the bilge.

"Can we get it out?"

"I been crawling around down there with a lantern. Couldn't find but a wee pile of coal. Looks like most of it got sloshed all over kingdom come by the bilge water."

"So we're down to four days' coal?"

"Yes sir, about that."

The captain feels an immense hollowness and nausea settle over him. "Goddamn ... it's not enough to hit New York."

"No, sir. Not if you aim to outrun half the Yank navy chasing us like a flock of valkyries."

"The crew's not going to take this well."

"We're bollixed four ways to Friday."

"How in all hell does such a thing like this happen, a hole in the bunker sole, on a spanking new ship? Tell me that, Mr. Freeman."

"I believe someone's played a Halloween trick of his own, sir. We maybe got our own troubles with them that go bump in the night."

41

DISTRICT OF COLUMBIA

November 4, 1862

Another Tuesday Cabinet meeting is over. Another two hours of debate and contentiousness.

First, Gideon Welles had to suffer the contempt of his fellow secretaries as they badgered him about more recent news about the depredations of the *Alabama* ... even though he told them that he has just sent more ships after Semmes—the *Dacotah*, *Ino*, *Augusta* among others. But he was still made to feel five times the fool for not having bagged the pirate yet. And that was just in the first fifteen minutes of the meeting. The rest of the time they spent debating—again—whether or not to fire George McClellan as the top field general. Attorney General Ed Bates wouldn't let the topic drop.

Now he's up in the White House attic with the president, Lincoln back to fiddling with the mane on Willie's rocking horse.

"It looks as though you have kept that wolf Semmes from New York, Gideon."

"It may be too soon to know, Mr. President."

"Maybe that turncoat got him after all. What was the name, Yount?"

"Yonge."

"Whomever. I am still rather pleased that man's letter is our little secret. Glad we haven't told Seward about it."

Welles strokes his beard, thinks that somehow this secret knowledge he and the president share about Yonge may someday serve them well.

"Just answer me something, Gideon. You've got some suspicions about Bill Seward, don't you?"

"You mean, do I wonder if he could be behind these threats I've been getting to leave town?"

"That ... or in league with the Rebs."

"Like tied-in somehow with Semmes' moll, Judah Benjamin's women agents, that gang?"

"Major Allen is back from another trip up north. He got something out of that Galway women's friend before he sent the two packing off to a jail up North."

"What?"

"She knows about the threats you got in those red envelopes."

"I should have guessed."

Fiona O'Hare confessed she knew that another one of Rose Greenhow's women friends was involved with the letters. It seems that the woman got the letters from an officer, passed them on for a fee to some Negroes to deliver to Welles.

"What officer? Who?"

The president says that O'Hare couldn't say. Never saw the man, but she guessed he's high in rank. Greenhow's woman friend travels in an elite circle.

"Who ... who's this woman?"

"Name of Sinclair. Abigail, Annabel. Something like that."

"Has Allen picked her up?"

"She's from a prominent Virginia family. Quite a few of the Sinclair men, as you well know, left our navy to join Jeff Davis. One or two of them may even be sailing with Semmes. Like them, she's gone south."

"Damn it."

"Yes, Gideon. Exactly ... but Allen learned other things."

The president says that the page of script from *Julius Caesar* that O'Hare carried came from a doctor in Richmond. A friend of Varina Davis and Judah Benjamin. O'Hare was supposed to give it to a fellow in Catonsville, Maryland. A man named Booth.

"I don't see how this connects to Bill Seward."

"Booth, it seems, is one of the family of actors. Word has it that among other young ladies, the daughter of J. P. Hale, Lucy, may be having a flirtation with him."

"Senator Hale, from New Hampshire?"

"And Bill Seward's friend." Lincoln gives Willie's wooden horse a hard push. It jumps more than rocks a step or two across the floor. "I've been thinking about this strange network of people, Gideon. Will you please follow up on this business with E. J. Allen? Tell him your suspicions about Bill Seward? See where this leads him."

$$\text{\&} \qquad \text{\&} \qquad \text{\&}$$

It's early afternoon when Welles climbs into the carriage ordered to meet him outside the executive mansion, the side curtains pulled over the windows. Finds Allen inside, warming his hands over a small brazier. For once the Secretary of the Navy feels almost glad to see the rat.

"The President said we should talk, Mr. Welles."

"Mr. Lincoln told me about your trip up North, about things you've learned from the Irish tarts."

Allen calls to the cabby. Tells him to head on down toward Foggy Bottom. *Take the back streets, please.* It's clear that he does not want to be followed or call attention to this interlude with Welles. There's a hard jerk as the horse tugs on the carriage yoke.

"So you know it's an officer who seems behind those red envelopes you've been getting."

"But who?"

Allen shrugs. "Most like somebody you've buggered in your navy."

"That could be a lot of people." He's thinking of all the so-called Curmudgeons, the older flag officers he has finally retired in favor of younger men like Porter and Farragut.

"Exactly."

"But a person with ties to Rose Greenhow and some Sinclair woman, ties to Richmond?"

"According to them Irish slutties."

Welles runs through what he's heard about the script page from *Julius Caesar* that O'Hare carried from a mysterious physician in Richmond. About the Varina Davis and Judah Benjamin link. About an actor in Maryland.

"You don't see any way, Major, that Seward could be involved? The man makes my skin crawl."

Allen hocks up a throat full of phlegm, pulls back the side curtain, spits. "I've been through his office and his house, up and down in some pretty righteous ways with his staff. Nothing in the way of red stationary. No suspicious rendezvous with any of your navy boys."

"You think he's clean?"

"As far as threatening you with the letters and that stuff in the tree by the Naval Observatory? Probably."

"How can you be so sure?"

"I've had someone following him for weeks. He hasn't gone near anything that has to do with you or yours."

"But there haven't been any threats in weeks."

"Bloody hell, man. Did you ever think maybe this stuff about Seward is all in your head?"

42

CSS *ALABAMA*
November 4, 1862

Yonge and Forrest are lubricating themselves again in the sail
locker. They've stolen a gallon of whiskey off a recent prize. As
usual, the rest of the crew's on the main deck now during the second
dog watch, lost in their smoking, music. Galt's black boy David is
wearing a dress, jigging with one of the gunners.

It has been two nights since the *Alabama* captured and seized the
whaler *Levi Starbuck* just four days out of New Bedford, fully loaded
for thirty months of hunting sperm whales in the South Pacific. The
Confederate *Alabama*'s now east of the Gulf Stream. If she continues on the rhumbline she will pass near Bermuda, fetch the West Indies in less than two weeks.

As is his custom at these meetings, Yonge doesn't speak until he
feels the magic of the whiskey smoothing the waves of care from his
mind—oil spilled on a troubled sea. Right now he's lying back on a
sail, staring at the deck ceiling over his head. Wondering when it was
that he stopped feeling so beset with guilt over becoming a turncoat
for the Yanks. Stopped feeling so angry at that saucy wench Lorraine
and her handler for bagging him. Angry at himself for letting bitter
Liverpool swill and cheap pussy get the best of him. Damn it all, he
usually has better taste. He had not intended to shit on James Bulloch and the Confederacy.

Or my miserable wife and child neither.

No question, the anger and the guilt put him off his gimbals for
a spell. But lately he has begun to feel just fine. He thinks it's Old

Beeswax that's drove him to it. The man is one fastidious, arrogant, self-deluded fuck, if he's ever met one. And Yonge has sailed with some real prince cocks. What kind of a man counts the gold in that chest stashed beneath his berth every day, or wants to recalculate his paymaster's ledgers to a trice? Who would wear such a ridiculous mustache or imagine himself capable of single-handedly attacking the largest city in America with impunity?

Man is daft. Just like James Bulloch, Bobby Lee and Jeff Davis.

Yonge now sees that there is no way the South can win this war. The Yanks are too rich in men, ships, industry. They are bleeding Dixie to death. Like it or not, Lincoln's boys are the future. And one of these days they are going to blow Semmes and the *Alabama* into a thousand little pieces, and his sorry ass with it ... unless he puts a stop to Old Beeswax's ridiculous, inflated dreams of glory.

And if he can do it, if he can deliver Semmes to the Yanks without a battle?

Why should I not be paid? Why should I not expect the rewards due any good facilitator?

First things first. Unlike Semmes, he does not believe he can move mountains by himself. He needs to build and school his team. Forrest is the lynch pin.

⚓   ⚓   ⚓

"I wanted to give you this." Yonge pulls a ten dollar gold piece from his pocket, passes it to Forrest.

"Thankee."

"I liked what you did with Beeswax's coal," says Yonge. "Fucked that old boy's plan to get us killed in New York right smart."

"You can be thanking John Latham for that."

"The stoker?"

"Aye. I just told him what we needed. Some kind of mess with the coal to bugger Semmes' plans for New York. He done the rest."

"Did you give him something?"

"Bottle of that brandy you let me have."

Yonge takes a long swig from the gallon of whiskey. Nods. Sure, give away brandy. He's got near two cases buried up here under the sails. "Did you tell him about me?"

"I told him there was an officer with us is all. Told him you said that with no coal we'd have to sail south to some tropic island fast-like to meet up with a collier."

"*Agrippina.*" Yonge says Semmes has the coal carrier under a long-term contract to supply the *Alabama* at all manner of far-flung, dark little places.

Forrest laughs, grabs for the jug. "His coal slut."

"What did you promise Latham?"

"Same as you promised me. Chance to get off this prison ship alive before Beeswax gets us shot all to hell by the Yanks."

"That did it? Fear?"

"Told him if he stuck with me, he could leave this ship with enough money to set himself up for life. Man's got a young wife back in Liverpool he's some proud of. A looker, I guess."

Yonge laughs. "And he fears she'll be fucking every sailor comes ashore if he doesn't get his skinny ass home right soon."

"The thought of pussy can make a man do amazing things."

"What's the mood in the fo'castle now?"

"Foul as hell."

"Good. You recruit anybody else?"

"Latham got four or five others on the black gang, sick of the heat, smoke and the shite they been taking from the engineer."

"How we doing for deckhands?"

"Bunch of topsmen. Waisters. Gunners too. Gill, that mean-assed Scot in the port watch."

Yonge snickers, seizes the whiskey. Takes a long swallow. "Beeswax and Kell are never going to figure out who's screwing them 'til its too late. Too many of us now for them to catch."

Forrest says he counts at least twenty men who are ready to tear the ship apart, plenty more who will go along once Yonge adds a bit of rum to the fire and his boys make their big move.

"We need to watch our step a bit. I heard Beeswax and Kell talking last night."

"They suspect something?"

"Wouldn't you after the coal just sort of vanished?"

"Fucking officers."

"Their time's coming."

"Pass me that jug."

43

NEW HOPE, PENNSYLVANIA
November 5, 1862

Maude feels the wagon bump over a stone, feels sun warming her cheeks. She opens her eyes. Thinks she has never seen a more beautiful morning, a more lovely place.

A golden sunrise. The mist lifting off the Delaware River, off the pale, green fields in the bottom land. Groves of maples and oaks on fire with red, yellow and brilliant orange. Leaves spiraling down in easy pirouettes, coating the grass around large, well-kept stone farm houses. Roosters crowing. Red fox, deer on the move.

All night long on this wagon ride north from the Brandywine Valley through the fog, she huddled with her back to one of the Negro women, her head on the shepherd Minty Tubman's shoulder. Smelled the sweet scent of the femaleness around her and thought about Fiona. Remembered the gunshots she heard as she fell from the train. What else could those shots have meant other than that her best friend had been killed? Her best friend gave her life so that she can start again, keep looking for Raffy. She should cry, beat her chest with grief. But she feels dead herself, except for the child in her. She wonders whether she has seen too much death in the hospital and on the fields outside of Sharpsburg to have any tears left.

"You gone to be alright, Missy?" Tubman.

"Look at this. Look at this perfect day."

"It ain't that New York you yearning for, but it something. It freedom. We safe here. Quaker country."

She looks around, sees the other ten or so people in the wagon waking up, staring at the fantastic morning.

"Lord of Mercy," someone says.

"Praise be to God."

As if by some unspoken signal the wagon veers into a grove, stops. There's a spring of water running from the hillside into a small, rock-lined pool. The blacks scramble out of the wagon, cupping their hands in the pool. Taking drinks, washing their faces and their children. An old couple is crying and hugging each other. A young man on his knees kissing the ground, laughing.

"Let me help you down." Minty Tubman stretches her hand up to Maude.

She takes the hand, rises on her haunches to ease herself out of the wagon bed. But something pops in her loins. Then the inside of her thighs, her knees, her calves feel warm, wet. The hem of her dress too.

"Oh dear," she says. *I bloody peed myself.*

"You best lie back down." Tubman squeezes her hand. "Your baby coming ... hallelujah."

☙　　☙　　☙

"Push, Missy." She feels the pain rising in her again. *Holy Mary Mother of God!*

It's after dark. The wagon has not moved from the side of the spring. A chill has settled over the river valley. The Negroes have two campfires burning. The men and children are huddled around one on the banks of the Delaware, cooking fish and Johnny cakes. Further away, next to the pool, five women surround Maude and a small fire. Making a wall against the night and the cold with their bodies, quilts slung over their shoulders. They sing in low, slow wordless tones. An incantation wrapping a web of spider silk around Maude.

She squats—elbow on knees, hands on cheeks—over a freshly washed blue shirt, naked except for the quilt the women have wrapped around her. Minty Tubman is on her knees facing her, pressing her forehead to Maude's. Arms wrapped around the white woman's lower back. Rubbing, kneading her muscles as another contraction rolls through.

"Push, Missy."

She wants to scream. This pain's ripping her in half. As it has all day. Into the night now. The last three hours divided between kneeling on all fours like a beast between contractions, and then rising— as the mothers have taught her—onto her haunches to push. Tubman's hands never stop, warm circles of energy are flowing into Maude's back just when she feels ready to collapse.

"Pain is power. Work with it."

"Lord Jesus." Her words breathless bursts.

"Rise above it, Missy."

A new jabbing through her hips make her eyes freeze. "Minty!"

"Push."

"The baby coming now," says a midwife, feeling beneath Maude. "Push again."

The women have begun to chant in an African language. " ... *Llale omalte allava omio* ..."

Maude grits her teeth, tightens. Bears down. Hears the women ululating. Chanting the name Yemanjá, again and again. Far off. Faint as a half-forgotten dream.

Minty has told her the moment would come tonight when the old African way of birthing would be like this. The dream state coming on her as Yemanjá, ancient goddess of the sea and the moon, the primal mother, mounts her freckled, pale body. Freeing her from everything except the power of motherhood and an overwhelming love for this child. Loosing her to shout, to scream, to squeeze new life from her body.

And now she's feeling this Yemanjá. This force. Bones lightening, muscles melting. Head and heart swelling. Bursting into a million pieces. A strange, shuddering ecstasy beyond any moment with Raffy. Yemanjá howling within her. Singing. Dancing. Guiding her hands between her own legs.

To catch the slippery, squirming child.

"Cry baby." Her voice weeps.

It does.

"A girl," says Minty Tubman. "You have a daughter of Yemanjá."

"I will call her Fiona."

44

MARTINIQUE
November 18, 1862

The captain of the *Alabama* has been catnapping fitfully since sunrise after a night on watch. Since the disappearance of the coal off New York, he's felt the need to sleep with one eye open. An ear always tuned for uneasiness in the crew. Especially now since *Alabama* made her first landfall in months yesterday. Even the greenest officer knows the ability to manage a crew shrinks in proportion to a ship's proximity to land.

But for just a few hours he tries to rest from his vigilance. Last night he saw his ship safely around the northeast tip of the island of Dominica. Saw her safely into the Caribbean Sea with no Federal gunboats in sight, no signs of rumbling in the crew. He's on course to his appointed rendezvous with the *Agrippina*. He and James Bulloch hired her to meet *Alabama* at Martinique during the second week in November. He's just a week late.

Now he hears the sounds of tiny feet on the deck over his berth, the melody of little girls' laughter. Feels a wave of sadness rushing through him.

Damn. They are preparing to go. Must go. Must get off as soon as I can land them today.

Yesterday he wrote to Maude about these children. In the letter he will actually be able to post to her today from Martinique. He's furled his sails, lowered the propeller. Is steaming south on nearly the last of his coal along the west coast of the French island now, bound for Fort de France. For the mailbox.

He has written how he savored the last nine days with these three young prisoners and their mother aboard. The *Alabama* has enjoyed warm, fair weather and easy breezes since she passed Bermuda off to starboard. There have been no more strange incidents, no more dirty tricks aboard. A carefree time. But a time for vigilance, too.

The ship has taken two more prizes. The second, the East India-man *T.B. Wales* bound home to Boston, five months out of Calcutta loaded with saltpeter for Yankee gunpowder mills. He condemned and burned her right quick. Signed ten of her seamen to his crew as well. But not before he stripped her of rigging and spars to replace all that his ship had lost in the October hurricane. Not before he did all he could to make these females among the prisoners from the *Wales*, Mrs. George Fairchild and her daughters, at home on his cruiser. Gave them two of his lieutenants' staterooms. Salvaged their entire wardrobes so they might have things to give them comfort on this ship of sea-weary men.

Since then these young ladies, ages four to eleven, have had the run of the wardroom. He's taken to calling them Muffin, Crumpet, Truffle ... as they have transformed the deck into a place for games of tag, the guns into mazes for hide-and-seek. So many mornings he has rested in bed listening to the fresh laughter, even singing, of the girls and their mother, an elegant English-born gentlewoman. Closed his eyes and dreamed of children, domestic tranquility. Home sweet home. As if he has one anymore. Anne and his younger children are probably still with her brother, the Yankee sympathizer in Cincinnati. That is surely no home for him. Yes, there is the empty Semmes' house in Mobile, but a house is just an assemblage of four walls.

When his mind drifts to a home, he pictures the one he talked with Maude about. The cottage in São Luís. In Brazil. The one he hopes she sees in her dreams, too. A tidy little place. Freshly painted in pinks and blues. Straw carpet. The shuttered windows open to the scents of acacia, bougainvillea. Opening on the sea, too. A big bed where they can make love and watch the sailing *jangadas* reaching into the harbor. A place to raise the baby. The baby she never wanted to tell him about. The one he pictures as the youngest Fairchild girl now. As Muffin. A bold little imp, with strawberry hair like her mother. A selkie too ... who he could most surely abide.

A knock on his cabin door.

"Seven bells, sir," says Bartelli, his steward. His standard wake-up call. "Mr. Kell says we shall be at Fort-de-France in three hours."

Something twists, tears in his chest. Rises into his mouth. He tastes blood. Tries to clear his throat. Can't.

"Sir?"

He reaches for the mug of cold tea on the cabin sole next to his berth. Drinks to wash the taste of blood away.

"Tell our favored guests they must make ready to be landed," he says at last. Then he buries his face in his pillow ... to muffle the sob rising in his throat.

⚓   ⚓   ⚓

"This cannot bode well," he says, eyeing the governor of Martinique over the full glass of champagne he has just been served.

His Excellency, M. Maussion de Condé, nods. "It is so good to see you again after a year, my friend. And with such a fine, new ship. I had truly hoped to give you better news. Or at least have some mail for you."

Just as a year ago, Semmes and the governor stand at the sideboard in His Excellency's office at Fort Saint-Louis. Last November when he was here with the *Sumter* the Frenchman had presented him a letter, a light blue envelope, reeking of Maude's lavender. Even as he remembers the letter and the scent of her, his heart begins to breathe. He sees her curls, the freckles on her shoulders. Can almost taste her mouth. Sees the cottage by the sea. The little muffin with her nest of strawberry hair. Skipping, singing in the yard ... as the sob starts rising in his throat again.

"*Chaque chose est-il bien*? Are you alright, *Capitaine*?"

He swallows a bit of blood.

"I fear war makes us desperate men," he says. "Tell me again, please, what sorts of things exactly Captain McQueen has let slip in my absence."

McQueen is the old Scottish master of the *Agrippina*. His ship has been anchored here at Fort-de-France for more than a week waiting on Semmes. According to the governor, McQueen has been drinking none too lightly in the coffee houses of the town, boasting of his secret cargo for the *Alabama*, predicting her arrival to fellow merchant captains. Yankees among them. Already some of those masters have taken leave of this French port, headed up or down the island chain of the Eastern Caribbean. Wilkes' Flying Squadron is hereabouts somewhere. Other Federals as well.

"News travels fast in these islands, *mon Capitaine*."

It will not take the damn Yanks long to hear that my ghost ship aims to coal at Martinique. Not long for the sharks to gather. They may well be on their way.

"I think I must excuse myself, Your Excellency." Already he's starting to write an order in his head for McQueen and his collier to leave Martinique today, head for Isla Blanquilla off Venezuela where they will transfer coal in secret. He must leave this island, too. Before the crew chooses liberty for itself and the officers be damned. They are already trading frantically with the bumboats that have surrounded *Alabama*, for who knows what kind of contraband. They will throw a fit, certain, when they learn they will not be going ashore. As is their due.

Damn. Double damn, McQueen.

The governor gives him a pained look. "Surely even a famous corsair has time for a drink with a friend and fellow man of the sea. This is very good champagne."

Semmes realizes his rudeness. Remembers a similar indelicate moment on this beautiful island a year ago after he first arrived here in the *Sumter*. "Please forgive ... "

"*De rien.*" The Frenchman, dismisses Semmes' apology. "My island is your island, *Capitaine. A votre santé, mon ami.* To the ships we love ..."

Semmes raises his glass of wine. Feels the blood rising in his throat again. Darkness settling over him, as he recites the hard final words of this worn English navy toast. "... And the women we wreck."

45

DISTRICT OF COLUMBIA
November 18, 1862

"This is not a good moment, Major Allen." Welles is on his feet, adjusting his wig with both hands. Dragging on his coat, clearly in a hurry to leave the Navy Department even though it is just after ten o'clock in the morning. His office is a small city of papers, plans, books. Piled on the floor in neighborhoods.

The grubby Scot glares from the doorway. "You may think I'm at your beck and call, Mr. Secretary, but I can assure you that is not the bloody case. You want to talk to me, it is now or never."

Welles wants to kick the man in the shins, whack him with his walking stick, tumble him on the floor. Bury him beneath some of this infernal paper. He requested a meeting with the mercurial Allen almost two weeks ago about Seward's most recent and new suspicious doings. Heard nothing from the ferret until this moment when the fellow marches right into his office unannounced. As if the little bastard enjoys surprising him, putting him off balance. Sometimes he wonders if this arrogance and unpredictability is just about Allen's only talent. A heathenish source of power. Like picking through people's garbage for juicy morsels. It feels awful to need such a creature.

And right now, Allen's arrival could not have come at a worse time. Forget these mounds of paper Welles must finish sifting through before he can write his annual report on the navy for the president, congress, press. Forget Allen! The secretary has just gotten a message to come home. His young son Hubert, four-and-a-half, has taken a turn in his long fight against an illness so like what cut down Willie Lincoln. He hears the president's keening rising in his head for his dear, sweet son. Feels the dread. As if there's a plague on all their houses ... on the nation, too, unless he can stop it. Unless he can put aside his revulsion for this Allen.

"I have a pressing need to be with my wife and son, Major. If your cab is waiting, can you drop me home? We can talk on the way. Of treason."

⚓   ⚓   ⚓

A harsh wind cuts through the cab as it turns onto Pennsylvania Avenue, a sign that winter is about to settle over Washington. Welles hugs his shoulders, talks fast. His breath bursts of steam in the cold air.

He tells Allen that a few weeks ago he got a letter from Seward asking that he instruct naval officers seizing blockade runners not to open the mail they carried. That the mail should be forwarded with all due haste to its proper destination. To do such a thing is an illegal, abject, unauthorized, unwarranted surrendering of the Union's maritime rights.

"So?"

"So listen to me, Major. Seward is attempting to make not just policy, but law here. He seems to suppose himself the government, his whims supreme authority."

"This sounds like envy talking."

"More like fear."

He thinks about those red-letter threats again and the nebulous cabal of enemies that has begun to take shape in the last month. Semmes' Irish moll and her tomboy friend. Rose Greenhow. A woman named Sinclair. A mysterious Richmond doctor. An itinerant actor. Varina Davis. Judah Benjamin. A high-placed Union officer. Who knows what Rebel evils may be in those mails? Why would Seward want them overlooked?

"Is everything drama with you, Welles?"

My God, man. My son is dying! I thought Ed Bates was just goading me when he stood on my front porch watching those thousands and thousands of boys marching toward their deaths at Antietam Creek. When he told me to go back to little Connecticut. When he said the nation is expiring ... and maybe it is too late for anyone to stop it. What if Bates was right?

Welles runs the finger of his right hand up under his beard, feels the blood throbbing, hot in his neck. "Who does Seward fraternize with?"

"According to my men? Fellow name of Stuart at the moment. The British *chargé*."

"Doesn't this strike you as suspicious?"

"The man's the Secretary of State. It's his job to befriend our allies."

"Not if the English diplomats are as in league with the Rebs as the Liverpool shipyards are."

Allen nods his head. "Maybe you've got a point."

"Do you think you could see what else you can learn about secret plotting against this administration from those two Irish strumpets you've arrested?"

"That won't be possible. They had an unfortunate accident on their way to prison up north. One got shot to death, the other drowned."

Black spots are pooling before Welles' eyes. "Now what?"

"I don't know, Mr. Secretary. Let me think on it. As you say, it is our legal duty in a time of war to look at overseas mails, Mr. Seward's included ... but right now it seems like you have important company."

Welles looks out the cab window, sees his house. The presidential carriage parked in front. Then he sees Abraham Lincoln step out onto the porch. The tears are just rolling down his cheeks as he covers his face with those enormous, pale hands.

My dear Hubert ... he was a treasure garnered in my heart.

46

———≈⁓∞⁓≈———

CSS *ALABAMA*
November 18, 1862

"It's time," says Yonge. He can't help smiling a little at George For-rest. Sees the glow of Martinique rum on Forrest's cheeks and nose as he ducks into the sail locker to make sure everything is all set for tonight.

"We're almost ready."

The decks are clear. All the prisoners from the prizes—including the little girls, and visitors from shore—left the *Alabama* three hours ago. The cooks have gotten out supper for officers and crew. Old Beeswax is stewing below somewhere. The officers on deck are mostly back aft smoking their pipes on the quarterdeck. Sunset's just a moment passed. The sky already tending from violet to indigo. A black night coming.

Some of the crew are bartering with islanders in the bumboats for orange water, tobacco. *Ganja* and spirits, too. Many of the men are huddling down below in the fo'castle. Swilling from a five-gallon car-boy of rum. Paid for by Yonge with money lifted from the ship's treas-ury, bought surreptitiously off a bumboat by Forrest. The Jacks have been listening to Gil, the tough-talking Scot, build his case for seiz-ing the *Alabama*. Everybody feeling the boldness of cane liquor as Gil tells them the ship has never been legally commissioned because she has never touched Southern soil.

Seizing this ship will not be mutiny, Gil has told them. Just a sim-ple transfer of ownership. And a thing easily accomplished. He and his mates on a Spanish ship have done it once already. On just a night such as this. Lured the officers of the deck forward by staging a fake fight. The men surrounded the officers. Took the ship. Grabbed enough plunder to live like princes ashore for more than a year. And that ship had nothing like the strong box of gold that Old Beeswax keeps in his cabin. Nothing like the military value of this corsair beneath their feet. Nothing like this captain and officers, who can be ransomed to the Federals.

"Are your men armed?" asks Yonge.

"Latham and his black gang have their shovels. I passed out belaying pins from a bag of spares we got from the carpenter's shop. Everybody has a rigging knife. Quite a few of the boys have slings."

"Can you get us some guns?"

He shakes his head. Semmes has all the ship's weapons under double locks in the wardroom. Only God knows who has the keys.

"Shite."

Is this a loss of will?

"We only get one chance at this, man."

He can't stop thinking that this is his moment to give freedom, a little dignity, a little peace, a little plenty to these mariners. Maybe even his chance to bring an end to this damned war. To get free, once and for all, of the self-impressed glory boys like Thomas Dudley and Raphael Semmes. By this time tomorrow he shall be gaily intoxicated ashore with a prime piece of West Indian chocolate flesh to feast on. No worries.

"Some of us got scores to settle with the dandy bastards."

"Listen to me! Tell your men. No one must die."

"You mean let the Yanks do that for us?"

"Why live with blood on our hands?"

Forrest hocks up a mouthful of tobacco phlegm, spits into a corner. "Because it feels so sweet."

⚓   ⚓   ⚓

"What the hell?" Semmes hears Kell shout. The words piercing through from the quarterdeck down into the great cabin.

"Fight," says someone.

The captain hears feet running forward.

"You better get the guns, Armstrong."

⚓   ⚓   ⚓

By the time Semmes reaches the deck, there's a mob shouting, pressing toward Kell, two lieutenants, the quartermasters forward of the bridge deck.

"Mutiny. Mutiny, men. Take the ship." Forrest and Gill are leading the charge.

A boatswain tries to stop the rioters, but a topsman beats him to the ground.

A belaying pin wheels through the air, just missing Kell's head. But he doesn't retreat. He draws his side arm, begins pointing it randomly at different Jacks as Lieutenant Armstrong passes out muskets to the officers.

"Load and aim." Kell barks.

Lieutenants Armstrong, Sinclair, Howell, and the petty officers train their guns on the crowd that has now become fifty or more men, brandishing shovels, pins, sheath knives. Slings loaded with lumps of coal. The officers spread out, start marching toward the mob. Backing them away from the bridge toward the foremast.

Kell seems to immediately sense that this is a revolt fueled by rum.

"This is an order, men. Unless you all want the lash, the sober among you take hold of the drunkards. Now!"

"Fuck you, pussy face." Forrest's cheeks are red with anger.

"Put down your weapons, men ... and no harm will come to you."

A flight of coal stones from the slings peppers the officers.

"Come and get us." Forrest's eyes dart around among the collection of officers and up on the bridge deck as if he's looking for someone. His eyes lock with Semmes, who has just scrambled up onto the bridge for a better view to take charge.

How dare you, damned devil. I'll send your soul to hell directly. He does not remember unholstering the marine pistol Sam Colt gave him in Connecticut two years ago, but he's drawing a bead on Forrest now.

"Drop your weapons, boys, or I'll shoot," Semmes shouts.

"Eat my shite, you ruddy prick." Gill shakes his huge fists at the captain.

"Seize that man." Kell barks.

A gunner tries to grab the rowdy Scot, takes a bludgeoning to the jaw.

But somebody drops Gill from behind with a capstan bar. He hits the deck with a thud. For a second there's quiet on the ship.

"Beat to quarters!" Semmes shouts to his fife and drum boys. Thinks he has not sailed across an ocean and back, left family and love in wreckage to be brought down by a gang of malcontent drunkards. He pulls pack the hammer on his pistol and sights it right on Forrest's nose. "Beat now, drummer!"

The drummer does. A hearty cadence. A shrill, piercing fife joins in.

It's as if the music makes puppets of the men. They have been so conditioned to respond to the rhythm, the simple melody. One by one they scuttle to their fighting stations, to the ship's massive cannons.

And now Semmes has it all his own way. Thirty armed officers fan out over the deck. He walks from gun crew to gun crew. Sniffs for rum, searches faces for the glaze of spirits in the eyes. Orders the quartermasters to haul off the drunks and put them in irons.

When he reaches Forrest, Paymaster Yonge is at his side. The mutineer tries to spit in Yonge's face, which is a sickly shade of pale. "Cowardly prick!"

The insolence!

Semmes raises his pistol at Forrest's head again. Would dearly love to pull the trigger. Love the instant release of tension that comes with the crack of a weapon, the scent of powder.

"This is going to cost you, sailor," he says and holds the pistol there.

"Your end is coming, Beeswax."

He feels that horrible wind again. The seething sea. The flash of lightning, the rumble of thunder, the rig crashing down. Men in the water. Selkies shrieking. The *Somers* ... and everything, everyone else he's damaged scattering on the water.

Most merciful God.

Slowly he releases the hammer of his pistol, lowers it. "My end will come, no doubt. But not today ... not from the likes of damned drunkards like you."

"Nobody knows tomorrow, old man."

47

LIVERPOOL, ENGLAND
November 18, 1862

Lorraine's half-sister Bet, fleshy mistress of the Jezebel den on Endbutt Lane, leans over the bar and grabs for Dudley. She has the lapels of his wool coat in both hands the instant he bellies up for a pint with his mates Maguire and Federal.

The moll pulls him so close he can smell the reek of pickled herring on her breath as she shouts loud enough for half the bar to hear. "Has Lorraine been with you?"

He bristles. Doesn't really think this is any of her business. Doesn't like that his friendship with Lorraine has become common knowledge. Thinks it's nigh on time to change the locus of his rendezvous with his agents. But no, damn it, Lorraine has not been with him. He's been in Scotland for the last week spying on a new ram the Rebs are building on the River Clyde. Just back this afternoon.

"I'm worried, Thomas. I ain't seen her in three days."

A chasm opening in his guts. "The devil you say, Bet."

"Was bloody Wednesday afternoon, before the docks let the men go, she lit out of here."

"I don't understand."

"Like a banshee loosed from Hell she was," says Bet.

She was at the bar washing glasses when Lorraine came running into the pub swearing a blue streak. She charged up the stairs to her room. Two minutes later she was running back out the door. No winter coat on her back, but a plump carpet bag in her hand.

Dudley looks around. The pub is full of sailors, longshoremen, doxies of every shape and size. Lots of them he's never seen before. Any number of them could be Bulloch's boys or girls. He can't talk in here. *Jesus Christ, what next?*

"Can we go somewhere private, Bet?"

"To tumble or talk?"

"What do you think?"

He wants to mash someone in the face. Himself most of all ... for ever being stupid enough to get involved with people like Bet and Lorraine. People who are always for sale. For all he knows, Lorraine may have taken a notion to barter herself to Terry Sinclair, James Bulloch. Or their betters. Taken his heart in the bargain.

"We could go into the brewery." She nods to a door near the back corner of the public room. It's the place the girls take their sailors to get their helmets polished for a shilling.

He flashes her a dark glare.

"I got a key to her room."

He turns to his agents who have heard everything. "Wait here for me, boys ... would you please?"

"Fucking Christ," says Maguire. "You think the Capulets got to her, Thomas?"

      ⚓   ⚓   ⚓

"Come on," he says to Federal and Maguire, leading them out of the pub, out into the cold and foggy night. "I need to see something."

He doesn't know much more than he knew before going upstairs to Lorraine's room with Bet a half hour ago. Except that Lorraine thought she was coming back shortly. Her stash of money was still tacked to the back of a dresser drawer. *Wuthering Heights*, the novel she had coaxed him to buy her so she could show off her ability to read, lay open and face down on her unmade bed. Beside her diary full of notes on Terry Sinclair. The last entry—Wednesday.

A sudden chance. Tonight I think Terry will risk soul and country for Cinderella.

Her dress boots are missing from the closet. Along with her stockings, most of her jewelry, and the silver silk dress Dudley bought her for her night in London with Raphael Semmes. *You ain't seen none of this*, she told Bet as she left, *unless I never come back.*

"Seems like she had to be someplace fancy. Some place secret. In a hurry."

"Fancy? Lorraine? Without us putting her up to it?"

Dudley turns on Maguire, gives him a hard look. "She was working a Southern boy for me. New guy in town. Terry Sinclair. Not one of the regular Capulets."

"The one who's contracted with James and George Thomas to build him the new cruiser they're calling the *Canton*. Federal and I've been all over that game for two months."

"She was onto something else?" asks Federal. The men are following Dudley through a maze of streets, heading uptown toward where the gentry live.

"I can't talk about it."

Maguire spits. "Have it your way ... but how are we supposed to help?"

"Can you help me find Allerton Hall?"

"The bleeding old fortress in Merseyside, on the park like?"

"Lorraine said that's where Sinclair has been staying."

Maguire says the eighteenth-century stone mansion is the new home of Charles Prioleau, the manager of Frazer, Trenholm & Co. Obviously the old boy is doing quite well for himself fronting for the Rebs. He's renting a bloody palace.

"I think she may have been invited to a party there."

"And not come home for three days?"

His chest tightens. "Something could have gone wrong."

"You think she's still in there? Against her will?"

Dudley gasps for air. "We have to see."

"How we going to bloody do that, Thomas? Tonight?"

"I don't know." His lungs shudder, collapse. It's as if all of Liverpool is tumbling down on him in the fog.

"Neither do I mate. The place will be crawling with Capulets. Carrying bloody guns."

"So ... we're stifled. Lorraine's stifled?"

"What in fuck's name was she thinking going into a place like that alone?"

"Maybe she really wanted to help."

48

DELAWARE WATER GAP, PENNSYLVANIA
November 18, 1862

Maude feels the warm pinch as the babe Fiona takes her right breast. Immediately the worries churning in her head begin to drain away. Her eyes close. She tries to forget her long, lost sailor. Forget the blowing snow howling down from the north between the steep hills on either side of the Delaware River. The wind cutting her. She and five of her fellow travelers press together beneath the wagon for warmth on the river bank, the wagon and horse serving as a feeble break against the weather.

No ferrymen have been willing to take Minty Tubman's party of Negroes across the Delaware near New Hope. Despite the issuance of the Emancipation Proclamation, there is debate among the Federal marshals as to whether they must still enforce the Fugitive Slave Act. None of the boatman wants to risk becoming one of the last slave smugglers punished under the harsh law.

They've told Minty and her party to wait a bit longer. Surely, the marshals shall cease the vigilant patrol of the river soon. But winter is coming on. At night, standing water freezes. Three days ago snow began to stick to the ground in swollen, white clumps. Minty needs to get her people to safe shelter—to Canada—before the snow and cold come in earnest.

The band of escaped slaves, Maude, and her baby have been moving north by wagon again, waiting for the river to recede after the early November rains. Looking for a place to ford. Today they have found the spot. The first half of their group has already begun wading out to an island in the center of the river, belongings and children on their shoulders. Their scout says the island offers easy access to the eastern bank, to New Jersey and the road to New York where Minty knows more Quakers who can help them.

As Fiona nurses, Maude slips into her favorite little dream of a seaside cottage in Brazil. But the dream seems hazy, more gray than it used to be. She's squeezing her eyes as tight as she can, trying to see it clearly, when she hears a woman's cry, shouts from the river.

"Sally's down."

She opens her eyes, sees one of the women thrashing in the water about fifty yards off the river bank. The current's got her, sweeping her downstream, tumbling her as she tries to hold her five-month-old baby boy above the water. Already she's more than ten yards downstream from the others in the party who are clinging to a rope strung for their safety, tied between a tree on the bank and tree on the island.

"My baby!"

One of the men in the river lets go of the rope and tries to wade to the mother. But he hits a deep spot; the current sweeps him off his feet. He would be gone, except that he lets go of the bundle on his shoulder, lunges for a friend's hand. Finds it.

The mother with the baby has gotten to her feet again. Leans into the current, holding her child over her head. The current rips by her at chest height.

"My baby. Get my baby." Her voice is shrill, panicked.

All of the party ashore are on their feet, shouting advice to the people in the river.

Maude suddenly sees the problem. Not only are the people in the river weighed down with belongings and children, but none of them can swim.

"Make a chain." Her voice is so loud baby Fiona shudders, loses her grip on the breast for a second.

The people in the river seem to freeze, stare at her as if she's speaking a language they don't understand. But then one of the men heaves his bundle into the river, grabs the hand of the woman next to him and lets go of the safety rope. She hands her child to one of the others, takes a hand, and swings downstream tethered to her neighbor's arm. A third person does the same.

"My baby. My sweet baby." The lone mother seems to be on the verge of losing her footing again. The water's almost up to her neck now. She's still ten feet from a helping hand.

"Throw him, Sally." The man at the end of the chain. "Throw me the boy!"

She does. She launches the infant as if tossing a watermelon.

The child lands wide and short of the man waiting with open arms. He dives for the baby, scoops it into his arm. Just as the woman who had his hand seizes him by the pant leg.

"Pull him in, y'all. Pull!" Shouts from the shore.

They do.

But when all the thrashing and splashing is over, when all the members of the chain, along with the baby, are back hugging the rope, the mother in the river is gone. The river just a hazy plain of rippling current beneath the driving snow.

"What we gone do with baby Leviticus now?" The old man standing next to Maude sucks his cheeks in bewilderment.

"Give him to me," she says. *I have two breasts.*

49

CSS *ALABAMA*
November 19, 1862

"What do you imagine our enemy thinks of Forrest hanging up there yonder, boys?" The captain of the *Alabama* looks to his officers, twist the tips of his mustache. Feels the seeds of a plan swelling in his chest.

"I think he wonders why we seem more concerned with meting out punishment to our crew than preparing for battle with him."

"Exactly what I hope, Lieutenant Armstrong. We're sending a message to both our Jacks and the Yanks, eh?"

Just after sunrise this morning the USS *San Jacinto* came steaming into the harbor at Fort-de-France, gun ports open, crew at quarters, armed detail of marines with weapons primed and loaded, immense stars-and-stripes flying from her peak. Clearly feeling smug that she has tracked down the Confederate ghost ship, clearly daring Semmes to come out and fight. The *Alabama*'s Jacks have been all astir, and Semmes knows that they are spoiling for a brawl to relieve the tension they feel after months at sea, a failed mutiny, their secret stashes of alcohol confiscated last night, no shore leave today. But he's not going to give them a battle, not if he can help it.

That's why he's called his full complement of officers, except Yonge who says he has some accounting to attend to below, here on the bridge deck. Just now Forrest has been triced up into the mizzen rigging—two hours on, two hours off—for the second time this morning. He hangs his head, a devil sick of sin.

"Our job today, gentleman, is to keep order, to exact our punishment of the head mutineer in a most thorough and public way ... and to go about our ordinary business."

He says let the *San Jacinto* fret and strut around the mouth of the harbor as much as she wants. Let her sling her yards, stopper her topsail sheets, rig preventers on her braces as if she were the HMS *Victory* before the battle at Trafalgar. He will not risk his ship or his mission for the sake of misguided honor. The old Federal wagon is too heavy for him to consider engaging. She has a crew twice the size of *Alabama,* a battery of fourteen eleven-inch guns. Can throw more than two pounds of metal for every one from his ship.

"But we have the speed on her, am I right?"

Nods from the officers.

"Then tonight, men, shall we show Abe Lincoln's penny boys how the fox can run?"

A general chorus. "Aye."

Semmes smiles. "Any man who is not on the watch may go ashore in the gig until the first dog watch ... and damn the Yankees."

⚓   ⚓   ⚓

Semmes mounts the bridge, sees a dark, rainy night beginning to settle over Martinique. Only a hint of the southeast trade winds. No sunset this evening, just a gathering pitch. He has been resting in his cabin since dinner ended. Lying in his berth, going over every detail of his escape plan. Writing the obligatory "If I die" letters to James Bulloch, his wife, and Maude, care of Frazer, Trenholm & Co. in Liverpool.

The one to Maude gave him the most trouble. Every day it seems he has been losing a little more of her as he tries to remember how she looks. He can picture details of her face, the pattern of freckles across her nose, her green eyes, her broad smile. But when he tries to picture all of those details together, the image blurs, dissolves in his mind. Surely his failure here is just temporary. Surely he is just weary from this nomadic life, from the worries of command. From thoughts of mutineers and *saboteurs* and a Flying Squadron of ships who might surround him at any moment. Weary, too, from this hole in his heart he can talk to no one about.

Duty first, man.

He turns to Kell, who is smoking his cigar with his back to the light rain.

"We used to call this a smugglers' night back in the old navy, Luff. A good night to disappear."

"The gods have smiled on us again, sir."

"What of the *San Jacinto*?"

Kell says the enemy is hove-to three miles offshore. She's got her cutters posted at the north and south corners of the harbor. No doubt with signals ready to fire if they see the *Alabama* heading their way. A Yank cutter has also been back and forth to a Maine merchantman loading in the harbor, no doubt arranging for the Mainer to send some sort of signal if he spies the *Alabama* getting under way.

"History repeats itself, eh Kell?" Semmes is alluding to how the situation is so like the night a year ago when he and Kell were here at Martinique in the *Sumter* and escaped the USS *Iroquois*.

"Aye."

"But tonight we're in a ship to outstride even Neptune's Car."

"Freeman has his steam up. The crew is ready, sir. Excited, even."

"Very well then," he says. Send the mail ashore. When it is full dark, call the crew to quarters. Silent as cats. Rig a spark arrester on the funnel. Ready the guns. *Alabama* has less than two days of coal. She must catch the wind as soon as she can clear the lee of Martinique. So ... men aloft to lightly gasket the courses, topsails, top gallants. Jibs and staysails ready to go. No lights at all.

"I mean to fetch *Agrippina* off the Spanish Main tomorrow."

If I live.

⚓　　⚓　　⚓

Four bells into the evening watch, it's ten o'clock when the phantom slips her cables, turns to the northwest and gathers speed. The low pounding of the engines is hardly audible over the sound of the rain that is coming hard now.

Three rockets go up from the Maine merchantman. In the glare, Semmes, on the bridge, sees his gun crews; men stripped to their waists, bandanas tied on their heads. They stand attentive at their loaded weapons, lock-strings in hand, his officers spread among them with their side-arms in hand if any man should shirk his duty. Then the flares fade, leaving the night darker than ever. Leaving *Alabama* last seen heading northwest.

Semmes descends to the quarter deck, pokes his head down the engine room skylight and catches the chief engineer's eye. "Give her hell, Mr. Freeman." Then to the Quartermaster. "Come left. Sou'west is your new course. Stick to it."

He finds Kell on the bridge again. From up here the ship beneath his feet is hardly visible beyond a few yards. The shore, the other ships in the harbor, the enemy? Nothing at all. There's only the smell of coal smoke and the sound of the hull hissing through the water at twelve knots to tell him he has not left the planet. In twenty minutes or so he will either be safely on his way toward his rendezvous with his collier at Isla Blanquilla ... or he will be in a hell of lightning and thunder from the *San Jacinto*'s eleven-inch guns.

The rain runs off his cheeks in little streams.

"Into the unknown again, Mr. Kell."

The luff scrapes the rain from his beard with both hands.

"I thought you should know, sir. Tonight the men have a new name for you. *The Flying Dutchman*."

He thinks on Wagner's opera and the legend of the ghost ship that can never go home, doomed to sail the seas forever. "Let us pray 'tis not so."

5 0

DISTRICT OF COLUMBIA
November 23, 1862

Lincoln holds a letter in his hand. "What am I looking at, Major Allen?"

"Possibly a death sentence," says the agent. "For treason."

Allen, Lincoln, and Welles are in the White House attic. Again. It's one of those rare, warm winter afternoons that Washington gets, and Lincoln leads the others through a trapdoor onto the roof to escape the mustiness. From here they can see a tug drawing a new ironclad up the river to the navy yard, hear the fife-and-drum cadences and songs of new Federal recruits drilling on the mall.

"A letter to Secretary Seward we've intercepted. It's from our consul in Liverpool, Thomas Dudley.

"The spy?"

"You better have a read, Mr. President."

The letter says that one of Dudley's agents has befriended a Confederate naval officer and agent in Liverpool named Terry Sinclair. The Reb has revealed in bits and pieces a plot against the president. The spy's dispatch confirms the story Allen wrenched from Fiona O'Hare at the Hessian Barracks outside of Frederick, Maryland ... and adds new details. Dudley's agent has learned from Sinclair that persons of note in the Federal and Confederate governments are conspiring to drive Gideon Welles and Abraham Lincoln out of Washington. One way or another. The dispatch says that Sinclair's cousin Arbella has been a messenger traveling between Judah Benjamin in

Richmond and a ranking Naval officer in Washington. The Naval officer has the initials C.W.

"C.W?" Lincoln.

"We think it could be Rear Admiral Wilkes," says Allen.

"The Flying Squadron man?"

"Who has done worse than nothing when it comes to finding Semmes."

Welles says the only thing Wilkes has accomplished so far on the cruise of his Flying Squadron is raise hell with local authorities out in the islands. He's already tried to bully the governors of Bermuda, Nassau and St. Thomas. The man has single-handedly cast the image of the United States of America as arrogant, ignorant, selfish, and lawless almost everywhere he stops. And, just as bad, Wilkes is hunting for Semmes in all the wrong places ... if he's hunting at all. Now Wilkes is in Venezuela wining and dining the government there on a diplomatic mission of his own design. Instead of spreading out his ships to guard the passes in and out of the Caribbean against the *Alabama*. It's as if he doesn't want to find Raphael Semmes.

The president rolls his eyes. "You think, Major Allen, that Wilkes is connected to those threats Gideon was getting? Connected to the Greenhow woman and her crowd of two-faced hens? To Semmes' lady friend?"

"If C.W. is Charles Wilkes, yes sir. He's a treasonous bugger, certain."

Allen say the proof lies with Terry Sinclair's female cousin, whom they have discussed previously. With this dispatch from Dudley, they have word from two very different sources, Terry Sinclair and the dead Reb agent Fiona O'Hare, that Arbella Sinclair has been a link between Richmond and C.W.'s threats to Welles.

"Wilkes has hated me since I reprimanded him for causing that ruckus with England when he seized the *Trent*," says Welles. "He's one of the last of that group calling themselves Curmudgeons in the ranks who has not yet been retired. And he clearly has ambitions as a diplomat."

Lincoln has begun to pace, stroking his beard. His eyes cast far off on the Potomac. "But perhaps all of this is water over the dam. Treason or not, Wilkes can be no immediate threat any longer ... off gallivanting around the Caribbean as he is. Semmes' tart and the O'Hare woman are dead. The Sinclair woman has gone South. That coded message—the page from that Shakespeare play, we intercepted it. It never reached its intended destination."

Allen says that he has started to come around to Welles' way of thinking. This dispatch from Dudley clearly suggests a well-developed Reb conspiracy at work to destroy the Lincoln government. A plot engineered through a nebulous collaboration between the Davis-Benjamin crowd in Richmond, this C.W. and a shadowy figure well-placed in the Federal government who Terry Sinclair mentioned only once to Dudley's agent. Someone he referred to as Iago.

"You've both come here to tell me someone close may well betray me," says Lincoln. "To tell me beware of this Iago within my circle or some such thing?"

For some reason, maybe thoughts of implacable fate, Welles pictures his dead son Hubert, that flawless four-year-old gone off to Connecticut in a box for burial with only his mother at his side. While Hubert's ridiculous old man of a father is stuck here in Purgatory facing ghosts of a different sort.

"I think we need to talk about Mr. Seward."

"You think he's Iago?"

"All we have is circumstantial evidence," says Allen.

Seward has been a loyal advocate for Rear Admiral Wilkes, has more than once disrupted government affairs with underhanded tactics. To wit: the diversion of a key ship in the defense of Fort Sumter last year that cost the Union the fort. Now he's attempting to prevent the Federal Navy from screening mail seized off blockade runners and keeping nearly daily counsel with an English diplomat.

"I want to try something, Mr. President," says Allen. "I want to try to bait a rat. Let's let this dispatch from Dudley get to Mr.

Seward. Then let's see if he brings it to you ... or whether he buries the information."

Lincoln closes his eyes as if this is all too much. "Spies on spies. Has public service come to this?"

Gideon Welles barely hears the lament. Just now his mind has stuck on a thought.

Suppose C.W. is Charles Wilkes. Wilkes? Where has he heard that name before in connection to treason?

51

ISLA BLANQUILLA, VENEZUELA
November 25, 1862

High noon and hot. Yonge feels shaky, dizzy as he huddles in his berth ready to scream. Scream at the stupidity of Forrest, Gill, Latham and the other mutineers for cowering before a few officers with guns. Scream that he somehow could not find the right moment to use his own gun in their behalf during the melee. Scream from his current sense of hopelessness.

He has felt this way since the day in Martinique following the mutiny when Kell and the petty officers found and seized his supply of brandy in the sail locker along with all the other alcoholic contraband on the ship. And he's sick to death of feeling wretched, powerless. During the night that *Alabama* dashed through the rain away from Martinique, he hid here in his cabin hugging himself and praying that the *San Jacinto* would rise out of the murk and blow this hell ship to the devil.

But such was not the case. Old Beeswax has done the impossible again. Escaped clean away from his enemy during the night without so much as a possible sighting, a momentary change of beat from Freeman's beloved engines. *God damn.*

Now they have been at Blanquilla for four days, rafted with the *Agrippina*. Transferring coal, basket by basket. Semmes found the Yank whaling schooner *Clara L. Sparks* trying out blubber here and detained the vessel, saying he will not burn the ship because Blanquilla is the territory of Venezuela. He's just going to hold her captive until the *Alabama* sails.

Yonge has been hoping that he might sneak off to the whaler and get passage to the Spanish Main, her *aguardiente* and her *senoritas*, but the schooner's captain has gotten so friendly with Semmes that he's afraid the man would turn him back over to the demon he yearns to flee. Even now, Semmes and the captain of the schooner are miles up the coast together on a sailing and fishing expedition in the ship's gig.

And he has been charged with the task of preparing George Forrest to be cast ashore with hammock and kit. This means the coaling is almost ended. *Alabama* will be weighing anchor shortly. Quite possibly bound off into the deep blue for three more months. With no more goddamn liquor than the captain is willing to mete out during dinner in the wardroom. Unless Yonge can steal some now from the steward's stash while most of the crew is ashore enjoying their last day on a beach for who knows how long.

⚓   ⚓   ⚓

The paymaster stands with two armed guards outside the barred door to the ship's brig. He would have preferred brandy to help him with this task. But British navy rum works in a pinch. And now he has three bottles buried deep in his kit. One, alas, nearly half empty. He needed a few jolts to clear his head. Before coming here to the brig for Forrest. Before writing a letter he wants Forrest to smuggle off to the first American consul he can find.

⚓   ⚓   ⚓

"Take your hands off me." Forrest spits at Yonge's face, misses.

They are standing by the portside entry port. Yonge has the mutineer by the elbow—ostensibly to guide the man, hands still bound, down the Jacob's ladder to the waiting boat that will cast him ashore. But Yonge's using this moment to slip his letter into Forrest's shirt.

"I have saved you from hanging, man." A whisper. A lie.

"The fuck you did." Old Beeswax just didn't have the balls.

"The men have taken up a collection for you." Hiccup.

"You think I need money on a desert island?"

"Get yourself to the Yank schooner yonder. The money can buy you passage."

"You sold me down the river, you worm."

"Do you want this money or not?"

"What do you think?"

"Then deliver this ... or your life will be a living hell." Yonge slips the letter beneath the mutineer's shirt, into the waistband of his pants.

He has just pressed the money wrapped in a kerchief into Forrest's kit, when he sees Semmes striding toward them. Old Beeswax must have come back from his sail in the gig. Got aboard on the starboard side when Yonge was not noticing.

"Shove it along, Mr. Yonge, if you please. I don't want this traitorous scum fouling our decks a second more." Semmes makes it a point to not even cast so much as a glance on Forrest.

"Aye, high, sir." Hiccup.

Aye, high?

Semmes gives Yonge a careful look, steps close, sniffs. Whispers. "Tell me you have not been at the bottle, man."

Fucking hell.

52

LIVERPOOL, ENGLAND
November 28, 1862

"The bloody bastards have her, Thomas." It's morning and Matthew Maguire's on the street in front of the U.S. consulate at 22 Water Street as Dudley arrives by cab at his work. "They've got Lorraine in their bloody Allerton Hall ... or at least, they did."

"Almighty God." Dudley feels a release then a new tightening in his gut. "Get in the hack, Matthew."

When both men are in the cab, Dudley tells the cabby to head toward the docks in Waterloo, then reaches a gloved hand over to the shoulder of the man facing him. "I haven't slept in days. Tell me everything."

Maguire says one of his men has been able to get to an upstairs maid working at Allerton Hall, Charles Prioleau's mansion in Merseyside. It's as Dudley imagined. Prioleau had a grand party ten days ago for his socially elite friends, for Southern supporters and partisans, for Confederate officers and agents working in England. People came from all over Britain.

"How is it that we did not know of this?"

"Lorraine was keeping tabs on the social side of Reb activities. The rest of us were busy trying to learn about all these new ships they're building."

"I was a fool to let her try managing all this on her own."

Maguire shakes his head. "She wanted it that way."

"But now they've got her. My god, is she alright? Do the Capulets know she works for us?"

The agent says what the enemy knows is unclear. But according to the maid, Lorraine is unhurt. The Rebs have had her under something like house arrest since late the night of the party.

"She must have pressed Terry Sinclair too hard for information, and he divined her real intentions."

"More like Jame Bulloch smelled a skunk. The maid says Sinclair has not been around since the night of the party, but Bulloch has been at Allerton Hall every day to talk with Lorraine. In a locked room for hours. You can hear her sobs."

"This could be a disaster for us, for my government. For the war."

"I think I could put an end to it before things get worse."

"Have her killed?"

"Just something in her drink. She wouldn't ever feel a bloody ..."

Dudley thinks about her sweet lips, the musky scent of her skin. Feels his head exploding. "We have to get her out of there."

"You're the boss. ... But for what it's worth, I think this is a mistake."

"Let this be on my head," he says. "You, Federal and I are going in there for her. My God, she's one of us. She's a soldier." *And the woman I love.*

"If you give me a few quid, I believe I can get the maid to leave the servants' door unlocked some night soon."

.

53

CSS *ALABAMA*
November 30, 1862

"Look how she dies, Kell."

A calm night off the north coast of Hispaniola. Bright moon. Silvery sea. Semmes and his first officer are back aft, both with one foot upon the flag locker as they watch the flames rise from their twenty-fifth prize, the *Parker Cooke* out of Boston.

Generally, Semmes has shared the spectacle of these bonfires at sea with the unfortunate captain of the seized vessel. But tonight he cannot bear to be near another man's grief. So he keeps only his Horatio, the trusted luff, at his side to watch this monumental waste and destruction. There was a time, a year-and-a-half ago aboard the *Sumter*, when he could watch the immolation of a ship with the calm eye of a philosopher. Now each burning brings feelings of inexpressible anger, self-hatred, regret.

These executions seem a recurring nightmare. The one that comes upon him so often these days, just like the memory of the storm-wrecked *Somers*. Day and night, waking and sleeping. As if something within him yearns to return to these ghost ships. Yearns to reclaim some part of the man who once labored face-to-face with the gods of fire, wind, water, war. The part of the man who loved a selkie.

"It was her time," says Kell.

He's speaking of the *Parker Cooke*, but to Semmes he may just as well be speaking about the wives, the daughters, the lovers they have left burning, sinking in their wake.

The *Cooke* lies a few hundred yards to leeward. A silhouette beginning to spark and flare, an empty hulk. Just a few hours ago she was a treasure ship laden with tea crackers, ship's bread, cheese, butter, salted beef and pork, dried fruits bound for sale in the markets of the West Indies. Now her cargo is securely stowed below aboard *Alabama*, provisions for months more of cruising. Months more away from hearth, home. Land even. Away from a selkie. Though, sometimes on dark quiet nights, he dreams that she comes for him. Comes swimming alongside in her seal skin disguise. Singing to him of peace, of plenty, of forevermore.

The flames have begun rising into the air at three parts of the ship at once. The draft of air sucking into the ship seems like the deep whir of a winged creature beating against the sky. The *Cooke* points into the wind, her spanker set, her square sails clued up, but hanging. Fire races up the rigging into the tops, then to the topmast heads. To the t'gallants and royals. Other currents run out along the yards, igniting sails. One by one, all aflame, the sails fly from the yards, landing on the sea, burning as if the water itself is afire. Yards flare like immense logs, drop. They hit the sea with wails and hissing. Red, green, as they dive down beneath the oily surface.

The entire web of the *Cooke*'s rigging appears as golden thread against the night sky. The threads part, twisting and whipping. The ship cries as the mizzen mast crashes on the poop, shatters, cartwheels over the side, taking the flaming spanker with it. The foremast sways, collapses with a loud snap. The mainmast falls. Thundering as it hits the ship below. A swarm of sparks wheels hundreds of feet into the sky.

"Do you think the Jacks gain much pleasure from these funeral pyres any longer, Kell?"

"You want a straight answer, sir?"

"I must know."

"Then, sir, I believe the Jacks crave something new. I think they're desperate for some new glory."

"Like mutiny?"

"If we supply them with nothing more exciting."

"Busy hands are happy hands then."

"Something like that. At least a third of the crew stood behind Forrest in Fort-de-France."

He thinks back on those weeks beating against the west wind and the Gulf Stream, the nearly endless chain of fall gales off the Canadian Maritimes. The hurricane, the chasing of every ship spied on the horizon. Twenty-five seized. More than seventy boarded.

"This has been a grueling cruise."

"You cannot blame the men too much who have turned to drink to relieve themselves of fret, fatigue, endless routine."

"I have seen it in the officers, too. I know Pills Galt and that Negro boy of his have been getting into the medicinal bitters when they think I don't notice."

"I've started watering down the grog to temper the lure of the demon rum."

"Don't you know, our paymaster was three sheets to the wind when we cast off Forrest the other day?"

"A new enterprise would suit us all."

Semmes nods. "Aye ... It may be that I have just the thing."

He says that he has gleaned strong indications of two opportunities that lay before the *Alabama*. From newspapers taken off recent prizes, he has learned of the sailing of a Vanderbilt packet from Panama for New York with a million dollars' worth of gold aboard. She will come this way within the week, most likely leaving the Caribbean for the Atlantic via the Windward Passage between Cuba and Hispaniola.

Kell's eyes suddenly catch the glow of the flaming *Cooke* off to leeward. "You aim to seize her."

"If there are no Yanks guarding the Windward Passage to stop us."

"A ship of gold would get the Jacks' attention right smart."

Semmes tells his luff to let it be known among the crew. They're no longer after treasure such as they can seize from the likes of the poor old *Cooke* yonder.

"Let's get us the stuff that glitters, Kell. The stuff that can make Jack rich ... and set the folks in Liverpool building three more like our bride."

"You mentioned two opportunities, sir."

"One adventure at a time, my loyal friend."

And, Jesus Redeemer King, may the women forgive us.

54

MILBROOK, NEW JERSEY
November 30, 1862

Minty Tubman comes through the front door of the grist mill with tears in her eyes.

"We have to talk, Missy."

Maude has just put little Fiona and Leviticus down for their naps in the corner next to the wood stove, wrapped them in blankets in a grain hopper. The mill, owned by a Quaker family, has sheltered Tubman's band for almost two weeks since their deadly crossing of the Delaware. With the corn and grain milling season largely behind him, the miller has let the travelers rest and recuperate here in this three-story, creekside building. Maude has relished the routine of tending the large iron stove, learning to cook cornpone, pigs feet, quail. Relished the end to traveling and living out-of-doors. Relished meandering in the woods and meadows of this lost little valley just a few miles east of the Delaware while one of the other women looked after her babies. The low and steady rumbling of the water wheel and the soft splashing of the stream below the flume have made her feel a calm and permanence she has not known since leaving Ireland four years ago.

But now, Holy Mary mother of God, something is wrong.

"Tonight we must leave ... you must make a decision."

Minty says that the miller has been hard pressed from his Huguenot neighbors to move the Negroes on or bind them in indentured servitude to the valley farms, where the tradition of keeping black labor in subjugation has been slavery in all but name for generations.

"Emancipation Proclamation or no, things ain't changed for the Negro. We got to follow the drinking gourde all the way to Canada. Only there we be free, sure enough, 'til Mr. Lincoln win his war."

"What are you saying?"

"I'm saying if you want to go to New York to find your sailorman, the miller has a friend who can take you there tomorrow morning. Take you to Irish folks from your home country who can help you ... but you must know you cannot go to your countrymen with a black baby. They will not have him or you."

The rumble of the water wheel shakes more than the floor, the walls. It shakes the muscles in her arms, her chest. Only in the last few days has she had the luxury to imagine that she would ever have a choice again, that these dozen people she has been traveling with would no longer be her only world. That this sweet Leviticus who nuzzles her breast would be anything other than hers to raise. Forever, really.

She thinks on her sailor, on Raffy. She has read in the papers that he is suspected to be somewhere in the West Indies. A fleet of ships chases him.

The mother closes her eyes and leans against one of the posts supporting the grain floor above. Lets her mind drift. To afternoons of love in the District, in the Bahamas. The cottage by the sea. The man's broad back, the muscle in his hips. The image of Raffy as a Roman warrior rises in her mind. The memory of the top sheet bunched between her legs as if that could ever stop the aching in her throat or bridle her desire.

And then she pictures him as she has never seen him. With his other girl. With the *Alabama*. His mistress now. She's the one. The one he worries over, cares for, maybe kills for. Maybe killing him, too. She can only imagine his ship as something like the bark that brought her and Fiona from the West Country to New York. But a ship taller, fresher, stronger. All gleaming paint, clouds of white sails, polished brass.

And he is very much with his new girl.

For just a second she sees him poised before one of the big guns on the *Alabama*. He's wearing a long double-breasted coat, tailored tight to his chest and waist. Fastened at the top, hanging open at the knees. The gold buttons and the epaulettes flashing in the light. He has one foot in front of the other as if he's about to dance a two-step. One elbow leans casually on the gun. *He owns it.* But his face is turned away, fixed on the horizon, the setting sun. She cannot see the mustache that she always thinks of as a tomcat's whiskers ... or those cool blue irises she loved to drown in. Even as she watches, the sunset paints him crimson, then a deepening purple. Until he's just a silhouette. A shadow.

It's then that she hears a voice in her head. *He may not ever want to see me with a baby. He surely would not want to see me with a black baby.*

"You look like you in a heap of worry, Missy." Tubman opens the wood stove and tosses in two logs.

Maude crosses the room to the grain hopper she's fashioned into a crib, tucks the blanket a little tighter around the tiny faces.

"Missy?"

The water wheel churns deep in her core. "My sailor's on a long voyage ... and I can't leave my babies, Minty. Not either one."

55

LIVERPOOL, ENGLAND
November 30, 1862

A little after half-past two in the morning. Three men leave their boots on the stoop, open the door at an obscure end of the massive stone mansion, Allerton Hall. They start up the stairs with bats in hand, pistols tucked in waistbands.

Third floor, fourth door on the left. That's where they will find the pretty thing, the maid has told Maguire. She has given him a key to unlock Lorraine's door in exchange for two quid.

Maguire is on the second floor landing, leading the way, when they hear something like the creaking of footsteps on the floor overhead. All three men press their backs to the wall, freeze. Wait for minutes. There's no other sound except a case clock down stairs in the public rooms chiming three a.m.

Dudley presses a hand against Maguire's chest and steps into the lead. The stairs to the third floor are noisy. He moves slowly, stepping close to where the tread meets the wall to limit the sound of his movement. It takes him minutes to reach the third floor. Moonshine coming through a window at the far end of the hall casts a steely light on the right side of the corridor. The men's shadows look like goblins on the walls.

Sounds again. This time on the floor below. Like four quick steps, then nothing.

"Shit." Federal's voice just a hiss, his eyes are swollen, empty.

Dudley signals for him to wait here at the landing to keep watch, beckons Maguire to start down the hall with him. Backs against the wall in the shadows. They pass two doorways with open doors. Tiny, unused servants' bed chambers inside. The third door is closed. Dudley can hear the sound of snoring inside.

They move on. When they reach the fourth door, Dudley motions for Maguire to stand guard, then keys the door. Softly. Slowly. He can smell the scent of strawberries and honey, the perfume Lorraine wore at the London ball with Raphael Semmes. Her party dress was over-laden with it; it scented her room on Endbutt Lane, too.

The lock clicks open. A loud clunk. For a second Dudley feels petrified by the noise, by the fear of discovery. But then he tells himself time is of the essence and throws open the door. He's two steps beyond the threshold when he sees her bound to a bedpost in a nightgown. A musket lashed beneath her chest. Her hands bound to the trigger so that the slightest movement will fire the weapon. Eyes round as plums.

"Get out of here, Thomas." Her voice a banshee's shriek. "It's a trap!"

A man leaps out of a shadow a yard away, waving a pistol at him. It's all so sudden he can't think, can't fear, can't even take his gaze from Lorraine. It's as if he's seeing her heart reaching for him as he swings the bat … it connects with the elbow of the man's gun arm. A hard crack.

Someone grabs Dudley from behind the door, wraps arms around his neck, squeezes. He drops his bat, tries to tear the arms from his neck. But they are crushing his Adam's apple in a vice, cutting off the last of his wind, when Maguire clocks the strangler.

"Help!" An old lady has appeared in the hall from the snoring room. "Thieves."

Running men are coming down the third-floor hall. With guns. Federal has already started for the stairs.

Maguire grabs his boss by the wrist, tugs. "Come on, Thomas. You can't help her."

He looks to her face, for a sign from her. But she has already closed her eyes, bent over the barrel of the musket, her hands starting to move . . . maybe starting to spring the trigger.

56

CSS *ALABAMA*

December 7, 1862

"My god, sir. She's loaded with women and children." The luff's voice has a deep tremble as he stands the bridge deck next to his captain. He surveys the object of this Sunday morning chase. The gold ship they have been waiting for.

"Hold your fire, men. Sheer off, quartermaster!" Semmes feels the old fears howling deep in his stomach. The guilt that he's doomed once again to be the bringer of thunder and lightning into the lives of women.

Alabama veers sharply to port. The immense packet *Ariel*, her side wheels churning, walking beam thumping, crosses the cruiser's bow less than a hundred yards off, light gray smoke trailing from her funnel. Her rails are completely lined with cheering women and children dressed in the Sunday finery, bonnets, veils, waist ribbons flirting with the morning breeze. The Windward Passage seems a tropic landscape to be painted. Cuba's Cabo Maisi a brilliant green just off to the west. Hispaniola and Jamaica blue and hazy to the east and south.

The *Ariel*'s passengers are cheering because Semmes' ship masks herself beneath the Stars and Stripes. They think *Alabama*'s a new Federal cruiser come to escort them, protect *Ariel* from a Confederate pirate. But now she must drop her disguise or let the prize go.

"Show the Stars and Bars, signal officer. Fire the bow chaser."

Immediately, the Federal flag drops from the mizzen peak. Up goes the flag of the Confederacy. The small swivel gun in the starboard bow barks a blue cloud of smoke. A signal cartridge to stop the packet, no projectile fired.

An audible chorus of screams rises from the *Ariel* as the passengers realize that they're face to face with the pirate Semmes himself ... with designs on their ship, their gold, themselves possibly. Immediately the smoke from the *Ariel*'s stack changes from light gray to great black billows. The packet surges ahead as *Alabama* wheels back starboard to give chase.

Semmes rings the engine room telegraph for full speed ahead. The race is on. From the bridge, just beneath the funnel, he can hear the roaring of the fires as the stokers lay on the coal. Yet the cruiser has lost a lot of speed making her sharp turn, and the gold ship is pulling away.

"She has the heels of us, Kell. Ready the persuader."

Women and children or not ... I will not lose her.

Kell to his forward gunnery officer. "Clear 145 for action."

The Jacks who work the seven-inch Blakely rifled pivot gun just forward of the bridge scramble to load their cartridge, haul on the gun tackle to rotate the gun toward the *Ariel*.

"Take aim on her foremast, at the crosstrees."

The chief gunner sights along the top of his cannon while the gunner's mates adjust the elevation screws.

Semmes sees that on this course his gunners will be firing too close to the starboard shrouds of *Alabama*'s foremast.

"Gunner, I will yaw the ship to port to give you a clear line. Quartermaster, come left one point on your card."

The ship falls away from her parallel course. On the *Ariel*, women and children are scurrying below decks. Crew and men seem to be gathering on the rail with muskets.

"Fire at will, gunner. Stop the bastard ... but, god damn it, don't hurt any ..." *Of those lovely ladies.*

The Blakely flashes. A curl of smoke from the barrel. A puff of splinters high on the foremast of the *Ariel*. The screams of women seem to rise from the air or, perhaps, the inside of Semmes' head.

"Hit." Lieutenant Sinclair's watching the gold ship through his long glass. "Gallant shot."

The foremast of the *Ariel* has been nearly cleft in two. The top of the mast hangs aloft largely by the force of the head stay and triatic.

"She's stopping." Kell has his glass on her now.

Semmes feels himself breathe for the first time in a minute. "Tell me we haven't killed any children or women."

⚓   ⚓   ⚓

The captain's pacing in his cabin before his first officer, listening to music drifting down on the *Alabama* from the *Ariel*. After an initial panic, Semmes' most dashing boarding officers, Armstrong and Sinclair, have so won the favor of all the gold ship's passengers that they are throwing a grand dinner party in honor of the gallantry of the officers and men of the Confederate ghost ship. The two vessels are hove to drifting slowly on the current in the Windward Passage. The moon already high and nearly full. A night for lovers, a calm tropical night to tuck away in memory for a lifetime. On the *Ariel*, pretty women are snipping gold buttons from the uniforms of the handsome young Southern officers as mementos.

"This is an elephant I had not bargained for, Kell."

"Would you like me to have the gig row us yonder? A party might do us well, sir."

Semmes shakes his head. No. Part of him deeply yearns to make an entrance on the *Ariel*. Experience has taught him that almost every man will want to shake his hand, every belle want to kiss his cheek. And he has seen one woman, waving from the bulwarks when he first crossed the packet's wake, who had the flowing copper hair, the winsome green eyes of his selkie. *Or was I just imagining again? My God.*

But tonight he dares not leave his ship. Dares not give the crew any chance to see his weakness, his need for the company of women. His need for approval. The Jacks are nursing their grog rations, smoking their clay pipes, grumbling up on the foredeck. They know this past morning's dreams of wealth are now faint fantasies. They have already heard from the boarding party that the *Ariel* is not the northbound gold packet from Panama. She's bound the other way. From

New York. Empty of treasure except for ten thousand dollars in her safe. Her much richer sister has likely slipped by the *Alabama* and is even now exiting the Caribbean via the Yucatan Passage at the western end of Cuba. No doubt with an escort of Federal warships.

He wants to confess that he shares the crew's disappointment. That he feels overwrought with the idea that now he has about five hundred women and children to look after. But he cannot air these emotions. He fears that his heart has already been too much on his sleeve with Kell. The success of his command is to always appear strong. And optimistic.

"I should go check on the ship and Jacks, sir."

Suddenly Semmes does not want to be alone tonight. "Stay, my friend. Sit. The officer of the deck is at his post. Let's open a bottle of good wine ... and talk of the future."

"The second opportunity you have spoken of?"

He says that the newspapers seized off recent prizes say that the Yanks are sending a flotilla of thirty thousand soldiers with General Banks of Massachusetts to Galveston to attack the South this month.

"Yes, sir."

"I missed my chance to sting the Yank's navy at New York. I believe I have a better chance now."

"How so?"

"I aim to ambush them by night as the transports lay off the bar at Galveston. We could sink them by the dozen. Enough of civilian targets ... and these ships of women."

57

———∿∿∿———

DISTRICT OF COLUMBIA
December 20, 1862

Gideon Welles is surprised that he's not feeling more satisfaction. Seward, the man so long his gadfly, may at last be on the verge of toppling from his self-made throne. Welles should be overjoyed. But right now everything about Washington feels stale, rotten. Bones.

It's near midnight in the executive mansion. Another December with the White House decorated in wreaths, bows. Fir trees dripping with silver bells. The entire executive mansion, maybe all of Washington, smells of ginger, cinnamon, hot cider. And ghosts. This is the first Christmas for the president and Welles without their sons Willie and Hubert.

The city itself seems a gallery of the dead and nearly dead. For the last five days ambulances have not stopped rolling into the District with the casualties from Lee's horrendous defeat of Burnside's army at Fredericksburg. The Union army has suffered over twelve thousand casualties. More than one thousand killed, nine thousand wounded, seventeen hundred captured or missing. And just yesterday word arrived that Raphael Semmes escaped the *San Jacinto* at Martinique. The Reb pirate has already destroyed about ten million dollars in shipping. Meanwhile, Charles Wilkes fails to give chase.

Welles and Lincoln are alone in the East Wing, having endured a meeting with a caucus of Republican senators that has lasted half the night. They were demanding William Seward's dismissal from the Cabinet for his abuse of power, his arrogance ... Seward has tendered his resignation to Lincoln as a result. But the president has not yet decided to accept it.

Welles is putting on his coat and hat, preparing to leave, when Lincoln stops him. "A word, Gideon. Please."

The president looks on the verge of tears. He closes the doors to the parlor behind them. Seems in a bit of a fog as he wanders over to a ravaged tray of sweets put out for the senators. His right hand toys with some ginger snaps absent-mindedly. Finally, he picks one up, raises the cookie to his mouth. Then sudden rejects it, gives it a sharp and violent toss into the fading flames of the fire in the hearth.

"If there is a worse place than hell, Gideon, I am in it."

Welles wants to say something. *But what? I too know this hell? That it seems we are indeed witnessing the advent of End Times? That the rending of flesh and the gnashing of teeth has begun in earnest? The four horsemen are riding? The anti-Christ looms? The terrible swift sword?*

"I must believe the Lord is testing us, this nation, for greatness, Mr. President."

"Would that I could believe you, Gideon."

"These are hard times."

Lincoln rubs his eyes with the tips of his fingers. "You think the senators are right? You think we should be finished with Bill Seward."

"He has not yet mentioned to you that he received the dispatch from Dudley about the Iago's plot?"

"No."

"So he's failed Major Allen's test of loyalty?"

"You really think he could be Iago?"

Welles shrugs. "The man has often made my life an inferno."

"But perhaps if I leave him in the Cabinet, we can better keep an eye on him than if I turn him loose."

"He's a maverick no matter where he is."

"These intrigues are all too complicated. We have a war to end. Seward is not a man without talents in diplomacy."

"I believe we must do whatever it takes to preserve the Union."

"Then grant me a favor, please, Gideon."

"Anything."

"Major Allen be damned. Go to Seward one more time. Sound him deeply for his patriotism and staunchness."

"Tonight, sir?"

Lincoln lays a hand on his shoulder. "We don't have all the time in the world."

58

LIVERPOOL, ENGLAND

December 21, 1862

"Who goes there?"

Dudley has just been locking the door for the evening at the U.S. consulate on Water Street when he hears a noise at his back. A little screech. Like a hinge or some awful weapon. It's only five o'clock, but it has already been dark for two hours. Darker than dark. No moon. No stars. The lamplighters have not gotten to the streetlights yet.

"Thomas, you better come with me ... a ferryman's found something." Matthew Maguire is leaning out the open door of a tattered hack, nearly lost in the pitch of the night.

"What do you mean, something?"

A pause. The clearing of a throat. "Lorraine."

His lungs freeze. It has been weeks since Dudley and his men botched their attempt to free Lorraine from Allerton Hall. Weeks of worry and self-recrimination for Dudley. A time when he has gone about his consular duties in fits of dread of what the Capulets might do to his lover and his network of agents next.

⚓ ⚓ ⚓

A stone wharf. A small wooden ferry boat that carries shipbuilders between Toxteth and Birkenhead. The body's lying on the deck wrapped in the crumpled riding sail the ferry uses for stability when the winds come strong northeast down the Mersey. A gray, bloated lump of flesh, bed-clothing, tangled blond hair. One side of her face has been eaten away by crabs and eels. The eye just a socket.

"Lord of Mercy." Dudley starts for the rail of the boat to heave, but doesn't make it. Spews into his hands, onto the deck.

"Aw, Jesus bloody fuck me," says the ferryman.

"That's not Lorraine." Dudley tells himself he doesn't see the scar on her right shoulder where the Capulet's bullet pierced her earlier this year.

"I'm sorry," says Maguire. "I thought you would want to see her. Want to say goodbye. She's still wearing that silver ring you gave her in London."

He staggers to the rail, vomits again. Mutton and mint jelly. "That's not her."

Not the girl I fished out of the river last March. Not the girl whose sternum I pounded back to life. Not the girl whose wounds I bound with her own soaking shirt. The girl in a silver gown of brushed silk. My Jenny Lind.

"I'm sorry, Thomas. She had a way about her."

That hair. Burnished blond, twisted, clasped up on the back of her head, baring a long, creamy neck. The immense, blue eyes. The bow of pink lips. The easy curves of her slender body beneath the bodice. The dress, tight at the high waist, flowing over shadows of hips, thighs, ankles.

Maguire says the ferryman is a friend. He found Lorraine this afternoon snagged up under a dock over in Birkenhead. She's been dead weeks. Would have been swept out to sea long ago except for a stray current that carried her up under that dock. Probably nobody would have ever found her, but there has been an unusually low tide today.

"The Capulets murdered her."

"I don't think so. It's not how they would kill a woman. She's shot through the heart."

She's bound to a bedpost in her nightgown. A musket lashed beneath her chest. Eyes wide as plums. But when I look again, she has already closed her eyes, is bent over the barrel of the musket. The fingers of her bound hands starting to move … starting to spring the trigger.

"I think she fired into herself to create a distraction, to save the network, save you, save your president."

For some reason he thinks of the fool turncoat Yonge on the *290*. Then of Terry Sinclair and the night he tried to stop Lorraine from going to see him.

Are you jealous?

It's just that what you're doing is so dangerous.

Your president could be in real danger.

Dudley feels like a man of wood, can't move. Can't stop seeing the play of candlelight on the ceiling in her bedroom. Can't stop feeling the silkiness of her hair as he strokes her head. Can't stop remembering that all the while downstairs in the pub the sailors and doxies were singing "Rolling Home."

He tosses again over the side.

After a while he feels Maguire's gloved hand on his back. "If we give the ferryman a few quid he'll take us out into the Mersey. I thought we ought to give her a proper burial. Say a prayer for her and such. She'd a liked that, you know? It being the Christmas season and all."

Dudley rises, stares at Maguire. "This is my doing, Matthew. Her death is on me."

"There's a war on. Soldiers die. She was just a poor doxie soldier from the likes of Endbutt Lane."

His throat tightens. "And the Queen of the Nile."

59

DISTRICT OF COLUMBIA
December 21, 1862

Welles is back at the White House at eight-thirty in the morning, finds the president sitting droopy-eyed over his toast and coffee in the residence. Lincoln is still in the same white shirt and rumpled black suit pants he was wearing last night. No jacket or tie. Stocking feet.

"Tell me something remarkable, Gideon."

Welles say he has not slept. It has been a most astonishing night. Bill Seward sat down before him in his parlor last night and wept. Wept! The man was painfully wounded, mortified, chagrined by the calls from the senatorial delegation for his ousting. Not just because of wounded pride; he told Welles he fears for the president's safety. In this regard he produced not one, but *two*, dispatches from Dudley. The first being Allen's bait, the one the president has already seen exposing the Iago plot. And a second, more recent, dated November 19. It said that one of Dudley's agents is missing and possibly in the hands of James Bulloch, Charles Prioleau, their web of Rebel spies and sympathizers. The entire secret operation in England may well be compromised.

"Surely this news is not intended to make me happy."

"In substance it is bleak, sir. Yet remarkable nonetheless."

Lincoln gives him a cockeyed look that says, *You better explain.*

"Seward has to some degree passed Allen's loyalty test. He has produced the dispatch about the Iago."

"But he has had that dispatch for weeks. It seems to me he may well have been holding onto it for just such a moment as this. To use it to reassert my utter dependence on him."

"What about the second dispatch?"

"It adds another turn of the screw in his favor." Welles stands there with his hands out as if waiting to catch a pig or a bomb falling from the sky.

Lincoln motions to the chair opposite him at the breakfast table. "Have some toast and peach jam. You look like ..."

Death. I feel like death. I do not think toast and jam will change anything, he thinks. But he sits anyway, spreads some jam. Bites into the wheat toast.

"I wish I were more help, Mr. President."

"Well, then I must decide on my own this morning whether Seward stays or goes. Whether he may be our Iago. What is your counsel?"

Welles says that it is truer than true that he has been suspicious of Seward for about a year-and-a-half. That he does not like Seward as a man. Finds him pompous, supercilious, indiscrete, rude, manipulative, self-interested. A glory boy. But the man has a thousand loyal friends among ministers of state, foreign diplomats, secret agents, well-placed political cronies. He may well wish he were the president and had never lost the Republican nomination. Be that as it may, Seward may yet prove of value to preserving the Union. He has been deeply humbled and embarrassed by this call for his resignation. Finally, Welles says he is now willing to stake his reputation on the conviction that Seward is not the administration's Iago.

Lincoln closes his eyes, tilts his head back on his impossibly long neck. "How can you be so sure?"

"Two reasons, Mr. President."

Welles says that before he left Seward's house this morning, the Secretary of State showed him two things: The first was a letter that came via the U.S. consul in Colombia from Clarence Yonge, paymaster on the *Alabama*, detailing the poor morale of the crew, plans for multiple rendezvous with *Agrippina* in the Caribbean, Semmes' increasing sense of invulnerability and risky choices. Like taking his raider right into the Gulf of Mexico to engage Welles' navy.

"You and I have known about Yonge's hopes to make a present to us of Semmes for some time, but this new letter from the turncoat seemed totally surprising to Seward. He has only heard once before of this man in a dispatch months and months ago from Dudley. If Seward were Iago, he might unpack Dudley's dispatches to us for credence. But surely he would keep Yonge's report on the *Alabama* to himself. He would protect Semmes."

Lincoln has opened his eyes again, is scratching unconsciously with the fingers of both hands at his beard. "What else did he show you?"

Welles reaches for the inside pocket of his topcoat, pulls out a pack of letters in red envelopes. At least ten of them, dating back to the summer of 1861. Hands them to Lincoln. "He thought I was sending these to him."

The president opens one of the letters and reads.

GO BACK TO LITTLE NEW YORK.
YOU'RE KILLING YOUR PRESIDENT!!!

"What does this mean to you, Gideon?"
"Seward's another victim."
"So it seems."
"I've been fearing the wrong man."
Lincoln is suddenly electrified, rises to his feet, napkin in hand. Looks seven feet tall as he stares out the window. Seems to see something on the horizon, in this winter daybreak. "Here's what I think. Let us both pray for a little more clarity ... and that from here on out Mr. Seward stands united with us."
"Yes, sir."
"We must have faith the real Iago will yet reveal himself."
"Yes, sir."
"A great task remains before us. Our beloved and honored dead, our lost sons ..."

Welles feels Hubert, Willie—all the other boys—crowd in around him, around the president. A host of souls swelling here in the residence and outside on the frozen lawn, the mall. Along the banks of the tumid Potomac. Watching, listening as Lincoln finds words to match his vision.

"We must make an increased devotion to the rightness of our cause. The dead shall not have died in vain ..."

"Yes, sir."

"And, for Heaven's sake, send every damn ship you have after Semmes. He may well be on his way to slaughter all those poor New England boys sailing toward the Gulf with General Banks ... unless Yonge can find a way to stop him."

60

NEW LONDON, CONNECTICUT
December 22, 1862

"It's time, Missy." Minty Tubman stands in the doorway to the warehouse stockroom where Maude is bent over a wooden bucket washing diapers.

"One more."

"The ship gone sail directly."

"I'm almost finished." Maude wrings out the clean diaper, shakes it into shape.

"Come on, gal. That captain got bees in his butt to leave. Wants to be in Canada by Christmas Day."

Maude looks around for her bundle and the carpet bag a Quaker lady back in Milbrook gave her to carry the diapers and clothes for Fiona and Leviticus. Minty has already scooped up the babies into her arms from their nest of blankets on the floor.

"I gots to give you this before I forget." Minty Tubman slides a twenty dollar gold piece into Maude's hand.

"What's this for?"

"You gone need some money until you find work in Halifax."

Maude knows Minty cannot afford to be giving away money like this. "I can't. We ... you keep this for us until we need it in Canada."

Tears are welling up in the black woman's eyes. "I'm saying goodbye, Missy. I'm not coming with you."

"What?" Minty has been her shepherd, her only real friend now that Fiona is gone, Raffy gone. The godmother of her babies. The idea that her savior might not be coming on the ship north ... it never occurred.

"More folk waiting for me to lead them out of Egypt. Army general waiting, too."

"I can't go without you, I ..."

"People gone to look after you."

"I can't go." Something hard and violet bursts behind her eyes. Blooms. Red and purple. "I don't have to go."

"Yes you do. Somebody chasing you just like they chasing the rest of us."

"Let me stay with you."

"You talking crazy."

"Let me stay with you. Let me help you?"

The tiny little woman shakes her head. "What am I gone do with a white woman and two babies? One of them chocolate."

"Where are you going?"

"Back on down to Carolina. General Hunter and black folks on them Cambahee River plantations been waiting nigh on two months for me to get back on down there."

"Take me with you."

"I am not hearing this."

"Please. Pleeeeeeease."

"No. It too dangerous for all involved."

Another violet is blooming behind Maude's eyes. "Maybe the babies and I could make it safer."

The black woman gives her a look like *what kind of nonsense has gotten into that flaming head of yours*. But it's not a hard look. It's a curious look.

"Wouldn't it be less suspicious? Couldn't we travel faster? If we traveled as a couple of married ladies with their babies?"

"Like I'm your nurse or something?"

"I didn't say that."

Tubman shakes her head, her eyes now sparkling with amusement and a sense of whimsy, no longer tears. A plan's taking shape. "You really want to do this? A white girl like you?"

There's so much she wants to say but can't find the words for. She's not sure when she stopped seeing the war as a noble endeavor, a freedom fight. Not sure when the war became monstrous. Maybe it started when she saw the girls at the Pegram's school having snowball skirmishes with the young recruits in the streets of Richmond as if war were a game. Or when the *Alabama* ripped Raffy from her in Nassau. She saw how combat had crushed and torn all of those poor boys arriving at the Robertson Hospital. Felt the sting of war during those days she and Fiona were beaten in the Hessian Barracks. Tasted something sour inside her the day Fiona died. It all seems such a waste. A bloody heathenish way to solve people's grievances.

"If I can help you save some lives, maybe stop this war ..."

"What about your sailorman?"

"Until this war ends ..." She throws her hands into the air. "He and I are just as lost in the wilderness as everybody else. And now I have these babies."

Tubman gives her a long look, takes her measure of this mother. "Alright, Missy ... alright. Maybe you gots a point."

A fiddle song starts deep inside her.

"This war. Slavery. They like an awful snake right there on the floor of the house. We got to help Master Lincoln kill it dead, else it spring up and bite us again."

"You're going to let me help?"

"We gone give this thing of yours a try."

"Bloody hell."

The black woman folds her in a big hug. "We gone to lead some folks out of bondage. Then afterwards we all gone to go to the Promised Land up north."

The hug feels so right, so strong. As if this is all she ever needs in the world. A sister. But then her mind drifts to Raffy—*the cottage by the sea, his broad back.* And the longing starts again.

She hugs Minty tighter. "I'm going to need to write a bunch of letters."

About twenty-five of them. For each island governor in the West Indies from Cuba to Trinidad. Each a duplicate of the others. Each overflowing with love for my sailor. Each promising to meet him after the war ends ... none with news about my babies or my strange bond to this

Negro woman. None saying I'm heading to Carolina to kill a snake that I now see would bite us all.

When she finishes writing, she will scent the letters with rose water, fold them, seal them. Address them to Captain Raphael Semmes, CSS *Alabama.* Then she'll enclose each in an envelope for a governor. She'll hand over all her letters to the captain of a brig bound tomorrow from New London to the Virgin Islands with a load of clear, white New England oak. After that, all she can do is hope that the postmaster in St. Thomas will forward her mail via traders bound to the surrounding islands.

It may well take months for all of her letters to reach their destinations, but surely at least one will find her Raffy.

A girl must hope.

61

CSS *ALABAMA*
January 11, 3:30–8:15 p.m., 1863

Northern gales have been coming now every three to five days. Veracruz and the last resting place of the USS *Somers* lies just a hundred miles to the southwest. Night after night, the same dream for Raphael Semmes.

A roiling wall of wind and water from the north thundering down on the Somers. *The screech of the wind as it lays the brig on her side, starboard rail awash. The tips of the lower yards snagging in the waves. Mainsail dragging in the water. Men tumbling into the sea, scrambling from below decks.*

She's down flooding by the head. Sailing herself under. The foretop mast splitting down the middle. Sails shredding to rags. An explosion like the roar of a cannon as the main hatch blows from the building pressure. A geyser shoots into the air spewing salt beef, sacks of corn, sweet potatoes. Rats. Drowning men begging their god for mercy. Cursing the navy and the captain as whoreson floggers. The ship a cold-hearted sea bitch. Goddamn the ship. Goddamn this ridiculous war ...

Since paroling the *Ariel* to go on her way to Panama with her women and children, Semmes has been fighting weariness, dread. He has been keeping to himself in his cabin most of every day, writing in his journal of feelings he hopes no one, not even his selkie, will ever discover. While the *Alabama* was coaling again with the *Agrippina* at the Arcas Islands in the Gulf of Mexico, he remained aloof. Christmas had been particularly hard, when the officers and crews were frying fresh fish, enjoying extra rations of grog, singing—both aboard and on the sandy cays. It had taken him a bottle of wine on several nights to chase thoughts of family, the *Somers*, Maude, from his mind.

And there's one other worry that won't quit him. He has sailed into the Gulf, his enemy's backyard. There are only two ways to escape if Wilkes' Flying Squadron or Federal warships on blockade and picket duty should spot him—the Yucatan Passage and the Straits of Florida. For days he has been telling himself that success, as a general rule, attends the man who is vigilant and active, who has been careful to obey the laws of nature. Yet he is neither vigilant or active. He chides himself. He sits here pen in hand, unpacking his heart, doing nothing. Given the gales that have battered *Alabama* of late, he may well be in defiance of the laws of nature. For weeks his ship has been plowing against head seas and north winds day after day, heading toward a bloody rendezvous with the Yanks at Galveston. Which must surely lie just over the horizon.

It's seven bells into the noon watch when a knock sounds at his cabin door. A bosun. Kell's requesting the captain come on deck. The lookout has spied the lighthouse on Galveston Island. And five enemy steamers, ships-of-war anchored off the bar.

"What else, man?"

"The enemy seems to be shelling the town."

Holy Mary, Mother of God, be with us ...

⚓　　⚓　　⚓

The Gulf is strangely calm when he arrives on the bridge, waxing the tips of his mustache.

"Five warships, but no transports, Kell?"

"Aye, sir."

"But they were to be here. The transports. The newspapers said Banks would arrive ..."

"There appears to be a battle going on."

Semmes tries to make sense of what he's seeing, the shelling, the lack of the troop carriers he's so keen to attack, the five large enemy steamers. He tells the luff that Banks' troops must have been diverted to somewhere else in the Gulf. The navy's shelling of Galveston can only mean that Confederates have taken the port. Now what? To go against five of the enemy's best would be madness.

But he has promised his crew some action ...

"I believe they have seen us," says Kell, looking through his long glass. "Flags going up on the largest sloop-of-war. She could be our old friend the *Brooklyn*."

"Steamer coming out, sir!" A shout from the lookout.

Semmes spots the puffs of smoke from the enemy's funnel. Even from this distance he can see that the ship getting underway is a three-masted, side-wheel schooner. More or less the size of the *Alabama*. Neither one of the older class of steam frigates nor one of the new screw sloops. He feels something stir in his guts. A raw hunger. The seed of a dark idea.

"Wear ship, Mr. Kell. Get up steam. Lower the propeller."

"Yes, sir."

"We will lure our new suitor away from his gang. Flirt with him. Lead him out into the Gulf."

"As you wish." Kell's cheeks have begun to redden with excitement.

"When it is nigh on dark, *Alabama* will draw him close enough to kiss. Then show him a broadside of her hot metal."

He hears Hamlet in his head now. The old refrain, the call to duty. *Readiness is all.*

⚓   ⚓   ⚓

It's dark and the Yank is on her. A distinct and shadowy presence beneath the starry night ... less than a hundred yards off to *Alabama*'s starboard, steaming a parallel course.

Semmes, Kell, and the sailing master have the bridge. *Alabama* and her pursuer now about twenty miles offshore. An hour ago the Confederate beat to quarters, furled her sails, turned to meet the enemy. The junior officers—except Galt and Yonge who are below preparing to take casualties—are dispersed among their gun crews.

The captain orders the engine room to stop the propeller. For several seconds the only sounds are the low hiss of steam from the funnel and the patter of the powder monkeys' feet as they tote the last of the shells into position by their guns. The crew—bare-backed, bandanas on their heads, wax stuck in their ears against the roaring of the guns to come—stand by their weapons. Master gunners hold lock-strings in hand. Their guns loaded, elevation screws and quoins fitted to deliver fire at the enemy's waterline.

Semmes knows he must hit first, hit hard, hit low. If he is to survive tonight, he must mortally wound the Yank, render her a sinking hulk in minutes. The wind is blowing onshore, and as soon as the other warships see the lightning of his guns and hear the rumble of battle, they will be after him. A prolonged battle or a devastating wound from his opponent will leave him prey for the dogs.

Now in full dress uniform, saber at his side, the captain senses that his crews' eyes are on him. He pictures Nelson at Trafalgar, John Paul Jones of Flamborough Head. Stands as erect as a man of iron. Tries not to move or fidget. His officers and men are looking for cool leadership tonight. *Courage, confidence, man.* He makes a show of twirling the tips of his mustache. Slow, feline gestures.

How many times in his life has he stood on the cliff of battle like this? When he out-paced the *Brooklyn* while running the blockade at New Orleans in the *Sumter*? When he dodged the *Iroquois* at Martinique in the *Sumter*? Just six weeks ago when he escaped the guns of the *San Jacinto* at Fort-de-France? But each time he has stepped safely back from the brink of combat as the enemy failed to close on him. He has seen his share of blood and thunder, the eye-burning fog of gunpowder. But it was all during his days of soldiering ashore during the Mexican War, after he lost the *Somers*.

As an officer at sea, as the commander of a ship, he has never been tested by a hard battle. He does not fear death. It will come when least expected, that is all. But he fears the thought that a moment might arrive when the chaos overwhelms him as in that squall aboard the *Somers*. Fears he might somehow make a rash or clumsy choice that will cost lives, cost him this bride of a ship. He's trying to focus on the details of speed, position, the elevation of his guns, the state of his powder, the readiness of himself and his crew—all the little things that matter so much—when a voice hails him from the phantom to starboard.

"What ship is that?"

"Her Britanic Majesty's steamer *Petrel.*" Kell's voice echoes over the water, buying time with his lie.

No response. Just the distant sound of hasty and muffled conversation on the Yank.

"What ship are you?" Kell into is megaphone again.

No reply.

"I say, what ship are you?"

Semmes feels a strange clarity come over him. He can see both the *Alabama* and her adversary clearly in the star shine. Great black monsters, casting a red glow in the air above their funnels. He can see the open gun ports for two thirty-two-pounders aimed at him. A pair of what look to be Parrot thirty-pound rifles and some smaller pivot guns trained on the *Alabama.* Hundreds of men on both ships at their fighting stations. Gun crews at their ready. Scores of men at the rails kneeling behind the bulwarks with muskets aimed. Sharp shooters in the tops too, aiming across the water at each other and at the officers below.

"This is the United States ship ..."

The wind carries away the name of his adversary. Semmes smiles at Kell, knows the name of the enemy right now is of little consequence. What matters is that with every line of dialogue exchanged, he distracts the Yank from the choice to engage, the poise to defend. Suddenly, he's thinking about Hamlet again, feeling a wild humming in his blood. Hearing the voice in his head, saying *Let the foils be brought.*

"If you please," the Yank again, "I will send a boat on board of you."

Another smile between captain and luff. "We will be happy to receive your boat."

The bosun on the enemy calls his crew to the davits and the falls. There's a whine of rope through tackle as the enemy lowers his cutter. The creak of oarlocks, the splash of oars as the boarding party gets underway.

Semmes leans toward Kell. "I suppose you are ready for action?"

"Only waiting for the word."

The seahawk says they must identify themselves to the enemy, must not strike him in disguise. And when the *Alabama* has done so, give the Yank a broadside.

Kell nods, raises his megaphone to his mouth and his free arm over his head as a signal to the gun crews. "This is the Confederate States steamer *Alabama*!"

His raised arm slashes down through the night air. And, for a moment, the world ends. A blinding flash of light, the deafening bark of cannons. The deck jerking so hard beneath Semmes' feet he falls to his knees, clutching the bridge railing.

Hardly has the first flash ended when the enemy answers with his own broadside. The air buzzes with metal. The enemy is aiming for *Alabama*'s rig. But has so far missed hitting masts or spars. Missed critical shrouds, sheets, braces, halyards.

Rising to his feet, Semmes sees the Yanks side-wheels begin to turn, calls for Mr. Freeman in the engine room to give him all ahead, half.

"Fire at will, boys!"

62

—⁓—

CSS *ALABAMA*
January 11, 8:20 p.m., 1863

"Fuck it." Yonge's alone in the wardroom, "Just fuck it all."

An hour ago gathering bandages, sheets, medicines for the surgeon, he found Pills Galt's stash of medicinal Plantation Bitters in the sick bay. Now he's drunk on the syrupy spirits. And he can't stand the roaring of cannons, the scent of gun powder, the shrieking of men, the choking smoke. Even a second longer.

Being in the depths of the ship during a battle is like being a goddamned fish in a barrel. Every sound on deck is amplified tenfold down here. Every time the Yank unloads a broadside, he can hear the fracturing of wood. Somewhere in this ship, red-hot balls of fire are trying to tear *Alabama* to pieces. The sounds of the musket balls ripping into and through the starboard planking makes him cringe. Twice already he has seen Minié balls fly through the wardroom, tiny comets embedding themselves in the woodwork with puffs of splinters And the smoke is beyond belief. He can hardly see ten feet. This has to be more than gun smoke. *Alabama* must be on fire.

"I have to get the hell out of here."

"What's that, man?" The ship's doctor and his Negro boy have just entered the wardroom to set up their surgical pit with armloads of clamps, knives, saws, needles, thread.

"We're going to die."

"But maybe not tonight." Pills Galt's voice has the cloying sarcasm and world-weariness of a man who has seen it all, seen the likes of Yonge's battle hysteria before.

"Old Beeswax is going to get us all killed."

— 237 —

The doctor shakes his head. "Pipe down, Yonge."

He starts arranging his surgical tools on the sideboard, directing the boy David to organize the medicines according to the color of the bottle—clear on the left, blue in the middle, brown on the right. Bitters over to the side.

Another broadside thunders against the ship, scatters the surgical instruments on the floor. Bottles of medicine topple. One shatters on the floor.

"Don't you see? This is all about glory for Old Beeswax."

"Why don't you go on deck for some air?"

"Why don't you shut your trap?"

"I've had about enough of this ... if you can't help, Yonge, leave us alone."

He feels a fuming anger rising in him. Wants to sting this superior Nancyboy doctor to the quick. "You want me to leave so you can hug and kiss on your little black boy until Semmes sends us all off to oblivion?"

Galt picks up a scalpel and starts toward him. He's more shadow than substance in the smoky air. The boy David ... nothing at all.

Yonge draws his pistol. "Leave off or I'll shoot."

He knows what he must do. He can end this all. He can set fire to the powder magazine ... then swim for the Yank. A hero. To collect his just reward from Charles Dudley, William Seward, and Gideon Welles. His reward for bagging the pirate Semmes.

63

———— ✺ ————

CSS *ALABAMA*
January 11, 8:23 pm, 1862

The intermittent crack of muskets sounds from the foredeck and aloft. Semmes can hear the occasional zip of balls near his head, sees one strike the handrail to starboard, sending up a shower of splinters. He dusts the wood off his jacket as if it were a bit of snow, resumes shouting orders to the quartermaster at the helm. He's beginning to feel an odd giddiness creeping over him when his gunners start with their second broadside. After the thunder of the guns comes the clang of *Alabama*'s shells piercing the iron hull of the enemy.

"Give it to the rascals!" Semmes is pacing the bridge, shouting. "Aim low!"

They do. On the third exchange of fire, a shell from one of the *Alabama*'s pivot guns blows a hole in the Yank's waterline plating the size of a hogshead barrel. Another lights a fire deep within. The enemy is still moving forward, his side-wheels churning, but perhaps his rudder is not answering. He's veering toward the *Alabama*, the ships barely forty yards apart. Every inch of the Yank is now clearly visible except during the seconds after blinding fire from *Alabama* and her foe.

Kell and Semmes see that unless they do something quickly, the yards of their ship will be tangled with the enemy's.

"Hard to port." Semmes shouts an order down to his quartermaster. "Fire 145 at his walking beam. Go, boys. Damn it all. Stop him!"

The crew of the Blakely pivot gun up forward takes aim, fires into the huge walking beam mechanism at the center of the enemy, which turns his side-wheels. The air over the Yank erupts with a blizzard of wood and iron, and the side-wheels grind to a halt. Steam's blowing off from somewhere below decks in a jet of billowing vapor spewing almost to the main top. A fire's burning forward—but the Yank gunners pay no heed. They hit the *Alabama* with a fourth withering broadside. The thirty-two pounders splinter the oak bulwarks midships. Knives of wood fly in all directions, leaving almost the entire crew facedown on the deck wondering if this is the great death. A carpenter's mate staggers to his feet with a six-inch sliver of oak entering his face beneath his chin and exiting through his cheek. Semmes eyes his watch, realizes that the first yardarm-to-yardarm battle of two deep-sea steamers is but ten minutes running. It has felt like hours ... and the blink of an eye.

$$\text{⚓} \qquad \text{⚓} \qquad \text{⚓}$$

Two more broadsides and the Yank is sitting dead in the water, burning fore and aft, fire licking up through her decks even as she is starting to settle into the water.

"Strike, man. By all God's grace. Strike your colors and be done with it." Semmes is shouting into the night, shouting to his counterpart on the Yank. The rush of battle has swept over him, is passing off now, and the reality of the devastation he's caused begins to tear at him. The enemy is vanquished. To fight on is to only bring more human misery. Why does this man not strike his colors and ask for help? Even now his gunners are reloading for a seventh broadside.

Why will he not strike?

The answer comes from the masthead lookout. "Funnels glowing on the horizon, sir. Three, maybe four, ships coming our way. Fast."

So there it is. The Yank is sacrificing himself so that his comrades on the other Federal ships might reach the *Alabama* and maul her before she has a chance to escape.

"They come for us, Kell. Hungry wolves."

"We must finish him, sir."

The captain shouts again for his gunners to aim low, stops his own ship just thirty-five yards to port of the burning wreck. He knows this broadside will condemn much of the enemy crew to death. Does not want these ghosts on his conscience like the dead of the *Somers*.

Semmes looks to the deck, sees the gun crews just finishing tamping down their charges. They will be firing in seconds. He turns away, cannot watch the carnage that is to come. *Holy Mary, Mother of God, save yourself Yank. Save us all.*

"A lantern is going up." Kell.

A leeward gun on the enemy fires.

Semmes spins to look. Are these the signals of submission? At last? Or a desperate Yank ruse?

"Have you struck?" Kell's voice bellows over the water.

"I have ... can you help us?"

The Yank's words are cool rain. For a second, maybe three, the deck of the *Alabama* is silent. Then a cheer for the ship and Old Beeswax rises to the heavens. In just thirteen minutes the battle has ended.

"Cease fire, Kell. Launch the boats. Look to those poor men. We need to pick them up."

"Their friends could be here in two hours."

"So ... get them aboard. You've got half an hour."

"Yessir."

"And the schooner—can you make out the name?"

Kell has his glass trained on the Yank's quarter boards. "She's the *Hatteras*, sir ... sinking fast."

Forgive us. Almighty Father, forgive us all. This is what he's thinking when he turns and comes face-to-face with his surgeon.

"Wardroom's ready for the wounded, sir ... but I've had a bit of a problem."

"What?"

"Mr. Yonge got himself drunk, sir. Went a little hysterical. My boy David had to break a bottle of bitters on his head."

EPILOGUE

KINGSTON, JAMAICA
January 24, 1863

Semmes braces his legs and leans back. Tries to find his balance on this chestnut gelding as it ambles and lurches over the cobblestones on Kings Street toward the waterfront of the Jamaican capital. He thinks that on such a fine tropical morning as this—the air full of bird songs, the scents of peach hibiscus and red heliconia— he should not be feeling these pains. The stabbing in his gut, the dark tightening beneath his breast bone.

His mind drifts, circles back on the last few days.

Everywhere he has gone, people on the street have cheered for him. Crowds gathering just to stare. The British navy and the governor of this fair isle have honored him with grand receptions. A band playing "Dixie." He has been surrounded by fawning young women in silks who want nothing so much as to touch his hand or his cheek, marvel at the way his mustache twitches when he smiles.

The *Alabama* has been in Jamaica for three days, and the crowds still won't let her captain be. Here, they tell each other, is a mariner to rival the great Nelson, here's the man who has already seized forty-five enemy ships. The most successful sea king in history. The man who engaged and sunk the USS *Hatteras* in less than twenty minutes ... then vanished right before the eyes of four American ships-of-war. The man with the sympathy and nobility of spirit to rescue over one hundred officers and seamen from the obliterated American ship, tend to their wounds, parole them here in Kingston. Where they now sport arm-in-arm with the Jacks of the Rebel cruiser.

The spoils of victory are surely ours.

And he has avoided treachery once again as well. Two nights ago Kell discovered Yonge drunk in a bar, whoring on money pilfered from the ship's strong box. Plotting with the U.S. consul to sabotage the *Alabama*. It only took the seahawk half an hour to cast the reprobate bastard ashore with his kit and a promise to shoot him dead—no questions asked—if ever they should cross paths again. The ship's new paymaster is Galt.

My loyal friend. It's just his attachment to the Negro boy that makes a fellow a bit ...

"What a party they're having," says James Fyfe, the man riding at Semmes' side.

One of *Alabama*'s topsmen and a gunner off the *Hatteras* are emerging from a pub ahead, each with a pair of Jezebels in their arms, rummy grins on their faces.

Fyfe's a local planter. A friend of James Bullock's from England, possibly even a Reb agent. He's been hosting Semmes on his estate, Flamstead, in the Blue Mountains since the seahawk's arrival.

Seeing these two Jacks with their molls now brings to mind for Semmes the party in London when he first met Fyfe. A party at the French Embassy last May. The men had bonded over their shared sympathies for the Southern cause, fine cigars, sparkling wine, witty repartee, beautiful women. It was the very last time Semmes danced, whirling around the floor to the melody of violins. The swish of a young goddess in a silvery silk dress—a woman who smelled like strawberries and honey. A woman who, for some reason, reminded him of Maudie when he stared deep into her eyes. A woman, Fyfe says, who was an agent of the enemy. A woman who has suffered an unfortunate encounter with a musket in Liverpool.

The women we wreck.

"Half Kingston seems drunk and in love since you've arrived. The other half, working on it," says Fyfe. He's still eyeing the Jacks and the Jezebels as they turn a corner onto a lane lined with short-stay hotels.

Semmes nods. He should be amused, gladdened even, that his crew is finally enjoying well-earned liberty. But this stabbing in his guts won't quit.

"What say we find ourselves a couple of cool bottles of champagne and I treat you to one of the finest dollies in all of the West Indies, Captain?"

Part of the seahawk thinks that maybe a dolly is just what he needs to take his mind off his pains. It has been six months since a woman wrapped him in her arms ...

But another part of him remembers the emptiness and guilt that ensued from his brief and heedless flirtation with the Irish lass named Nessa. The daughter of a master sergeant gunner at Gibraltar who told him to get fucked.

Jesus. Enough of that.

Then there's his family to consider. Anne, who knows where? Tending to his daughters, fretting over his sons at war, fretting over him too. To spit into the face of kin for a half hour's flight into oblivion with a stranger seems beyond churlish and weak.

Finally, how could he be with another woman when he cannot ignore the web of feelings spawned by a letter tucked into the side pocket of his service jacket, a letter the governor gave him two days ago?

A letter that came most recently on a trading schooner with the mail from St. Thomas. A letter from New London, Connecticut, that seems to have brought with it these stabbing pains in his gut, the tightening in his chest, sometimes even blurring vision. He has read it over so many times he has already taken it to heart.

> *Please know that I love you with all of my heart and soul. But something that is simply beyond us has come up. Children. I have been blessed with two. They are the future, and I am responsible for them. So I will be taking them when I can to Halifax, to Canada, a place that is safe for them, beyond the terrors of war and hatred that we know all too well. It is not that little cottage by the sea in Brazil of which we have dreamed. But Halifax is something. I hear that the native people call it the land of the first light. The first place to catch the dawn. Look for me there. By the sea. I'm waiting. Will wait. Forever.*

"So ... will it be a dolly for you, Captain?"

He shakes his head no. "I must see to the ship and her repairs. Must get to sea again. Before the Yank's hounds sniff me out."

"Come again, sir?"

Semmes can't respond.

Words from Tennyson's "Ulysses" are rising in his head. They come like this sometimes—when he's staggering, desperate to find his balance, his focus. And just now—as the words start to swell in him—he begins to float above the pain in his guts, chest. He smells the salt air.

There lies the port; the vessel puffs her sail;

There gloom the dark, broad seas ...

Old age hath yet his honor and his toil.

Death closes all; but something ere the end,

Some work of noble note, may yet be done.

Not unbecoming men that strove with Gods.

HISTORICAL NOTES

———～✒✒✒———

Like *Southern Seahawk,* the first volume in this trilogy, this novel
is set against the backdrop of real events in the American Civil
War. The naval action, infighting in the Lincoln Cabinet, political
intrigue in the Office of the Secretary of the Navy, the clandestine
operations of secret agents like the Confederates James Bulloch and
Terry Sinclair, Thomas Dudley (U.S. consul in Liverpool) and Federal Allan Pinkerton in this novel are rooted in well-documented
facts. The turncoat Clarence Yonge and the mutineers Forrest and
Gill aboard the *Alabama* were actual trouble-makers. Harriet
"Minty" Tubman's work as a conductor on the Underground Railroad is well known. Even specific locales used in this novel, such as
the Ebbitt Grill and the Willard Hotel in Washington (which are
still in operation), the Pegram School and Robertson Hospital in
Richmond, the station on the underground railroad in Chadds Ford,
Pennsylvania, the pubs/docks/spy nests of Liverpool, the Federal
and Confederate White Houses, have been the subject of analysis
by scholars and internet coverage.

All of the major historical figures is this novel—Raphael Semmes,
Gideon Welles, William Seward, Abraham Lincoln, Charles Wilkes,
Allan Pinkerton, Rose Greenhow, Varina Davis, Harriet Tubman—
were real people. The dates, places and action of all major war-
related events in this novel are drawn from actual occurrences as revealed through the journals, published memoirs and correspondence
of the characters. Semmes' *Memoirs of Service Afloat* and *The Cruise
of the Alabama and the Sumter,* as well as the three-volume diary of
Gideon Welles, have been invaluable research tools.

Biographers have often revisited the lives of Semmes, Welles, Lincoln, Bulloch, Dudley, Wilkes, Seward, Greenhow and Pinkerton.

Among Semmes biographies, Stephen Fox's *Wolf of the Deep* stands out for its deep and meticulous research, as well as its courage to air guarded secrets about the man the Semmes family often refers to simply as "The Admiral." Specifically, Fox documents that Raphael Semmes' wife Anne bore a daughter, Anna, in 1847, who could not have been fathered by Semmes. He was away fighting the Mexican War during the time of conception. Fox also details the existence of a "romantic connection" between Semmes and a young English woman named Louisa Tremlett, a relationship that persisted through years of correspondence.

These discoveries led me to make an intuitive leap and imagine that Raphael Semmes may well have had a mistress at the outset of the Civil War. Maude Galway is that character in my novel and is an entirely fictional creation. Maude burst onto the page the day that I began to draft the first book of this trilogy. I immediately liked her spunk, admired her loyalty to her man. So she stayed, blooming in *Southern Seahawk*, evolving further in *Seahawk Hunting*. Fictional flesh-and-blood, heart-and-soul. Like Maude, Thomas Dudley's fictional spy consort, Lorraine, is an emblem for the many women caught in the deadly web of the war. These women kept company with secret agents and played crucial roles as spies on both sides of the Civil War ... often at great risk to themselves.

—RANDALL PEFFER
October, 2009

RANDALL PEFFER is an instructor at Phillips Academy in Andover, Massachusetts. His published books include *Southern Seahawk; Old School Bones; Provincetown Follies, Bangkok Blues; Bangkok Dragons, Cape Cod Tears; Killing Neptune's Daughter; Logs of the Dead Pirates Society,* and *Waterman.*